You Will Never Lose Me

STORIES
BY
TIM JEFFREYS

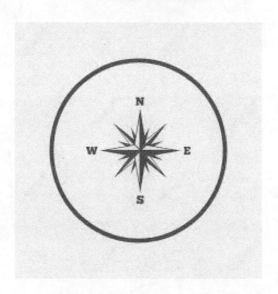

"YOU WILL NEVER LOSE ME: STORIES"

BY

TIM JEFFREYS

ISBN: 978-0-244-46595-7

www.timjeffreys.blogspot.co.uk

Cover art and design by Sally Barnett
www.sallybarnett.co.uk

Published by Dark Lane Books, 2019

Contents

"From childhood's hour I have not been
As others were—I have not seen
As others saw—I could not bring
My passions from a common spring—
From the same source I have not taken
My sorrow—I could not awaken
My heart to joy at the same tone—
And all I lov'd—*I* lov'd alone."

— Edgar Allan Poe, "Alone."

Raking Light

*T*HE REASON ROS assigned Marco the Sauvageon project was, she said, because his own paintings, or what she'd seen of them at least, were *in that field*. By this she meant Abstract Expressionism. Embarrassed at being given this news in front of the other conservators employed by the gallery, his response was typically self-depreciating.

"My paintings aren't Abstract Expressionist," he told Ros. "They're just bad."

Oblivious to the mutters and the sideways glances being thrown their way, Ros laughed, patted Marco on the shoulder and said, "We start work a week Monday."

Marco grinned despite himself and clapped his hands together. Of course he knew the real reason Ros had given the project to him; and he imagined the other conservators knew it too.

Back when the gallery was only *showing an interest* in acquiring the recently unearthed painting, some of his colleagues were already excited about working on it. For this opportunity to have been snatched from under their noses and given to the new-boy just because he'd had a bereavement was certain to be the cause of much resentment. Marco knew this. Still he couldn't help but feel glad. The work would give him something to focus on. Restoring a painting like Dryston Sauvageon's *Je T'Amene* was sure to be a challenge. Plus, the work was to be done in public which meant he'd occupy a cordoned off area of the gallery where visitors could chat with him and watch him work. Right now, for him, this was far preferable to working alone in some dusty backroom where he'd inevitably return to thinking about Dean. Clearly, Ros was throwing him a lifeline and for this he was grateful.

TWO DAYS AFTER being assigned to do the restoration, Marco got to see the painting. In the meantime, he'd done some reading up on the artist, and hoped to impress Ros with his new-found knowledge as they descended in the lift to the gallery basement.

"Did you know that Sauvageon only took up Abstract Expressionism after moving to New York from France following World War II? Before that he only painted portraits, most of which were of the same person."

Ros raised an eyebrow. "Esme Rochefort."

"Correct. They'd grown up together and he was besotted with her, but she ended up engaged to someone else. Then she was killed when Germany invaded France. 1940 I think it was. Tragic. Sauvageon was devastated. His most famous New York paintings—the Esme series—were thought by some to be attempts at a kind of abstract portraiture. Isn't that interesting? It was thought that in a way he was still painting Esme, that's why he'd named the pictures after her."

"Marco—?"

"Sauvageon actually denied any attempts at portraiture in his New York work, saying that he'd come to despise figurative painting. After Esme died he said he'd never paint anyone's portrait again. When they asked him why he'd named the paintings after Esme, he'd said something like: Because when I step back from the work, she is always there."

Ros gave him a tart look. "Thank you for that, Professor."

"What? I think it's a nice story. Undying love."

"Unrequited love."

Marco shrugged. "I just wanted you to know I'm serious about this, you know. That I've been doing some research."

"I know you're serious. Spare me any more lectures." She touched a hand to her brow. "I've had it up to here with Sauvageon's life story ever since we started planning the retrospective. It's a good thing I don't have a life outside of this place, huh? Now come on, shall we take a look at this thing?"

After all the reading he'd done on Sauvageon, Marco couldn't help but feel awed when Ros led him into the basement store room and uncovered the newly arrived *Je T'Amene*.

"Sensational, isn't it?" Ros said. "First thing it'll need is a good cleaning. It's been stuck in some New York attic for the past sixty years."

Marco studied the canvas. It had been executed in much the same style as the Esme paintings he'd seen in books: fuzzy-edged blocks of oil paint; blue, red and black on a mustard-coloured background. The ragged-edged blocks gave off a sense of uncertainty. There was certainly nothing figurative about the painting.

Mould had obliterated some of the oil paint in the centre of the picture, and clinging to the canvas was a thin layer of dirt and dust which would need careful removal.

"I wonder why Sauvageon kept this one hidden away."

"Lots of artists have paintings that are forgotten about or cast aside," Ros said. "Perhaps he wasn't happy with it. Although I can't see why. I think it's wonderful. It might even be his best work. Reckon you're up to the job of restoring it?"

"I think I am. You've got confidence in me, right?"

"Total confidence. Just don't balls it up. Newly discovered work is a big deal for any gallery, and we're going to milk this one for all it's worth."

"Now you're making me nervous. Maybe you should give it to someone more experienced."

"You'll do fine."

Marco smiled. "And the title? Where did that come from?"

"It's written on the back of the canvas." Carefully lifting the painting from its easel, Ros turned it so that Marco could see the words scrawled in the lower right-hand corner. "Actually it says: Je t'amené partout où je vais."

"Anyone around here able to translate?"

"*I take you wherever I go*, or words to that effect. My French isn't great."

"No, I'm impressed. What're those?"

Also scrawled onto the back of the canvas were various letters, symbols and icons, including a sun and a moon surrounded by what appeared to be rain or teardrops.

"That's just some mystical nonsense."

"What?"

"You didn't know Sauvageon was into the occult? I thought since this morning you were the world's leading expert on the man."

"Ha ha. And no, it wasn't mentioned in any of the books I read."

"I've seen this stuff on the back of some of his other abstracts. He was in some kind of creepy club. Like the masons." Ros set the painting back down on the easel. "Bunch of weirdos, basically."

"And the title? I Take You Wherever I Go. What do you think it means?"

"No sodding idea. Maybe if you stare at the painting long enough, all becomes clear."

Thinking she was serious, Marco stood and stared at the painting until Ros laughed and clapped him on the back. "How're you bearing up anyway?"

Marco drew a deep breath. "I'm okay. I just keep thinking about something Dean said before he...you know. He was angry because I'd starting seeing that Travis guy and I hadn't told him."

"Travis guy? What Travis guy? You never told me about any Travis guy."

"Oh, it was just a fling. Anyway, when Dean found out he kept asking why I hadn't told him and saying that all he wanted was to be the most important person in my life. To be honest, the only reason I didn't tell him was because I knew how he'd react."

"I could write the book on unrequited love."

"You?"

"I've had my heartbroken. It's never easy. For anyone."

"I know. I just wish I could've made Dean understand without hurting him. He was important to me, but I just didn't think of him in that way."

Ros nodded then took hold of his arm. "Let's talk about this over lunch. My treat."

MARCO EXPECTED ROS to take him to the new Bistro that had opened up across the street from the gallery, but instead she led him to a café a few streets away. The café was done out in Formica, and had plastic seating bolted to the floor. Under normal circumstances, Marco wouldn't have given the place a second glance but before he could complain Ros was leading him to a table by the window.

Ros surprised him a second time by ordering a plate of chips with baked beans, whilst he struggled to find anything on the menu that appealed to him. In the end he opted for a veggie burger, which he didn't like the colour of and nibbled at speculatively whilst Ros poured salt, vinegar, mustard and ketchup onto her lunch until her plate looked like a painter's palette before she finally tucked in with obvious delight.

"Don't tell anyone at work about this," she said. "Those pricks with their spinach feta hummus. This is our little secret."

"I honestly cannot believe you're eating that."

"Don't be a snob, Marco."

"It's not snobbery. It's just that it looks so...so bad for you."

Ros laughed. "Don't you just crave something you know is totally *bad for you* once in a while?"

When she raised her eyebrows at him, he smirked and diverted his eyes. "Stop it."

"More than once in a while, I'll bet."

10

Now they both laughed. They were silent for a short time then, watching the city traffic through the window until Ross said:

"Look at that sky. Looks like it's been painted by a Dutchman. Jan Van Goyen, somebody like that."

"I find all that golden age stuff a bit dreary."

"Like I said..." Ros pointed with her folk towards the sky outside the window. Then, after taking a deep breath, she said, "So were you and Dean ever an item?"

At the mention of Dean's name, Marco felt heaviness settle again in his chest. He noticed a few spats of rain on the window glass.

"Look at that. I was planning to walk home today. Do me good. I haven't been to the gym in weeks."

"I can give you a lift. You live Horfield way, right? Near the prison?"

"How'd you know?"

Ros shrugged. "Noticed it in your file. So?"

"So?"

"You and Dean. Were you ever..."

Under the café's strip lights, Marco could see threads of grey in Ros' hair. When she noticed him looking, he diverted his eyes. "We were. Years ago. I suppose you could say he was my first love. It was Dean that helped me accept it, you know, that I was..."

"A follower of Dorothy?"

"Uh, I hate that expression. But, yeah, Dean knew before I did, I think. He'd always been so open about it, even when we were at school. I really admire...*admired* him for that when I think about all the abuse he took. But he always gave as good as he got. He had this 'I am what I am' attitude, whereas I was terrified when I first realised I was attracted to men. I couldn't even admit it to myself for years. I lied to everyone, even myself. Dean helped me through that. Shone a light on it, I suppose you could say. Helped me face the truth."

"So why'd you guys break up?"

Marco gazed at his half-eaten burger. "I suppose once I was out, I wanted to explore this thing. You know, experiment. I did care about Dean but I just needed to see what else was out there. I hurt him. I hurt him a lot, I realise that. You know what he used to say? That we were soulmates. He said he knew it, and that I knew it too, I just didn't want to accept it. He thought we were destined to be together."

"That sounds a bit possessive, if you ask me."

"He was kind of possessive. You know that song by Diana Ross. I'm Still Waiting. You know that one?" Marco sang a snatch of the chorus.

Ros grimaced. "A gay man who likes Diana Ross? Whatever next?"

"Dean used to sing that song to me all the time. *I'm still waiting.* It was funny at first, but after a while it started to annoy me. He made me feel suffocated."

Having finished her meal, Ros wiped her mouth with a napkin and sat back with her arms folded. "You're not responsible, you know, for what he did. It was his decision. You shouldn't feel guilty."

"I do though," Marco said. "But mostly it's just that..."

"What?"

"Well...I don't know."

"Go on. You can tell me."

"I suppose I just...I miss him. You know?"

Ros nodded. "Well, it's almost the weekend. Go and let your hair down. You shouldn't be sitting around brooding at your age. Get yourself out there. Maybe you'll meet someone who can take your mind off things for a night or two."

"I doubt it," Marco said.

THOUGH HE KNEW Ros was right, Marco, in the end, spent the weekend alone. He set up his easel in the corner of the lounge and painted over a half-finished canvas, thinking to begin again but by the time the new undercoat was dry he'd lost interest. That image of Dean kept returning to him. The way Dean had looked when Marco had finally convinced Dean's landlady to let him inside the flat and they had found Dean lying white and bloated in a bathtub that looked as if it was filled with blood. The sight was etched on Marco's memory. There had been something considered in the way Dean lay, the razorblade still pinched between two fingers, as if even now he were posing. Marco couldn't help but see it as an exhibition Dean had put on just for him. He was sure he would never forget it as long as he lived. Never. And he would never forget the smell, or the landlady's piercing shrieks. He could hear them still, despite all the weeks that had passed.

He could not wait for Monday and the distraction of work. The beginning of the restoration.

WITHIN TWO WEEKS Marco had painstakingly cleared the dust and mould from *Je T'Amene* and was ready to begin the real restoration work:

reapplying paint to the worst affected areas. Visitors to the gallery would often gather around his cordoned off area to watch him work. Sometimes they would ask him about the painting or the artist, and he generally found them more receptive to his new found knowledge than Ros had been. There was one elderly woman, dressed in an expensive-looking horsehair coat, who visited so frequently that even Ros noticed.

"Think you've got an admirer," Ros said one day when they were lunching again in the greasy spoon café she loved so much.

"What?" Marco said, glancing around.

"Not *here*. Christ, you gay-boys have always got your radars up. I meant back at the gallery. That old woman. Well dressed. Very elegant. You must have noticed. She visits almost every day."

Marco nodded. "I know who you mean, but it's not me she comes for it's the painting."

"She must be eighty at least. Where's your cut-off point? Sixty? Sixty-five?"

"When it comes to women I don't have a cut-off point. They're all cut-off."

Ros appeared offended. "Such a waste. Have you never tried it with a woman?"

"I did have a girlfriend once."

Ros stopped chewing and glared at him. "*Did* you?"

"When I was young. And confused."

"What happened? You had to get rid of her when you realised you were gay as a maypole."

Marco laughed. "Will you stop it? No, she broke up with me actually. I never found out why. Not back then anyway."

"What do you mean?"

"I bumped into her years later in a club. She was out on a hen party— you know those things always hit the gay bars—and we got talking. She'd clearly had a lot to drink. She said she only broke up with me because of Dean. She claimed he threatened her. Really frightened her, apparently."

"Really? And you believe that?"

"No, not really. Dean could be possessive but he wasn't violent. Lizzie— that was the girl's name—Lizzie and Dean never got along. They hated each other, actually. She just wanted to blacken his name a bit, I think."

"I feel for poor Lizzie," Ros said with a sigh. "And that silly old dear dropping by every day at the gallery. Doesn't realise she's barking up the wrong tree."

"Will you give it a rest? She comes for the art. Have you seen the way she stares at the painting? Sometime I swear she has tears in her eyes."

Ros sat up and gave a bark of laughter. "I bet she's from The Hayek. You know they put a bid in for *Je T'Amene* and they're still so cut up about it they wouldn't loan us that early portrait work I wanted for the retrospective. They were planning their own, see? Have you spoken to her?"

"Only once. Had some kind of accent. French, possibly."

"What did she say to you?"

"Usual stuff they all ask. How was I going to go about restoring the painting? How did I know where to apply paint when there was no photograph of the painting to use as a reference? I explained to her that I could still see the shapes Sauvageon had mapped out on the canvas, and that it was just a matter of filling them in again. Even so, she did seem very worried about the whole thing, as if she had some kind of personal stake in it. There was one thing she said that I thought was a bit odd."

"Yes?"

"She said the painting should never have been found. Not yet. She said *not yet*. I wonder what she meant by that."

"Well did you perhaps think to ask?"

"Oh, she wandered off."

Ros shook her head. "I'll bet she is from The fucking Hayek. They're spying on us."

"Seriously?"

"They don't trust us to do the restoration properly. They always were up themselves, that lot."

"I'm sure she's not a spy from The Hayek, Ros. Probably just an art lover. Maybe she was a Sauvageon groupie, back in the day."

"Abstract Expressionist painters don't get groupies, Marco. Most of them were homo's anyway."

Marco rolled his eyes. "Now, now," he said. "Be nice."

IN THE DAYS following this conversation, Marco kept an eye out for the elderly French woman thinking to get to the bottom of whether or not she was a spy from The Hayek but she never reappeared. He put her to the back of his mind and concentrated his thoughts on the difficult job of touching-up the painting.

It took him a few days to mix his oil paint to the exact shade of blue Sauvageon had used. The difficult job then was matching the artist's brushwork, so he set up a raking light on one side of the canvas in order to better understand the thickness with which Sauvageon had applied the paint. Once this was done, he spent three days meticulously filling in all the missing blue. During this time, he couldn't help thinking about the strange symbols that were drawn onto the back of the canvas. At one point, finding himself alone, he turned the painting around and copied as many of the symbols down in his notebook as he could before, hearing footsteps at the end of the gallery, he hurriedly turned the painting around again. When he looked up to see who had entered, he saw an old woman stood by the barrier gazing at the picture. At first he thought it was the elderly French woman he'd discussed with Ros, but on a second glance he saw that he was mistaken. And there was no trace of a foreign accent when she spoke, unless you considered the north of England a foreign country and Marco knew people who did.

"Oh," the woman said. "There's a face."

"Sorry?" Marco removed his loupes and wiped his eyes on his sleeve, careful not to smear paint on himself.

"I thought it was supposed to be abstract expressionist. But there's a face."

"No, it's..." Marco turned to look at the painting. "It is abstract. It's..."

He took a step backwards so that he was closer to the old woman and narrowed his eyes. He saw at once that she was right. Something in the painting had coalesced now that he had filled in the blue areas, and he could indeed see within the composition a face. The face was not just a coincidence of the arrangement, but appeared to have been put there deliberately. Later, he would realise it was the shadows cast by the raking light which had exposed the face as when he switched it off he saw the face vanish.

"A young woman, I'd say," the old woman added.

Marco stood gazing at the painting. "The...the artist hated figurative painting. Did you know?"

"It's clear as day," the woman said. "There's a face."

THE DAYS WERE growing shorter. It was already dark when Marco left the gallery. As he walked home, he at one point noticed a car slowing alongside him. When he turned to look, the car sped up so that he didn't get to see the occupant although he had the impression that the driver was a woman. Later, as he nearer the entrance to his own building he heard the

15

sound of heels somewhere behind him but when he turned to look there was no one there.

Paranoid now, he thought as he searched for his keys. *That's all I need.*

As he entered the flat a sharp smell of turpentine hit him. Seeking distraction, and inspired by his work on the Sauvageon project, he'd began a new painting the previous evening. It sat on an easel in the corner of the lounge. Looking at it as he crossed to the kitchen, he suddenly saw Dean's face in the shapes he'd mapped out on the canvas.

"Fuck," he said, halting in his tracks.

He looked again to make sure it wasn't just some trick of the light. But there it was. The outline of Dean's face. He was certain of it.

He crossed to the picture, took one of the brushes from the pot of turpentine, dabbed it in some blue paint that had not yet dried and used it to try and eliminate the lines he'd painted the previous evening. Growing increasingly agitated, and unable to rub out the face with the brush, he picked up the pot of turpentine and poured it across the length of the painting. The only effect this had was to bring out the darker lines and make the face appear more prominent. Tears now spilling across his face, Marco turned and stormed into the kitchen, returning with a stake knife. He made to stab at the painting. He wanted to destroy it. Destroy it utterly. But the outline of Dean's face staring out at him made him pause and he broke down instead.

"Why'd you do it, you bastard?" he said between sobs. "Why'd you do this to me, you selfish fucking bastard? Why'd you leave like that? *Why?* Why'd you wanna make me feel so *guilty*?"

When he took a step back and saw the mess he'd made, he was horrified. Carefully, his hand shaking, he placed the knife down atop the stool he'd rested his mixing board on. He heard a voice in his head saying: *You're losing your shit, darling. Get it together. You're losing it.*

It was Dean's voice.

HE WENT TO bed and tossed and turned for hours, plagued by memories of Dean, until he finally fell asleep sometime in the early hours. The next morning he slept through his alarm. He woke around the time he should have been arriving at work, and leapt out of bed in a panic. The gallery had already opened by the time he arrived. When he got to his work area on the second floor he saw that there was a woman stood by the cordon gazing at the *Je T'Amene* painting. Though she had her back to him, he knew it was the French woman he and Ros had discussed. He recognised her long burgundy coat. Approaching her, it occurred to Marcus that he could perhaps make up for his lateness by finding out if Ros' suspicions were true and discover if the woman really was working for the Hayek Gallery. But before he reached her, the woman turned and looked at him and he was so taken aback that he halted in his tracks. At first he thought it wasn't the same woman, it couldn't be, but he was sure that it was. Only, she looked *younger*. It was as if someone had turned the clock back thirty years. Her hair was now blonde with only streaks of grey. The lines in her face had almost vanished. Before Marco could gather his wits the woman muttered something in French, turned, and hurried away towards the stairwell. He was tempted to call after her, but in the end he simply let her go.

Losing your shit, darling. Losing it.

Entering the cordoned-off area, he turned on the raking light and the face in the centre of the painting leapt out from the abstract shapes.

He stared at it for a few moments.

Didn't it look like the woman he'd just encountered?

He shook his head, deciding that he really was losing it. Before starting work, he decided to look for Ros, eventually finding her in the gallery's main room overseeing the hanging of Sauvageon paintings for the upcoming retrospective. Marco was stunned to see so much of the artist's work on display, from early portraits to his later abstracts. Many of the portraits were of a young blonde woman in various poses, and it was these that Marco couldn't take his eyes off. As he was examining one such picture, he was startled to hear Ros' voice close behind him.

"Put someone in a painting and they live on even after they die. Make that painting famous and they live forever."

"Huh? W-what's that?"

"A quote," Ros said.

"From who?"

She grinned. "Sauvageon of course. I might use that somewhere in the publicity."

"He said that?"

"Yes. And it's true, don't you think? Look at the Mona Lisa. She's still with us, still around, smiling enigmatically at multitudes of Japanese tourists. Da Vinci made her immortal."

Marco cast his eyes around the walls of the gallery. "It's true, isn't it? That's her. In all these pictures. Esme. Sauvageon painted her over and over again."

"Until he got to the abstracts."

17

"Even then..."

"Yes, I know."

"Listen, Ros, I think I need some time off."

"*What?*"

"I think I need a break. I think I'm...I don't know. I'm cracking up or something."

Ros' eyes widened. "Don't you fucking *dare*," she said in a hushed voice. "You've got a restoration to finish. It's going to hang right over there." Ros pointed to the far wall of the gallery, which was currently bare. "Pride of place. Don't let me down, Marco. We're counting on this exhibition being a success."

Marco shifted his eyes away from her gaze. "I'm not sure I should have taken it on. It's too much pressure. After Dean, I should have taken a holiday or..."

"Bullshit. Work is the best distraction."

"But I keep seeing faces. His face. Dean's."

"You're grieving, Marco. That's—"

"Last night I thought I was being followed."

"So you've got a stalker. Think yourself lucky."

"I can't do it, Ros. It's too much."

"Listen," Ros said in a low voice, drawing close to him. "I have absolute faith in you. You've done an excellent job so far. Now see it through to the end. Then you can have a holiday. Take yourself off to San Francisco, Barcelona, wherever. But finish the restoration first. This exhibition has to be a success. *Has* to be. I've...my job could be on the line here."

Marco turned from her, but meeting the gaze of the blonde woman in one of Sauvageon's portraits, he squeezed his eyes closed. In his mind's eye then he saw the face of the old French woman who had visited the gallery so many times to watch him work. But not so old. Not so old anymore.

"It's her," he said, opening his eyes again. "It's Esme."

"Marco," Ros said, studying his face in concern. "Get your shit together, okay?"

"She...she..." Marco stood for a moment with one hand pressed over his eyes.

"I need to leave early today. There's something I have to do. I'll make the time up tomorrow."

"Fine," Ros said, turning away. "But I need that restoration finished on time."

LEAVING THE GALLERY an hour early, Marco headed for the city library. He hoped to learn something about the symbols he'd copied in his notebook from the back of *Je T'Amene,* but as it turned out none of them appeared in any of the books he looked at. He could have gone home and done a search on the internet, but the thought of looking at occult symbols when he was alone at home made him uncomfortable. He could do it here, he realised, but all the library's computers appeared to be busy. Eventually, he went to the enquires desk where a small, rotund middle-aged man sat. The man's hair was a russet-red colour, obviously dyed, and he had a thin little moustache which Marco found repellent.

"Yes," the man said, looking at Marco over the rim of his glasses. Marco saw a glimmer of recognition in the man's eyes, then something in his face —a quick downward glance and purse of the lips.

"Ah. Do you have any more books on occultism? I was hoping to find out more about the meaning behind some of these symbols."

Marco laid his open notebook on the countertop. The man pushed his glasses up on his nose then studied the notebook for a few moments.

"It's your lucky day," the man said.

"How'd you mean?"

"I'm just what you're looking for."

"Sorry...?"

The man glanced up and winked. "I'm an amateur semiologist."

Marco shook his head.

"I love all this stuff. I find it fascinating. Maybe I can help."

"Oh I see. Well...great."

The man jabbed one of his stubby fingers at a page of the notebook. "This here looks like a scarab beetle. Ancient Egyptian. And see this over here—the snake eating its own tail? It's—ah yes." The man's finger moved. "This over here is called a Triqueta. It's a Celtic symbol. There's a real mix of iconography here—Ancient Egypt, The Celts, Chinese lettering, and—yes —there's even some Christian symbols. Some of these others I've never seen before, but I think I'd be correct in saying that the meaning's the same in all of them."

"The meaning?"

"It's pretty clear."

"Is it?"

"Yes. They're all symbols for life, death, and..." The man sat back in his chair and met Marco's eyes. "Resurrection."

"Resurrection? Really?"

"Quite. If you'd like to discuss it further, I get off in half an hour. We could..."

"No," Marco said, gathering up his notebook. "Thank you, but I have to...be somewhere."

"Oh well," the man said, with a rueful smile. "You know where I am. Anyway, it's resurrection. That's your theme there. Returning from the dead. I could do with a few of those symbols painted on me some mornings, you know what I mean?"

"What? Oh. Yes. Ha ha. Well...thank you." Marco clutched his notebook to his chest and stumbled away from the desk. "Thanks a lot."

"Any time," the man said, and winked again.

Once outside, Marco saw that the day had grown dark and it was raining hard. The city was all smudges of green, red and yellow light. His heart raced as he hurried down the library steps.

ONCE AGAIN, WHEN he went to bed, Dean filled his thoughts and he couldn't sleep. He was remembering the time when he and Dean had first entered into a relationship, how perfect it had been until Marco had decided he wanted to play the field. He saw now what a mistake that had been. He'd never known such a perfect fit again. He'd never been as happy as he had been when he and Dean were together. He tried to remember what had stopped him going back to Dean. Had he just been worried that it wouldn't work out, that he'd lose his best friend? Was that a good enough reason for them not to have given things another chance? Life could have been good again.

Now he'd never know. Now Dean was gone, and all Marco saw in his future was an endless series of one-night stands.

Kicking off the duvet, Marco got up and padded through to the lounge. There, his easel was still set up and propped upon it was the painting he'd started weeks ago. The canvas was stained from the turpentine he'd poured across it, and there were slashes of blue paint where he'd tried to obliterate the image of Dean's face, but his original intentions were still well mapped out and if he tilted the desk lamp he'd placed to one side, he could still see a rough outline of Dean's face in the centre of the picture.

Something took hold of him then. Fetching his notebook, he searched with trembling fingers for the pages on which he'd copied the symbols from the back of *Je T'Amene*. Then he turned his painting around and painstakingly began to copy the symbols from his notebook onto the back of the canvas.

20

"Crazy," he muttered to himself. "Going seriously fucking crazy."

But he didn't stop until he had covered the back of the canvas with all the different symbols. He set his paintbrush down and went into the kitchen to make tea. Cup in hand, he returned to the lounge, poured out new turpentine, squeezed fresh oils onto his palette, turned the painting to face front again, and set to work.

BY THE WEEKEND, Marco had convinced himself that he needed a night out. He wanted to celebrate completing the Sauvageon restoration; but he also hoped to escape thoughts of Dean if only for an evening. So he called some friends to meet for drinks and then a nightclub. By the time they arrived at the club, he knew it was a mistake. The friends were already tipsy but Marco still felt sober despite having matched them drink for drink. The alcohol only made him despondent. The spinning lights and pounding music were too much for him. And the first time a man tried to flirt with him he got a sick feeling in his stomach and turned his back. Then his friend Eddi appeared out of the throng on the dancefloor, grinning.

"See anything you like?"

"No, just basket shopping."

"Stick out your tongue," she said.

Marco put out his tongue without thinking and Eddi laid a tab of acid on it. Marco swallowed the acid but quickly regretted it. The music and lights soon became an even more bewildering cacophony. He kept thinking he saw Dean looking back at him from the mirrors behind the bar, but when he turned and tried to find him Dean was nowhere to be seen. He even followed one man to the toilets, thinking it was Dean, but after the man enticed him inside a cubicle, Marco realised it wasn't Dean at all—how could it be? It was someone much older. Some chicken hawk, as Dean would've said. Mumbling an apology, he fled. Immediately afterwards he said goodbye to his friends and headed home. He found himself weeping on the nightbus, not knowing exactly why. Arriving home, he went straight to bed and had a series of dreams about Dean. In between each one he woke briefly and found that his cheeks were once again wet. In the morning he wept again with the realisation that his dreams were now the only place where he would ever get to spend time with his oldest and dearest friend.

The next day he got up early and set to work on his home-painting. By evening it was complete. It was abstract, in the style of Sauvageon. A homage. But when he turned the desk lamp he was using to light the painting on and off, he saw the image of Dean's face appear and disappear from the centre of the picture, and he wondered to himself: *What have I done?*

THE NIGHT THE Sauvageon retrospective opened, as Marco mingled with the guests and tried to keep his nerves under control and his thoughts from carrying him away, he noticed a number of times Ros watching him with an expression of concern from across the room.

When Ros finally found a moment to cross the gallery and speak to him, Marco discovered the reason for her concern. He'd been at the buffet table refilling his plastic cup with wine when she caught hold of his elbow.

"Who're you, Richard Burton?"

Marco faced her and tried to smile. "I suppose I'm just nervous."

"Whatever for? Everyone thinks you've done a splendid job on the painting."

"I know. It's not that it's...Do you know much about Sauvageon's later life in New York?"

Ros rolled her eyes. "Not another lecture? Seriously. I should have got you up on a podium."

"He quit the art world in the early sixties, right? Just quit. *Je T'Amene* might've been his final painting."

Ros pursed her lips and nodded. "It's possible."

"But do you know why he quit? It was because of a woman. The books don't say a lot about her. She's like this shadowy figure. But Sauvageon quit painting, quit New York, and returned to France to live a pretty undisturbed life with this woman who had come back into his life. He gave it all up for love."

"Come back? Who was she?"

Marco glanced around then lowered his voice. "Could it have been Esme Rotchefort?"

Ros laughed, her head falling back. "What? You think he had her stuffed?"

"What if I told you he found a way to bring her back to life?"

Ros didn't laugh this time, but looked closely into his face instead. "I'd say it's time you switched to something non-alcoholic. Want me to get you a coffee?"

"What about all that occult stuff he was into? Those symbols on the backs of his paintings? Esme was his one true love, right? Would he have given up everything for anyone else? You *can* bring people back, Ros, I know you can. I...Sauvageon found a way."

Ros gazed into his face for a long moment. "Marco? Are you okay? Do you want me to drive you home?"

"Look," he said. "Look." He dug into the pocket of his jeans, taking out his house keys and his wallet and placing them on the buffet table before he found what he was looking for. It was a page torn from his notebook on which he'd copied some of the symbols from the back of *Je T'Amene*. He unfolded it and thrust it in front of Ros' face so abruptly that she drew back. "See? It's resurrection. That's what all the symbols were for. He resurrected Esme. Her face is in the painting. In *Je T'Amene*."

Ros glanced across the room to where *Je T'Amene* hung. "I don't see a face. It's abstract." She looked back at Marco. Besides concerned, she now looked confounded. "Is this about Dean?"

Marco tilted his head back, closed his eyes and drew in a long ragged breath. "I loved him, Ros. That's what I've realised. I can't stop thinking about him. He was the love of my life and now he's gone. I've realised too late."

Ros glanced to one side, noticing that some of those gathered were taking an interest in their conversation. "Don't say that," she said, facing Marco again. "There'll be someone else. You'll feel the same about someone else some day, I promise. Why don't you take a couple of weeks leave from tomorrow? You've earned it. Get some rest."

Suddenly irritated, Marco brushed her hand away as she made to place it on his arm with the clear intension of steering him towards the door. "Don't touch me. You're always touching me."

"I'm sorry. I only..."

"You need a raking light, Ros. You need a fucking raking light to bring out the shadows...the...the *truth*."

Ros turned to a group of people who had glanced their way and gave a reassuring smile, before turning back to Marco and saying in a hushed voice: "What are you talking about?"

"Nothing. Never mind."

Marco turned his back on her. He needed to get away, away from all those people crowding in on him. He made for the exit with Ros calling after him, but he didn't look back. A woman crossed his path, her eyes meeting his, and he realised it was *her* again. It was Esme. That face that was now so familiar from all the time he'd spent working on *Je T'Amene* under the raking light—there it was right before his eyes rendered not with

23

paint but in flesh and blood. To his amazement he saw that she had grown younger still, her hair now a lustrous blonde, her face free from lines and wrinkles, her eyes blue and bright. She was beautiful. And she was looking at him as if the two of them shared a secret. Marco opened his mouth to say something, but before he could she had turned and pushed her way into the throng. Ros was still calling after him, and the thought crossed his mind to tell Ros about the woman, about Esme. *She's here tonight. She's grown younger again. She looks just like she does in Sauvageon's early portraits. Look! Look!* But he knew Ros wouldn't believe him. She'd tell him again that he'd had too much to drink. So he ran.

It was raining outside, but he decided to walk home anyway. The walk would clear his mind and sober him up. He took the back streets. He didn't want to walk the main roads with all those faces glaring at him from the passing cars. He only headed back to the main stretch when he was almost home and happened to look over his shoulder and notice a man further along the street who appeared to be following him. He couldn't make out the man's face, but the sight was enough to unnerve him. He hurried on, taking a few turns until he reached a bypass busy with traffic.

Not until he arrived home did he realise he'd left his keys and wallet back at the gallery. The anger and frustration he'd managed to walk off rose in him again.

"Oh fuck fuck fuck!"

Glancing up at his building then, he saw that the bedroom window of his apartment was lit up. As he tried to remember if he'd left it on that morning, he saw a figure cross in front of the window, just briefly, too sudden for him to make out. His heart did a little back flip and his throat felt suddenly dry. He ran to the set of buzzers next to the main entrance and pressed the one for his own apartment. When he heard the click of the intercom, he shouted into the voxer:

"Dean? *Dean?*"

No one answered. There was a buzz and he heard the door release. The time he spent in the lift seemed interminable. His heart was hammering and a tumble of emotions coursed through him, making his head feel light. Was it true? Had it worked? Could it really be possible that his altering of *Je T'Amene* could lead to...

"Dean?" he shouted, banging a fist on his own front door. "Dean!"

A door across the hall opened and an old man put his face briefly in the gap before closing it again. Marco heard footsteps inside his own apartment. Someone was opening the door from the inside. Marco thought

24

in that one brief moment that his elation would overwhelm him. He'd done it. He'd actually done it. He'd brought Dean back to life.

A little fear crept into his heart as the door swung open.

But on seeing the face that greeted him from inside, Marco felt not fear or elation but confusion. Then a sudden anger.

"*Ros!*"

His disappointment was so acute he wanted to scream.

Ros, showing him a sheepish expression, shrugged. He noticed that she was wearing one of his own shirts and she had it unbuttoned almost to the navel. Part of him wanted to laugh out loud. What was she doing? Didn't she realise how ridiculous she looked? He took a deep breath, trying to contain his simmering emotions.

"Ros? Please explain. What...what are you doing here?"

She shrugged again. "You left your keys and wallet at the gallery. I thought I could wait for you."

"Why are you wearing my shirt? Where are your own clothes?"

"I got soaked through coming up from the car. You don't mind, do you? I thought you might need some company tonight. You know? You seemed so upset. I thought you'd left your keys back there as some sort of...I don't know...a sign. Like you were telling me you wanted me to—"

"That's the most ridiculous thing I've ever heard. Why would I do that, Ros? W*hy*?"

Behind him, Marco heard the door across the hall opening again. Twisting around, he yelled at the face pushing out through the gap.

"Why don't you mind your own *fucking* business, eh?"

The door snapped shut.

He was sobbing then, great heaving sobs, and Ros was leading him inside and then helping him off with his coat and then his wet clothes. She guided him towards the bedroom. Then she was lying him down in his bed and for some reason slipping in beside him and pulling the duvet up over them both.

"Ros," he said, hearing the bluntness in his own voice. "Go home."

"But I thought..."

"You thought wrong. Go home. Go. I don't want you here."

After a pause she got up from the bed. Marco lay staring at the ceiling.

In his peripheral vision, he could see Ros going about the room collecting up her clothes. Buttoning up her blouse, she stopped by the window, looking out at the street below.

"I really am sorry, Marco. I honestly thought..."

25

"It doesn't matter. Just leave. Please. I need to be alone."

Ros was silent a moment, still staring out of the window. "I saw your painting. The one in the lounge. It's good. Derivative, obviously. The *Je T'Amene* restoration's clearly had quite an impact on you. "

You don't know the half of it, Marco thought, wanting to laugh again.

"It's good though. Good work."

"Thank you. Now if you don't mind—"

"Shit," Ros said then. "He saw me."

Marco opened his eyes. He looked at Ros who had ducked to one side of the window. "What is it?"

"Just some guy. Hanging around out there."

Marco rolled over onto his side. He wrapped his arms around himself, feeling clammy and cold. He wanted to scream, cry, shout. But there was nothing left. Nothing. He felt numb. He got up from the bed.

"I'm going to take a shower. You can let yourself out. Right?"

Ros said nothing. She peered towards the window. "Do you mind if I stay for a few more minutes. That guy down there. He gives me the creeps. Can I just wait here until he's gone?"

"Whatever," Marco said over his shoulder as he moved towards the bathroom.

The hot water of the shower soothed him and he began to think perhaps he'd been too hard on Ros. He was the one after all, who'd let himself get embroiled in some ridiculous fantasy, thinking painting someone into a picture with silly symbols on the back could restore them to life. When he'd arrived home and seen the light on and the figure moving across the window, he'd wanted so much to believe that Dean was here. But how could he have ever let himself think that? Dean had killed himself. Slit his own wrists. Dean was dead. Dead, dead, dead. He wasn't coming back. Ever. And there was no use crying about it. The only thing to do was just to get on with life.

He decided he ought to apologise to Ros, try and explain what had been going on in his mind and why he'd been so angry, but before he left the shower he heard what sounded like the front door opening, and he was glad. A few days was what he and Ros needed to see how foolish they'd both been. They would laugh about it on Monday, he was sure of it: in the greasy spoon café over chips and beans and a veggie burger.

When he turned off the shower, Marco heard someone singing softly in the living room and he felt a new pang of annoyance. Why couldn't Ros just go home like he'd asked? Hadn't he been clear enough, or was she going to use some man wandering around outside as an excuse to stay for the entire night until he somehow miraculously stopped being gay and they could jump into bed together?

Opening the bathroom door a crack, he realised what he'd heard was actually music playing on the stereo system. Angry now, he yanked the door open further intending to storm into the living room and confront Ros. But then he froze, one hand on the door handle, the other clutching the towel around his waist. From the lounge he heard the voice of Diana Ross.

I'm...still...waaaaiting, she sang. *La la la la la la.*

Without realising what he was doing, Marco closed the bathroom door again and locked it. For a few moments he stood still, not knowing what to do. His gaze settled on the bathroom's one small window and for a second he actually contemplated climbing out of it.

What have I done? What the hell have I done?

No, he thought then. *I'm being ridiculous. Ros must have put that music on. Ros must be playing some kind of silly game.*

Thinking this, he immediately unlocked the bathroom door and pulled it open.

"Ros!" he called as he stepped out into the hall. "Ros, I'd really appreciate it if you'd just go home like I asked. This is—"

He glanced into the bedroom as he passed. Ros was not there. He followed the sound of the music toward the lounge. A jittery fear took hold of him again, so he called out, "Ros? Ros? Can you hear me?"

Before he reached the lounge he noticed that the front door stood open. Huffing to himself, and shaking his head, Marco went to close the door but then with a jolt he saw the body lying in the corridor outside. From where he stood he could see only the lower half, but he knew at once that it was Ros. He recognised her imitation Gucci leather pumps. Unconsciously dropping the towel, he ran naked to the door.

"Ros! Ros!"

She lay face down. The hair at the back of her head was matted with blood. There was more blood on the tiles beneath her head. He was startled by how bright it was under the corridor's strip lights, how red.

"*Ros!*"

Crouching beside Ros' still body, Marco sensed another presence nearby. Looking up he was alarmed to see that there was a man stood at the far end of the corridor, in the gloom at the top of the stairwell, staring back at him. The man was only there a moment, but Marco was sure that it

27

was Dean. The sight froze him to the spot and a wave of horror and disbelief passed through him. As soon as their eyes met, Dean had turned and scurried away down the steps, but Marco had time to notice the expression on Dean's face. It was an expression Marco had seen before, first long ago when he'd told Dean about his girlfriend Lizzie; and more recently when he'd started dating that guy Travis. It was an expression of anger, hurt and betrayal.

Before Dean fled he tossed something towards Marco which clattered loudly against the tiles. Startled, Marco glanced around and saw lying on the floor at his side a hammer. He picked it up and felt the weight of it. The blunt end of the hammer was wet with blood. Stuck in the blood were a few hairs.

Raising himself on trembling legs, Marco moved to the top of the stairwell. He could see no one, but he heard rapid footsteps descending.

"Dean? What've you...? *Dean!*"

At the same time Marco heard the door opposite the entrance to his apartment opening, and he was suddenly aware that he was naked, that there was a body outside his door, and—most acutely—that he was still holding the hammer.

Unwritten Songs

*I*T ALL STARTED when I wrote that one song. "Lily's Song." Though I'm not sure "wrote" is the right word. The song just came to me. Some songs are hard-won. You jam for hours until you stumble across a riff or a chord pattern or some kind of hook. Then you fine-tune it; add a bridge, maybe a middle-eight, then the words. Sometimes the words come first and you struggle for weeks, or months, or even years, trying to come up the right melody to go along with them.

"Lily's Song" came to me in my sleep. It was like a gift. I woke up in the middle of the night with the melody going around and around in my head. It was sometime after Destine and I broke up; after I'd sold the apartment and moved into a bedsit in the basement of that big Victorian house on Wellington Road opposite the disused railway line. Though I'd traded leafy Clifton for the inner city, I told myself that a bedsit room was all I needed. It meant I could continue to pursue music rather than go out and find a job, which was what Destine had wanted me to do. I'm just not cut out for a 9-to-5 life. I'm not some office-lackey. As I tried to explain to Destine, being a singer-songwriter isn't something you choose. It's a calling. "Some calling," Destine threw back at me. "You haven't actually finished a song in years." She visited the bedsit once with some of my old records, which she said had got mixed in with hers. Johnny Cash, *At Folsom Prison*—how could I not have missed that? But she didn't stay long. Days later when I spoke to her on the phone, she explained why.

"That place you're living in now...it feels haunted."

Had Destine and I still been together, I would never have dared get up from bed in the middle of the night and start strumming my guitar. We'd argued about my doing that too many times. Destine's job at the hospital meant she had to be up early every day, and looking presentable. She didn't understand what it meant to be a slave to the muses. But for our split, "Lily's Song" would never have been written.

Or maybe it would. There was something nagging, kind of insistent, about that melody and those words. They demanded to be set down. Once I'd got the chords worked out on guitar, the words were there on my lips right away.

The sun shone down into the room
The green grass invited me
A gentle breeze stirred the leaves
Of the eucalyptus tree

My heart it wanted nothing more
Than to be there in that day's long dream
Oh, my heart it wanted nothing more
Than to be there in that day's long dream

My name is Lily
Sing a song for me
A kiss like winter
Touch like frost
Sing a song for me

The sun shone down into the room
And touched me where I lay
I did not wake, I did not stir
A stillness lay upon that day
And settled on to me

And I am lost, forgotten now
A hundred years or more
Who will think of me and smile?
Who will speak my name aloud?

My name is Lily
Sing a song for me
A kiss like winter
Touch like frost
Sing a song for me

When I finished singing those words for the first time, I sat on the edge of my bed in stunned silence. I'd never had a song come to me so instantaneously and fully-formed before. I'd heard that Keith Richards dreamt the riff to "Satisfaction" and I'd had moments like that myself, especially back in The Glamour Drag days when my inspiration tended to be more chemical-dependent; but I'd never had a song presented to me out of the blue. I must've had the whole thing worked out in less than half an hour.

The words meant nothing to me. I didn't know where they'd come from. I didn't know anyone named Lily. The other odd thing was that most of my songs are written in C or G minor—those being the places my fingers always seem to find first on the guitar—but "Lily's Song" was written in B. I'd never written a song in B before. If you'd asked me before that night to find the B chords on my guitar, I'm not sure I'd have been able to.

I started scrabbling in the clutter around me for the old tape deck I always recorded my songs on to. I first began using it before I got involved with The Glamour Drag; back when my songs were just a form of expression, a way I found of communicating, not even songs really, words and chords and feelings that had to be exorcised, lanced out of me. Using that tape deck had become a ritual. I'd tried recording onto a computer, but it felt wrong somehow, sterile. And the songs I recorded that way always sounded shit once I listened back. So I'd stuck with my little tape machine. I'd hit those Play/Record buttons so many times it was a miracle they hadn't stuck.

The tape deck was under my bed all covered in dust. I took it out, wiped it over with my palm, and set it on my desk. There was a cassette tape already inserted, containing sketches of songs I'd been working on months ago. I rewound to the beginning and hit Play/Record. Then I got as close to the mic as I could and sang "Lily's Song" through from beginning to end. As soon as I was done, I rewound the tape and hit Play. I wanted to hear it. I wanted to know if the song was as good as I thought it was. My finger hesitated a moment over the button. What if the song wasn't any good? What if it was some rip-off? That'd happened to me before. You think you're on to a winner then you realise it's "Friday, I'm In Love" by The Cure

The only light I had on was a desk lamp set on the bedside table and turned towards the wall so that the glow was subdued. Sitting there, in that near-darkness I could hear the silence, almost feel it. It was that stillness you get at four or five-o'clock in the morning, when the streets outside are quiet and everyone's asleep. It was the perfect atmosphere in which to hear "Lily's Song" for the first time. A shiver of pleasure ran up my spine at the first strum of the guitar, then again when my voice began. I was singing a little higher than I normally did in order to fit the song's B-chord pattern. When it reached the chorus, I sat up straight and an icy wave flashed through my body. I stopped the tape, did a quick rewind, and listened again. There was another voice singing along on the chorus one octave or so above mine, at least that's what it sounded like. Stunned, I stopped the tape, rewound and listened again, thinking maybe it had been a fault with the player or else the tape was getting old and stretched. I must have done this eight or nine times. But there was no mistake. There was a female voice joining in with me, only on the chorus.

My name is Lily
Sing a song for me
A kiss like winter
Touch like frost
Sing a song for me.

Sitting on my bed, I felt the hairs go up on the back of my neck, as if someone had touched me there. I looked around the room and peered into all corners. I was, of course, alone.

WHEN I WAS TWENTY-EIGHT years old I died.

I actually died.

I overdosed on heroin after a Glamour Drag gig in Stockholm. They told me later that my heart stopped beating for three whole minutes. Any longer and I could have been brain damaged.

You could say I was lucky, but I think back then I wanted to die. I was at war with myself. I wrote this one song for The Glamour Drag called "Smear," which was about wiping myself out of existence, erasing myself, which is what I think I wanted. The band and the management were well prepared. They knew it was only a matter of time, so they had the Narcan on hand for just such an emergency. It's to this that I owe my life.

People ask me sometimes—usually these hippie chicks I've ended up in bed with—if I remember anything from those three minutes when I lay dead. I've often wondered about that myself. There was no tunnel of light, I can tell you that. I do have this freaky memory of lying on my back in the middle of a field, with the sun or some other very bright light high overhead, and people drawing in around me. The light was behind them so I couldn't see their faces, but I had the impression they'd been waiting. They began to reach down and clutch at me, all of them at once; but then I opened my eyes and saw the face of Dave Wren, The Glamour Drag's guitarist. Dave was the straightest man I've ever known to play in a rock and roll band. He should have been a bank manager.

"You fucking idiot," Dave said. "You selfish fucking bastard."

SOMETHING ABOUT THAT female voice, whether it was real or some kind of recording glitch on the tape, spooked me, so I erased the cassette and did my best to forget about "Lily's Song." The following Friday I had a gig lined up at Mr. Wolf's. It had been arranged by my sometime manager Ed. Ed had been a huge fan of The Glamour Drag, and he thought my artistic resurgence was just around the next corner. The hours he put in booking and promoting my shows were done mainly on goodwill and whatever percentage he took from the door, which can't have been very much. In the days leading up to the Mr. Wolf's gig, I avoided Ed's calls. I was becoming increasingly nervous, and his enthusiasm would only make me feel worse. Ed believed in me, and that was the problem. I always had a sense that if I stumbled I'd be letting him down, somehow soiling all the years he'd spent listening to The Glamour Drag and all the memories he had of seeing us live during our glory days. Back then, I obliterated my stage-fright with alcohol and drugs, but playing shows sober was an entirely different prospect. As soon as I knew I'd won the audience over, the nerves vanished, but getting to that point was often hard. Mr. Wolf's was a young crowd, students mostly, many of whom weren't even born when The Glamour Drag appeared on the front page of *NME*.

On the day of the gig, I felt self-conscious about my thinning hair, so went onstage in a white ushanka hat I'd bought in Moscow years ago when The Glamour Drag toured our first album. It was hot under that hat. Rivulets of sweat were already running down my face and dripping off my chin as I tuned my guitar. The floor was packed, but no one seemed to be looking my way; and the hubbub of conversation was so loud I didn't know how I was going to silence it. There were tricks I could pull out of course: open with a Glamour Drag song or a cover, something they might recognise; or else start with the noisiest and most confrontational of my solo compositions and force them to listen. For some reason, though, as I approached the mic, I found my fingers looking for those B chords on the guitar. Without any real thought, I started playing "Lily's Song." It came to me as easily as it had the first time I played it, and from the opening note a hush fell over the crowd.

It was as though I'd stopped time. All eyes were now turned towards me. As my gaze drifted over those faces before me, I saw Ed amidst the throng near the front of the stage. His mouth hung open and he looked mesmerised. Not in the fake, eager-to-please way he sometimes did when I played him a new song. This was genuine. As my attention drifted towards

33

the bar, I noticed a young woman with long red hair standing alone in a corner of the room. The stage lights were dazzling, so I couldn't make her out well, but I could see that she was swaying from side to side and I thought I saw her lips moving. When I finished the song and looked for her again, she was no longer there.

A moment later I was startled by the kind of applause I hadn't heard for fifteen years.

"YOU FUCKING IDIOT. You selfish fucking bastard."

Not exactly the words you hope to hear when risen from the dead.

I didn't know it then, but I would find out soon enough that it was all over for The Glamour Drag. The others in the band couldn't cope with my behaviour any longer, so they'd decided it was finished. And just when the record company thought we were about to go big-time with our third album, which never got released.

I was selfish.

At the time I just thought *fuck them*, and started another band straight away. For the first time in my life I had a voice. I was *somebody*, and I wasn't about to let that go. I was the star, not those fuckers in the background. That's what people had been telling me. I called the new band Lazarus. Geddit? But it wasn't the same. The chemistry wasn't there with the new players; I could feel it every time we stepped on stage. We were all pulling in different directions. The music press wouldn't get behind us. We released two songs on 7-inch vinyl then called it a day.

The comedown was horrible.

A week later I was down the job centre in flares and high-heeled boots hoping to find something that didn't involve getting up early. I never did.

ED CALLED. HE had good news.

He'd been talking, he said, to Yan Weir about my storming set at Mr. Wolf's.

"Who the fuck is Yan Weir?"

"Dove Tundra records."

"Who?"

"He runs it. They're a small label, but they've got prestige. Yan used to work for EMI. He was the one who signed Peculiar Church."

"Who?"

"Jazz-funk trip-hop fusion band from Birmingham. Never heard them? They're pretty good."

"Really? Because it sounds fucking awful."

"Yan's a cool guy. He's interested in putting out a single with a view to making an album. You've got new songs, right?"

"I...sure."

"Yan's going to drive down on Thursday so that you can play him a few numbers. Then he'll decide which one he wants to put out."

"He only wants one song?"

"At the moment. He said he'll consider putting out an album depending on how well the single does."

"Fuck."

"I know. You *have* got new songs?"

"I'll write some."

COME THURSDAY THE nerves were back, so much so that I considered going to the off-license and buying a bottle of vodka. It doesn't matter how much time you spend in rehab, that little voice in the back of your mind never really goes away. When the phone rang and I heard Ed's voice, part of me hoped he was about to tell me Yan Weir had cancelled. Instead he said:

"Seven, okay?"

"Seven o'clock?"

"Yeah. You got the songs prepared?"

"Yes."

Buoyed on adrenaline, I'd managed to finish two new songs in as many days. The one I was most confident about was a folksy ballad called "Sleepless," which I imagined having a discordant hum of electric guitar low in the mix on the recorded version.

"Brilliant," Ed said. "This is it, man. I can feel it. Rock star Loudon Waltz is about to get back in the game."

I cringed when he said that. At the same time, I had glanced up and caught sight of myself in the mirror above the sink: thin whiskered face; shadowed eyes; and long hair scraped sideways over visible scalp. I didn't look like anyone's idea of a rock star.

THE NEXT THING I knew Ed, Yan Weir and a young blonde, possibly Yan's girlfriend and possibly Russian as she'd shown a lot of interest in my ushanka hat, were sat on my bed drinking tea whilst I tuned my guitar. Yan was a youthful, fiftish man and very self-contained which didn't help my nerves. He wore a shirt and tie, but with jeans and trainers—I suppose to show that he was part business man, part rock-and-roller. It seemed to take me an age to tune up, but all three sat in silence and sipped their tea as they waited. When I was finally satisfied, I looked up and said, "Uh, this is called 'Sleepless.'"

Then, just as I struck the first chord on the guitar a framed copy of the artwork from the second Glamour Drag album, *Spitting at the Sky*, which I had on the wall above my desk, flew from its hook and smashed against the opposite wall. The Russian woman screamed so loud it sheared my nerves. Everyone in the room stood up and stared in disbelief at the bits of broken glass and picture frame lying on the floor at the foot of the bed. Ed started laughing under his breath and I stared at him.

"Loudon? What the...did you *see* that?"

"What just happened?"

"It flew, man. It just *flew*."

I was reeling. Desperation set-in. "It...it happens sometimes. When the trains go by. The house shakes. This stuff happens."

"Trains? What trains?"

"Didn't you feel it? The train...? They go right through here. Just..."

"Dude, it flew right off the fucking wall."

"It's the trains, man, I'm telling you."

It took some time to get everyone settled again, the Russian woman in particular. She kept pacing the room, crossing herself and muttering in her own language. I was unsettled myself, but I was determined that Yan Weir would hear my songs.

"Okay," I said, when they were all perched precariously on the bed once more. "Sorry about that. So...yeah...this is called 'Sleepless.'"

I hadn't even strummed the guitar this time. A cupboard above the sink flew open and a few tins and packets shot across the room as if they'd been fired out of a cannon. I saw it with my own eyes. One of the packets hit the Russian woman in the back of the head so that she screamed again and went on screaming. Ed wasn't laughing this time. All the colour had drained from his face.

"Loudon, man, what the fuck is going on in here?"

"I don't know, Ed. I don't know. Just...just sit down and give me one more chance, okay?"

"Yan's missus is freaking out. Look at her."

"Just one more chance. Please. Then you can all leave if you want to."

Ed looked at Yan. Yan nodded, but the Russian woman wasn't staying. She told Yan that she would wait in the car. When she was gone I picked up my guitar again, took a deep breath, and began playing "Lily's Song."

By the time I'd finished Yan was grinning and clapping.

"That's it," he said. "That's the one." He stood up. "Now if it's all the same to you I'm getting the hell out of here."

EVER SINCE I WAS a boy, I felt I didn't belong here. Something about this world didn't feel right to me. I couldn't understand it. I felt like everyone else was speaking a different language, like they'd all been a party to something I'd been excluded from. Nothing felt real. As I got older I became convinced that it was me, not the world, that was wrong. Drugs and alcohol were just something to hide behind. In a weird way I thought that doing those things made me like everybody else.

These days it's different. I don't feel like hiding any more; at least not too often. When I walk the streets, I ignore the traffic and the people and I listen to the birds singing instead. I look at the sky, and I feel at home. I look at the stars. There's something out there, something *real*, but most people don't see it. There's a barrier. I feel like it's my job to break that barrier down.

ONE FRIDAY EVENING the phone rang and it was Destine. It had been about three months since we last spoke.

"I've just heard it," she said. "I've just heard 'Lily's Song' on the radio. Loudon, it's beautiful. I almost cried."

"On the radio? Which station?"

"One of the local ones, I think. Loudon, congratulations! It's the best thing you've ever done."

I asked her if this meant we were getting back together. She laughed and hung up the phone.

Sometime later Ed called. He said that he'd heard from Yan Weir who'd told him the download sales for "Lily's Song" were into quadruple figures and the first vinyl pressing had already sold out. Not only that, but Radio 2 were putting the song on their playlist.

"You're kidding me."

"It's a hit, Loudon. A bonafide hit. Yan said he definitely wants an album."

"Did he?"

"Yeah. He wants more songs like 'Lily's Song.' More songs in that vein."

My enthusiasm wilted. I held the phone away from my ear and gazed towards the window. A line of stationary traffic was lined up along the road as it usually was at this time of day. Evening rush hour. I could feel more than hear the thrum of all those idling engines, vibrating up through the floor and into my body. I could see the glassy look on the faces of the people inside the cars as they thought about getting home, then getting back, getting home and getting back, doing it all again, over and over, endlessly. There was something terrible about the sight. It gave me shivers.

"I don't know, Ed. That song was kind of a one-off. It's not even about me, it's..."

"What do you mean?"

I tried hard to articulate what I felt. "It's somebody else's song."

Ed's tone turned serious. "What are you saying, Loudon? That you didn't write it?"

"No, I did write it. I did. Kind of."

"What's the problem then? Write some more like that. Yan wants an album's worth."

Before I could add anything, Ed hung up.

I THINK I know what Destine meant that time she said my bedsit felt haunted. I'd felt it myself, from the first moment I stepped inside the door. It had an odd atmosphere: kind of dank and sad. Sorrowful, that's the word. Perhaps at the time, I'd thought it was me giving off that air, what with the break-up and losing my apartment, which was the only thing I'd got to hang on to from the Glamour Drag days. One time, during the recording of *Spitting at the Sky*, Dave Wren was sitting in the control room watching as I did a vocal on a song called "Living with the Lost." I'd shot up before going in there and started nodding off half-way through the song. And Dave lost it. He started yelling and screaming, pulling at his hair and flailing his arms around, going totally bananas. He was so angry at me. Only, because I was inside the vocal booth I couldn't hear him. I could see that he was furious, but it was like his anger couldn't reach me. He was like a bottle that had been stoppered. I felt sorry for him in a way, that he hadn't realised I couldn't hear, that though his anger was so very real his voice had been cut-off. That's kind of the same feeling I had when I first moved into the bedsit, like there was a person here somewhere upset and angry and stuck behind soundproof glass.

38

Does that make sense? I suppose it doesn't. You'd have to experience it to fully understand. Only that weird, sad, stifled air is gone now. There's been a change in this room. Maybe it's the spring sunshine shining in the window, but it feels different now. It feels cheery, hopeful. *Satisfied?* It's an atmosphere that makes me uncomfortable. I feel as if I've had something stolen from me. That's another thing no one else could really understand.

ED LINES UP the interviews and every single journo wants to know who Lily is. I tell them I don't know. I tell them the song came to me out of the ether. This seems to make them even more curious.

There are royalties and door-takings these days. Actual money. I feel like a fraud whenever it's handed to me.

The venues I play have increased in size. No more Mr. Wolf's. Now it's academies and arenas. These are the kind of venues I always dreamed of playing as a solo artist, but never expected to. And the audience has swelled. At every gig the crowd heckle and jeer until I play "Lily's Song." Afterwards, half of the audience leave and those that stay start talking amongst themselves. They don't want to hear my own songs. It's always "Lily's Song," "Lily's Song." Well, I'm sick of playing "Lily's Song." If I spend the rest of my life playing "Lily's Song," what's going to happen to my voice? People don't listen to The Glamour Drag albums anymore. Who's going to break those barriers down and show people what's real. Where's my song?

Who's going to sing a song for me?

WE NEVER MADE the album. Ed keeps asking how the new songs are coming on, but I don't answer. It's not that there aren't any songs. There are. At least, there could be.

There are many nights now when I wake up in the early hours with these nagging melodies going around in my head. It happens time and time again, so that most nights I barely sleep. Either that or its fragments of lyrics about other people's lives, people I've never met. They all want a voice; they all want to be heard. They all want their story told. My fingers itch to pick up my guitar, but I don't get up. I toss and turn instead. It's torture sometimes: I can feel how much these songs want to be sung. I had to go to the doctor and ask for a prescription of sleeping pills. You should have seen her face when she asked what was keeping me awake at night and I said:

"Unwritten songs."

The Stench

*T*HE STINK WAS first noticed in the centre of the village, along Buxford's High Street. That morning, at exactly six minutes past nine, Mr. Pugh the bank manager paused at the point of declining a loan application and twitched his nostrils. His eyes left the computer screen and shifted towards the open window. The fragrant summer air drifting in to his office had suddenly become thick with a damp and earthy smell not unlike the one he always encountered in the basement of his house. In fact, so immediately familiar was the smell that his face flushed red and he had a moment of panic, imagining that his basement stood open and that this smell was emanating outwards from there. Then he reminded himself that his house was two miles away, the basement always kept locked, and he the sole key holder. Most obviously, he assured himself, the smell of a single basement could not be so pervasive as to travel such a distance from his home to his place of work. He got up to close the window, but when he sat down again he found that the fleeting grip of panic had unsettled him so much that he accidentally approved the loan application instead of declining it.

A few doors down from the bank, eighty-year old Miss Owen was standing in a short queue outside the baker's and muttering insults at everyone who caught her eye. When she inhaled the smell on the air, her eyes welled with tears. Before anyone else in the queue noticed, Miss Owen had begun sobbing inconsolably. Since she was well-known in the village as a bad-tempered spinster who preferred the company of cats to people and who had a not-entirely-pleasant odour all of her own, no one knew quite how to console her. She was eventually led inside the baker's where a chair was found so she could sit down. When Louise, the shopgirl, asked what the matter was, all anyone could make out of the words Miss Owen said between sobs were: "It was her perfume. See? I always loved it. Because you could always smell *her* underneath." When these words were only met with confusion, she yelled at the concerned faces gathered around her, and stamped one foot like a disgruntled child. "She wanted me to go with her. But I said no. I said no! I wanted to but it was wrong. Wrong, they said! Wrong!"

At that moment, from outside the shop, a horn blared. Robbie Bradbrook, having finished his paper round, was returning to the newsagents when the smell hit him full in the face. As he crossed the street, his feet slipped from the pedals of his bike and he toppled sideways into the path of an oncoming car. The car braked. Seeing the registration plate inches from his face, Robbie, in his confusion, laughed. Overwhelmed by the sharp locker room smell that had assailed him from nowhere, Robbie clamoured to his feet, picked up his bike and hurried off up the high street in the wrong direction from the newsagents, thinking about something Ben Waddle had asked him that one time they were alone together in the showers after football practice.

The car that had nearly run Robbie over was being driven by Mrs. Lancastle, or Doctor Lancastle as she preferred to be known. Doctor Lancastle had been in a something of a hurry. Such a trial had it been to get her two teenaged children out of bed and packed off to school that she was late for her first patient at the GP surgery. Incensed, she lowered her car window to yell at Robbie as he stumbled away and immediately noticed a strong not-unpleasant smell which she at first thought was that of some kind of fruit, possibly berries. Rather it was, she quickly realised, the smell of the codeine pills she had been prescribing herself, under an assumed name, for more than a year now. The exact same smell, but magnified. She hardly noticed the smell when she popped open the pill bottle; but evidently it had embedded itself into her subconscious. Feeling a flush of shame, she raised the car's window and went on her way, with only a toot for Robbie as she passed him instead of the verbal reprimand she had intended.

By mid-morning the smell had reached the outskirts of town.

They must be laying manure in the fields again, thought Mrs. Dobson, head of Buxford Church of England Primary, as she crossed the school yard after morning assembly. She ignored that it was the wrong time of year for muck spreading; plus the fact that the stink reminded her more of the inside of the care home where she'd incarcerated her elderly mother. This had mostly been done to satisfy Mr. Dobson, who'd said he wouldn't stand for his mother-in-law stinking out his home in her final years. Every time Mrs. Dobson entered the care home she felt the same mix of guilt and despair which had now become associated with the mixed aroma of shit and boiled cabbage.

Retired army corporeal, Mr. Ferlong, in talking to his neighbour and ex-vicar Mr. Beech over the fence, put the stench down to pollution. "I blame the French," he said. "Sending their whiff across the Channel." He was quite ignoring the fact that the smell in fact reminded him of the sulphurous stink of battlefields where he'd seen blood mingle with the mud underfoot; where he'd killed without mercy men like himself, men with wives and children waiting for them at home, men who just happened to be wearing the enemy uniform. Sometimes, when he closed his eyes, he could still see the fear-ridden faces of these men.

Mr. Beech, on the other hand, thought there might be a gas leak, and wondered if someone should be informed. He, for one, suspected that the rotten-egg smell was the stench of his own soul which he had befouled many times years ago with the wife of one of his parishioners. The woman's name was Rosie Dowler. She'd been prim and proper in company but cursed like a sailor in private and her mouth had always tasted of bourbon.

Though the day, as it went on, grew hotter, windows and doors were being closed all across the village. By evening most of Buxford's residents were grumpy and uncommunicative. If they spoke to each other at all, it was only to complain about the awful stench which they could not escape no matter what they did. Though they shut it out, it found a way to invade their homes. When it was time for bed, some took measures in order to sleep: filling their nostrils with cotton wool, draping blankets over their faces, splashing eucalyptus oil on their pillows in the hope that this smell might overpower the other. But nothing worked. The stench still found a way to reach them.

The next day some residents were seen packing up their cars. They were taking a last-minute holiday, they said to anyone who asked. Going away for a few days. The stench was unbearable. They simply could not stand it anymore.

Those who couldn't leave Buxford looked at those who could with envy. What they couldn't know was that though everyone who fled the village that day did indeed escape the awful stench, the memories and the feelings of guilt associated with it were harder to circumvent. They still lay awake in their bedrooms at the Holiday Inn, or on the couches of friends or relatives, mulling over their past, kicking at their blankets, and reassessing their lives. In the days that followed they found that their hometown had begun to make headlines.

MYSTERY STINK HOVERS OVER DARBYSHIRE VILLAGE.
TOURISTS TOLD TO AVOID SMELLY BUXFORD.

PONG IN THE AIR OVER BUXFORD IS 'EURO-WIFF' LOCAL MAN CLAIMS.

EXPERTS BAFFLED AS TO CAUSE OF UNEXPLAINED STENCH ASSAILING HISTORIC SPA-TOWN.

One journalist had even interviewed Owen Lloyd, a notorious village drunkard, and deduced from his proclamations that it was not a stench that afflicted Buxford but some kind of mass hysteria from which Owen himself —having not smelt anything remotely out of the ordinary—claimed to be exempt.

VILLAGE IN THE GRIP OF LUNANCY, the headline of this particular article read.

Those left behind in Buxford however were in no doubt that what afflicted them was not madness but an assault on the nasal passages. They prayed for a storm to clear the air, but the weather stubbornly remained fine.

Then things took a darker turn when the suicides began. First it was twenty-five year old Freddie Sizemore, who hung himself in the garage of his parent's house. He was no longer able to live with the memory of Filly Pishmore, a girl he and others had bullied so relentlessly at school for being overweight and for having body odour that one day she had climbed to the highest window she could find in the school building and jumped out. Filly hadn't died that day. She broke her back in the fall and was thereafter paralysed from the waist down. Freddie still saw her around Buxford from time to time being pushed along in her wheelchair. *Fishy Pissmore*, they had called her, *Fishy Pissmore, Fishy Pissmore,* having decided that her body odour had a particularly sea-shorey, urinary sort of tang. It was this same tang that had followed Freddie everywhere he went for too many days now until he finally decided he could no longer live with the guilt.

Following Freddie to a self-inflicted end was Mrs. Cousins, who for days had smelt the unique, indefinable smell of a newborn baby, something she had only smelt once in her life before handing the boy she'd given birth to at age seventeen over to his adopted parents. Not a day passed without Mrs. Cousins thinking about her son. Though at the time everyone had told her it was for the best, it had felt like giving part of herself away, an arm or a leg, and the loss had become heavier with each passing year. Hanging herself, though, was too violent an end for Mrs. Cousins to contemplate so she chose an overdose of sleeping tablets instead.

In the space of a fortnight three other Buxford residents followed suit, each with their own methods of ending their lives and their own reasons for doing so. An emergency meeting was set up in the village hall where it was decided that something had to be done. No one who attended the meeting wanted to talk about the suicides, because no one wanted to admit that it was the stench that was causing them. No one was prepared to say out loud what everyone secretly knew: that what they smelt was their own individual guilt. Buxford being a decent, church-going community it was difficult for anyone to comprehend that the whole town had been afflicted by a pall of secrets, indiscretions and festering remorse. Instead, they focused on issues of economy. The pubs and the souvenir shops were suffering from the lack of tourists, and—someone said—if the stench didn't shift soon house prices would start to go south.

Towards the end of the meeting, someone near the back of the room stood up and asked to know what everyone was getting so worked up about. He claimed he hadn't smelt anything unpleasant. Not a thing; and he had only come along to the meeting in order to find out if everyone else in the village had gone batshit crazy. Heads turned, and everyone saw that the speaker was Owen Lloyd. After noticing this, the people in the room began to look at each other. As one they had realised something. They did not speak about it, but it showed in their eyes, in their expressions, in the glances they gave each other. Owen Lloyd was well known in Buxford as someone to avoid. He was a crook, a criminal. He had spent time in prison. In the 1990s he had been behind a spate of burglaries which he had carried out in order to fund a voracious cocaine addiction. He was argumentative. He started fights and had once attacked a man so savagely that the man finished up in a coma. He was the sort of man who would burst a child's balloon for no reason then laugh about it, or kick a stray dog in the street merely because it was there. He had beat his wife and terrorized his two children before they'd had the sense to up and leave him. He sometimes drank himself into a stupor and spent the night on people's lawns; then when, in the morning, they asked him to leave he would kick over gnomes or water features and tell the owners of the lawns to go fuck themselves. Countless letters had been sent to the village council asking for Owen to be removed from Buxford. In short, Owen Lloyd was a nasty individual. And he was, as the people gathered in the village hall were slowly realising, a man without a conscience.

And so for him there was no stench.

From that day on, something changed in the minds of the residents of Buxford. At first it was just a vague idea, a suggestion, but over days it became clearer and clearer in their thoughts. They began to see the stench

45

hanging over their town differently. Rather than a curse, they started to see it as something of a consolation. At the very least, it was a reminder that though they weren't—any of them—perfect, at least they were not like Owen Lloyd with his casual acts of cruelty and criminality for which he apparently had no sense of contrition. This gave them hope. Then, over weeks, a strange thing started to happen. Mr Pugh the bank manager cleared out his basement and burned the contents; whilst old Miss Owen confessed to Jim Slader one day in the butcher's that she had once loved another woman. "Her name was Carol, and she was the love of my life," she said, before picking up the ten pounds of lamb meat Jim had wrapped for her, turning on the spot, and marching past the queue of people waiting behind her and leaving the shop. Robbie Bradbrook sent Ben Waddle a note in class saying he had enjoyed what happened in the showers after football practice and wouldn't mind doing it again sometime. Mrs. Dobson decided to convert her garage into a flat where her mother could live instead of in the nursing home, and when her husband complained she told him that she had made her decision and it was not up for discussion. Never again, she told him, would she suffer that awful shit-and-boiled-cabbage stink, and she wouldn't allow her mother to do so either. Doctor Lancastle confessed to her husband that she was addicted to painkillers, and told him she'd understand if he decided to leave her. Her husband held her as she wept and told her they would get her some counselling. Mr. Furlong, too, wept over the garden fence one day when he told Mr. Beech apropos of nothing about the men he had brutally murdered during the war, and how he sometimes still saw their faces in his mind's eye as clear as the day he had mercilessly machine-gunned them to death. Mr Beech, in the spirit of confession, then told Mr. Furlong about his long affair with Rosie Dowler, the woman who had drove him, as he himself described it, 'mad with lust'; and how even all these years later he still became aroused whenever he thought about how she'd said to him *fuck me fuck me fuck me.*

On and on it went, with a kind of domino effect, as the people of Buxford faced up to the things they felt most guilty about in the hope that it would free them from the stink of their own despair. And it happened. Bit by bit, the awful stench that was reported to hang over Buxford began to dissipate. There were no more suicides. The tourists returned, the house prices remained stable, and everyone in the village noticed that the air was that little bit clearer, that little bit fresher, than they had ever noticed it to

46

be before. All, that is, except Owen Lloyd; who of course had never noticed anything amiss in the first place.

Visions of the Autumn Country

*W*HERE HAVE YOU been? Her voice on the answerphone. *I've been trying to reach you for... where have you been?*

I can answer that. For the past few days, at least, I've been in limbo-land. Ha! Look at that. I've gone and created another of those paracosms my childhood pshychologist used to talk about. Another of Dolan's imaginary worlds, or subjective universes, as the pshychologist sometimes called them in the letters she wrote to my mother. I can picture her now. Susan, wasn't that her name? Doctor Susan something. *You can call me Soo if you like*, she'd said, that first time we met, though I never did. She was always Doctor Susan, because that's what my mother called her. *Did you have a nice chat with Doctor Susan today?*

I can picture Doctor Susan now with her loose smile and affable tilt of the head. I can imagine her saying, with that faux-enthusiasm adults so often use with children, "So, Dolan, tell me all about Limbo-land."

What would I tell her? One glance out of the window and I can see it's springtime, and that seems appropriate. Isn't spring, after all, the season of waiting? Waiting for the weather to improve, waiting for those buds to grow, waiting for the lambs to be born. Waiting. A pale grey sky. A nothing sky. And silence; broken only occasionally by the trill of the telephone which I don't answer. This is limbo-land.

I try to occupy the time with things I've been putting off for months— mending furniture, pulling weeds from the small flower garden at the back of the house, or clearing out my cupboards—but all I really want to do is paint. I can't paint of course because a few nights ago when the noises woke me I locked the door to my studio, and I can't open it again because there's something inside. Or someone. I'm not sure which. Whatever or whoever it is, I know it's still in there because whenever I go and put my ear close to the door, which I find myself doing more and more often, I sometimes hear shuffling on the other side. There are no other noises. No shouts or pleas or scratches or hammering. Just shuffling. I imagine what it must be like to be trapped in there surrounded by so many of my paintings, both finished and unfinished. How one might move around the room and try to decipher them, wondering what kind of lunatic you've gone and got yourself imprisoned by.

But something tells me that's not how it is.

I thought to try and speak through the door, to see if I could get a response, but something stops me. One time, without thinking, I almost said, "Gangel? Is that you?" But I couldn't get the words out, so I went and sat in the lounge, staring out of the window at that blank expanse of sky. That was when the phone rang. It must have been ringing for some time before I became aware of it, as just when I thought to pick it up I heard Beth's voice on the answerphone.

Dad...where have you been? I've been trying to reach you for... where have you been?

"WHO'S THIS BOY who keeps appearing in your drawings?" Doctor Susan asked me once.

I didn't want to tell her. I remember that. I didn't want her to know, but I worried she'd tell my mother I wasn't cooperating.

"Gangel."

"And who's Gangel? Is he your friend?"

"He is. Kind of my friend."

"Kind of?"

"He acts like he's my friend. But I don't trust him. Not really."

"I see. And is Gangel from The Autumn Country?"

"He is. But sometimes he's...here."

I CALLED IT The Autumn Country because everything I saw there looked dead or dying. It was a brown decaying world, a world moving towards winter. A place on the brink, eternally ending. I first started drawing scenes from The Autumn Country when I was eight years old. It was shortly after the death of my father, around the time my blackouts started. I didn't occur to me until much later in life that these three things might be linked.

Drawing and painting was in my blood. That's what the biographers always say. *Art was in his blood. His father was the great Irish-born abstract painter, Sheehan Foley, known for his bold emotionally-charged imagery, who sadly committed suicide in 1972 at the height of his success, aged just 46.*

In saying this, I often think these writers are trying to explain or even excuse my own paintings which are frequently described as weird, bleak,

49

and disturbing. Or dark. How I hate that word, *dark*. But it's true that I started drawing almost as soon as I could hold a pencil. Like most children I drew grassy scenes of family outings, with big yellow suns, or colourful chaos straight from my imagination. But after my father died I would no longer draw rainbows or pirates ships or rockets headed for the moon. From then on it was stick figures trapped in empty landscapes or crowded together in odd sinister gatherings, crooked skeletal trees drawn in heavy black crayon, and barren landscapes littered with rocks and pebbles and broken bits of machinery.

"What's this?" my mother said once. I can still hear the ring of horror in her voice. "What is all this?"

That's when I told her, for some reason thinking she'd understand. "It's The Autumn Country."

Soon after, I paid my first visit to Doctor Susan's office.

NOW IT'S NOT the phone that's ringing but the doorbell. Someone's banging on the wood with their fist. I hear Beth's voice.

"Dad? Dad, are you in there? Dad?"

What's she doing here?

What time is it?

Clamouring out of bed, I put on my dressing gown and slippers. As I approach the front door, I can here Beth talking on the other side of it and I briefly wonder if she's brought more people with her. Thinking of the locked studio door, I start thinking about what I can say, how I can get rid of them. But then I realise it's a one-sided conversation. She must be talking on her mobile phone.

"Hang on," I hear her say, as I unlock the door. "Someone's coming."

When I open the door, she gives me the same low look of condemnation her mother used to use. She shrugs, glancing about as if waiting for an answer to some question she doesn't need to ask. She's looking more and more like her mother those days; thin and colourless. Washed-out, like the landscape at her back. Her hair is pulled into a tight bun, from which the wind teases strands loose, and she's wearing some kind of constricting outfit that makes me think of boardrooms.

"Beth?"

"Never mind, he's here," she says to whoever was on the other end of the telephone. Lowering the phone from her ear, she looks me over. I know she's seeing the unwashed hair, the week's worth of stubble, the ratty dressing gown.

"What's going on?" she says. "What is it? Are you working?"

"Working?"

"Painting. I know you like to shut the world out when you're in the middle of something."

"Not at the moment."

"Then why won't you answer the phone? I've been trying to contact you for a week or more. I was worried. You could have had a fall or...I don't know...got stuck in the bath or something. How would I know?"

"Now you're making me feel old."

"Well, you're no spring chicken." She moves forward so that I have to step back and open the door wider to allow her to enter. She starts taking off her jacket. I remain by the open door, looking out across the empty yard.

"Did you drive here, love?"

"Of course."

"Where's your car?"

"I parked it behind the barn where it'll be safer."

"Safer?"

"It's a Merc, Dad. I'm not going to leave it stuck out front."

"Are you staying long?"

"How many times have I told you to sell this place and move to the city where I can keep an eye on you?"

"I told you, Beth, love. Don't like the city. Too many distractions."

"Is it fair that I have to drive all this way just to check on you? It keeps me awake at night thinking about you living all the way out here on your own."

"I'm fine. You can see I'm fine."

"It's so silent out here."

"I like the silence. It helps me think."

"I need a drink. Do you have coffee?"

"I'll look."

On my way to the kitchen, I pause for a few seconds to listen at the studio door. I hear no sounds from inside. *That's good*, I think, *maybe he's gone. He could have opened a window and climbed out. Fled.* I wonder why I'm thinking it's a he. Surely I don't still believe it's Gangel I trapped in there? Gangel, my imaginary childhood friend. Gangel, who I've drawn and painted so many times he seems real to me. Maybe Beth's right; maybe I am getting old, losing it, losing my mind.

Beth isn't surprised when I tell her I'm out of coffee. I make tea instead.

51

"There's no milk. Just the powdered stuff."

"That'll do," she says, not without a roll of the eyes.

I'm always surprised by her, surprised that someone so straight—isn't that the word, *straight?*—could be my daughter. When she was a girl I waited for that artistic blood to show, but Beth never had any interest in art. She was keener on making tallies of everything. *Six dolls. Seven cups. Eight dresses.* Marching around the house with a pencil and a clipboard, drawing up itinerates, bossing all her friends around, always making them play shop when they wanted to do other things. It was no great surprise that she became a banker. It was a relief of sorts, for what is this creative compulsion if not a curse? How many times have I heard that question: *why do you paint this stuff?* I have no answer, other than that I'm compelled.

It's like that same question of my mother's all over again.

What is all this?

Why not portraits or seascapes or colourful abstracts, paintings people might want to hang in their living rooms? Why all this dark, disturbing stuff?

It turns out some people like the dark disturbing stuff. The dark, disturbing stuff has made me a living for twenty-five years.

Beth makes small talk as we drink our tea. Eventually, she becomes annoyed that I keep asking how long she plans on staying.

"It's like you can't wait to get rid of me," she says. Then before I can say anything, she sets her cup down and stands. "Well, I'll just use the loo and then I'll be on my way. Will that make you happy?"

"Beth, love..."

With a huff, she's gone. I sit and finish my tea. When I realise Beth seems to have been gone a long time, I feel an inexplicable rush of panic, and I get up to look for her. Maybe I'd caught the smell of turpentine. In the hall I see the studio door standing open and it feels like my heart drops as far as my feet.

"Beth."

I start to run, but then I halt. She's standing at the far end of the studio. She has her arms folded and she's examining one of my paintings which stands propped against the wall. I enter the studio looking everywhere in the room at once. When she notices this, Beth knits her brow. I'm relieved to find that there's no one here but the two of us, at least physically. But all those figures in the paintings—they're here too, and it suddenly feels as if all those eyes are watching me as I cross the room to stand next to my daughter.

I can't help but look at her, marvel at her.

Beth's mother badly wanted a child. I understood that urge to create, but her urge seemed purer, less hollow than mine, so how could I refuse? It took six years of IVF treatment for her to fall pregnant. Maybe that's why we always treated Beth like she was doubly precious, and perhaps we spoilt her, or maybe that's how every parent treats their child. How would I know?

"Beth, what're you doing in here? The door was supposed to be locked."

"The key was in the door," she says, looking at me as if I need sectioning. "Why? What's the big deal?"

"No big deal. Just that I thought I'd locked the door."

"Why lock it?" she says, throwing her arms out to indicate the surrounding paintings. "Are you worried some of these guys might make a run for it?"

I know it's supposed to be a joke, but for some reason it makes my blood go cold. I can see them in my mind's eyes, the figures from my paintings, trooping out over the fields, finding the road, leering at passengers in passing cars, causing the drivers to veer off the road, to crash into each other, descending on the occupants as they fall, bloodied, from their vehicles.

"Don't be daft, love."

She looks to my face. "I'm not intruding, am I?"

"Of course not."

"I like seeing what you're working on. You're still painting The Autumn Country, I notice."

"Yes." I know what's coming next.

"You never feel like painting something a bit cheerier?"

"This is just what comes out."

"They're always so..." Here it comes. "...*dark*. What's this one about?"

The painting she's been looking at shows a group of figures wearing hooded robes. Their faces, just visible inside the hoods, look like death masks. They crowd together around another figure knelt on the floor before them. This kneeling figure is only roughly sketched in, since I haven't yet completed the lower half of the painting.

"It's the Council," I say. "The Council of Eight."

Beth noticeably shivers. "And who's that down there?" She points at the figure outlined into the bottom half of the painting. "I wouldn't like to be that person."

When she looks at me, I shrug. Then after a moment, I say, "So? Shouldn't you be heading back?"

"You know I always thought of your paintings as...snapshots."

"Really?"

"Yes. It always seemed to me like this was a place you'd actually visited. You went there and saw these scenes and you brought back these snapshots. Does that make sense?"

"I suppose it does."

"Where's Gangel?"

Shocked, I cast my eyes about the studio. I think I see a shadow shift behind a large canvas set at a wide angle from the wall. *There you are*, I think.

"Well?"

I twist to face her. "Huh?"

"Where is he? I thought he always appeared in your paintings. He's like your...our...guide or something. Our guide through The Autumn Country."

"Oh, he'll be there somewhere. Hiding. You'll see when it's finished. So —what was it? Don't you have to be somewhere?"

Beth lets out a long sigh. "You know what—I don't feel like driving back today. Maybe I'll stay with you tonight." Perhaps seeing my expression change, she adds, "That's okay, isn't it? I mean, you're not doing anything. Are you?"

"No, love. Of course, love. I always enjoy seeing you. I'll make up the spare bedroom."

As she follows me out from the studio, I make sure to lock the door behind us, this time taking the key out from the hole and dropping it into my dressing gown pocket, before ushering Beth through to the lounge.

DOCTOR SUSAN IS holding up one on my drawings. It shows a figure squatting on a rock. Using a biro, I've given him big black eyes and a scribble of hair, but I've used a red crayon to draw dots all over his face. I've also scribbled his clothes in black, so that it looks as if he's wearing a suit jacket and a long ragged skirt. I've drawn his mouth in such a way that he appears pleased with himself. On the ground at his feet lies a litter of broken objects.

"Is this your friend Gangel?" she asks.

54

I nod.

"Why do you say that you don't trust him?"

For a moment I can't speak. Then I say, "Because he's always stealing my things."

"Things?"

"Toys. Books. Anything. He takes them back there."

"Back? You mean back to The Autumn Country?"

I nod. "They don't have nice things there. Mum doesn't believe me. She thinks *I* lost them."

"Are these your things?" Doctor Susan asks, pointing at the various objects strewn about the ground in the picture: a teddy bear, a book, a model train, a jar of marbles.

I nod.

"He stole all these things from you?"

"Yes," I say. "He always takes something. Even Mum's things sometimes. He shows it to them and they decide what to do with it. Usually they just break them. They like destroying things."

"And who're they?" Doctor Susan asks.

Leaning forward, I scrabble through the sheets of paper set out on the low table between us. I select one sheet and hold it up for her to see.

"Them," I say.

Doctor Susan takes the paper from me and frowns at it. "Who are these scary-looking people, Dolan?"

"The Council of Eight," I say.

BETH AND I stay up late, drinking wine and talking. Beth likes to talk about her mother. She likes to remember her mother. Though I try to be attentive, my mind keeps returning to that locked studio door and I can't help listening for sounds: a footstep, a jar of brushes being knocked over, or a painting being overturned. I'm terrified Beth will hear something too —although it's unlikely anything happening in the studio could be heard from the lounge where we sit. A couple of times, when the TV is momentarily silent, I notice Beth glance towards the hallway as if something has caught her ear. But she says nothing; and I hear nothing myself.

"Mum never liked your paintings, did she?" Beth says.

"I think she hoped—like most people—that one day I'd paint something a bit jollier."

"Have you ever tried?"

55

"Not for a long time."

"Did you ever paint Mum's portrait?"

"No," I lie. There was that one painting, done after Jayne died. It was a crowd scene, full of blank-faced figures in hoods all shuffling forwards against a late evening sky. The light was low along the horizon. The impression the figures gave was of endless, silent suffering. And there amongst the crowd was one face I recognised. It surprised me to see her there. I hadn't intended to put her in the picture. But there she was.

I don't know why, but I painted over that picture with emulsion. I suppose I just couldn't bear to the see my Jayne there amongst that crowd of damned figures.

As Beth goes on talking I feel a sudden sense of frustration with myself, a loathing. What could possibly have compelled me to paint my dear departed wife into such an ugly scene?

Maybe some kind of insanity.

At some point I must have fallen asleep. I dreamt of my own mother. I see her that sunny spring day when she was tending the flower bed which bordered our garden. She was there most days after my father died, yanking up weeds and coaxing chrysanthemums into bloom. Perhaps she had an urge to see things grow and live. That day, as I sat on the grass watching her, her hands found something buried in the dirt and pulled it out. I see her rising up onto her knees and turning to me, her face flushed with shock and anger.

"Dolan?" she says. "Why do you do it?"

WHEN I AWAKE it's daylight, and Beth is no longer in the room. I feel ravenously hungry, and my hands are black with dirt I don't remember touching which makes me think I've suffered another blackout. I'm not certain what day it is because I haven't been keeping track. Though I look, I can't find Beth anywhere in the house. The bed in the spare room is neatly made, as if no one slept there and I wonder if Beth was ever here at all or if I'd simply dreamed it. I hurry around the house, up and down the stairs, calling her name. If she had been here, why did she leave? Could I have done something, said something, to force Beth to hightail it out of here? Something I now can't remember? I'd been so keen for her to leave, but now that's she's gone I want her here. I need her here. All I can think about is a day long ago when I was woken by a grinning six year old in green pyjamas, who thrust a bundle at me and said, "Happy Birthday, Daddy!"

Remembering that she wrote her mobile phone number down for me on a scrap of paper, I hunt it down and dial the number. There's no answer, just a few rings before the phone goes to voicemail.

"Beth," I say. "Call me back, please. Let me know you're okay. I hope I didn't...you know I love you, right? I just wanted to say...you know...?"

A bleep signals that I'm out of time. I set the phone down and, after gazing at it for a few moments, head to the kitchen to wash my hands and prepare some breakfast. It's only now that I realise—to my horror—that the studio door is standing open. Sliding one hand into my dressing gown pocket, I find the key is still there. Could Beth have taken it whilst I slept, or had I opened the door myself during my blackout? I take a tentative step inside the studio and look around. But for the paintings, it's empty. Feeling braver, I cross the floor, tilting to look behind paintings, lifting some away from the wall. I find nothing, and no trace that anyone has been here. Of course, I tell myself, there never was anyone here. It was all in my imagination. Or perhaps I dreamt it too. Maybe I'm cracking up. Maybe all this dark stuff I keep painting is finally getting to me. Maybe I'll start painting bright things instead. Sunflowers, perhaps. Okay, not sunflowers. Something happier, sunnier, like the stuff I used to draw as a child before the darkness set in, before my first visit to The Autumn Country. A seascape—yes! What a challenge that would be. And what a change. The sea has never featured in my paintings before, although there have been boats. Landlocked boats stranded on dry rockbeds, occupied by bizarre, lost figures clutching oars and rowing fruitlessly at the ground in some impotent bid for freedom or escape.

I find myself standing in front of the half-finished painting Beth had admired. *Admired*—is that the right word? Perhaps not. I remember how she'd shivered as she looked at it. The Council of Eight cluster in judgement around the sketched-in figure knelt at their feet. Looking at the picture I feel a familiar itch—not a literal itch—something deeper, beneath the skin. My fingertips prickle. My heart picks up. The anticipation builds in me, as if someone's just placed a luxurious meal before me and I can't wait to tuck in. I tell myself there'll be plenty of time for seascapes. I'll finish this painting first.

Why?
Why do you paint this stuff?
What is all this?
Dolan? Why do you do it?

MOST OF MY father's paintings are kept in the storerooms of galleries the world over. On occasion they are brought out for a retrospective. One, and only one, is owned by me and hangs on the wall above my staircase. My father named the painting Dun Sky IV. Though my father's paintings were meant to be abstract, I always saw them as landscapes, and this one is no different. He used a familiar pallet of brown, black and orange with slashes of red and pink here and there like open wounds or mouths crying out in torment.

Though I've never admitted it to anyone, in my heart I've always thought that my father too was painting The Autumn Country. That muddle of angry lines and blotches of brown were my father's attempts, I believe, at rendering this place we both knew.

Or perhaps they are merely abstracts. Perhaps I'm merely projecting my own ideology onto his paintings.

Either way, I wish he'd stayed around. I wish I could have known him better. He would have understood, I think. He would not have been one of those asking *why*.

DOCTOR SUSAN THOUGHT my blackouts were caused by stress, possibly brought on by my father's death. It was I who had discovered him, after all, racing into the house ahead of my mother, eager to tell him all about my day at school. The smell of the PVA primer my father used is still associated in my mind with the image of a kitchen chair lying on its side and my father suspended silhouetted against the big window of his studio. That's why I've always primed my cavasses with rabbit skin glue.

My mother thought otherwise. She thought I lied about the blackouts. She thought they were a way I had of not taking responsibility for the destructive things I did.

I SET TO work the next day. I don my overalls and lay out my paints. Then I place the Council of Eight painting on the easel and study it for a while. I like to listen to classical music when I paint: Bach or Beethoven. There's something about the rise and fall, the swell and sweep, of the music that mirrors my emotions as I paint. I slide a CD into the little boombox I keep in one corner and then begin. Very quickly, something else takes over and I become lost in the process. Hours go by before I stumble out of the studio, smeared in paint and bleary eyed. It's dark outside. I'm hungry but too weary to prepare food. All I can do is slip off my overalls and collapse onto the sofa. The painting has taken all my energy. I feel drained, emptied out in a way that is not entirely unpleasant. The phone rings as I lie there, but as much as I want to answer it—hoping that it might be Beth —I'm too exhausted to get up. I let the answerphone take it. There is no voice, just odd sounds, a kind of distorted metallic warble as if someone's calling me from the bottom of the ocean. After it ends, I close my eyes and am soon asleep.

I DREAM OF my mother again. Of that spring day when she tended the flower beds and I paused in my lawn games to watch her. What is it about that day that makes it return so often to my subconscious mind? Doctor Susan would know.

My mother finds the sack buried in the dirt and with some effort she drags it out into the open. She seems surprised by how large it is, but equally at how easily it comes free from the earth. Loose dirt spills onto the grass. A flush rises in me as I watch my mother open the sack. After a pause she begins to take things from it: broken toys, torn up books, ripped t-shirts and a few items of her own, jewellery and such, now damaged beyond repair.

My flush deepens when she turns to me.

"Dolan," she says. "Why do you do it?"

I START AWAKE remembering something Beth said, that day she arrived.

It's a Merc, Dad. I'm not just going to leave it stuck out front.

Why was that suddenly so important to me? Of course. She said she'd parked behind the barn, a spot that couldn't be seen from any of the windows in the house, and when I looked for her I hadn't thought to check if her car was still here.

Why would her car still be here? She's gone. She's gone.

Something compels me to get up and go outside. The day is a grey void. Land and sky seem equally ambiguous. As if in a trance I move around the side of the house. As soon as I turn the corner I see the car's bright red tail sticking out from behind the barn.

Still here. Still...

I run then, back to the house and into the studio. Something awful is forming in my mind. I stand in front of the newly finished painting and take it in. There they are, The Council of Eight. And that figure knelt at their feet wearing a tight grey suit with her blonde hair pulled back into a bun...

59

"Beth," I say, my hand instinctively reaching out to her. She's a small figure before The Council of Eight in their long dark robes, cowering, her head bowed. Beth was not the sort of woman to cower, but there she was, cowering before The Eight. I squint at the painting, noticing something else. There, peeping out from the robes of one of the standing figures is a pale face covered in red markings—they are *burns*—a face framed with badly cropped and unkempt black hair. He appears to be looking directly at me. And he is smiling in a way that I know well—an evil mocking little smile.

He always took the things that were most precious to me.

I think of Beth saying: *Where have you been? I've been trying to reach you for... where have you been?*

The Hole

*A*S JOSH HAD said on the day of the viewing, the house was everything they were looking for in a starter home. Though Marion agreed, having herself fallen in love with the place from the moment she stepped through the front door, something about it hadn't felt quite right. It was nothing she could put her finger on. The kitchen was small, but since there was a separate dining room this didn't worry her. The garden too was small, but as Josh said that would make it easier to manage. The other rooms, including the bedrooms, were of a reasonable size. There was even a downstairs toilet.

Perhaps it was the price that bothered her. "The owners want a quick sale," the Estate Agent had told them, which Marion—seasoned house-hunter she'd become—had thought to be an excuse. She imagined all would become clear at the viewing, as was usually the case, but on arriving at number 28 Arcadia Street she could find nothing to explain the low asking price. Perhaps it was true then. The owners only wanted a quick sale.

The owners were a thirty-something couple named Carrie and Wayne who had two children in their early teens, both girls. The girls sat in silence on the sofa for the duration of the viewing. They didn't even look up when Marion said hello to them, though she noticed how their hands wrestled in their laps. It was Carrie who showed Josh and Marion around the house. She seemed weary and put-upon, but determined to show a brave face.

"Marion's obsessed with finding her dream home," Josh told Carrie as they climbed the stairs. "You wouldn't believe how many hours she spends on the internet every evening searching."

"It's true," Marion said, smiling. "Josh has been feeling neglected. He's about ready to divorce me, aren't you, honey?"

They laughed, but Carrie only showed them a thin smile and indicated the master bedroom.

Marion was resolved to uncovering something to explain the asking price. "Such a lovely home," she said to Carrie. "And such a steal. You must be going somewhere amazing after this."

"We want to get away," Carrie said. "Get our lives back."

"Get your lives back?"

"It's for the children mainly. They need a fresh start."

61

"Oh," Marion said, though she didn't press for further information. She imagined this meant trouble at school, or a bad crowd. Drugs or boyfriends or bullying or peer pressure, or *something*. Nothing to do with the house then, after all; only some hardship this particular family wanted to get away from.

The husband, Wayne, had spent the duration of the viewing looking at his mobile phone; until the visiting party returned from upstairs and his wife snapped at him to put it away. Her reprimand, which seemed overly harsh, and Wayne's expression of shame set Marion's imagination into gear again. She thought maybe there had been some infidelity in the relationship, perhaps with a neighbour or someone else close by, which would again explain why they were moving. Secret texts and sexy photos stored on a hard drive. The exact same thing had happened to her friend Natalie. *That* had been an ugly divorce.

The house had a basement for storage, which Carrie only showed them after Josh insisted, and then only from the top of the steps. First she'd had to find a set of keys to open the padlocked door.

"Light's broken," Carrie said as the three of them stood in the doorway peering down into the gloom. "Sorry."

"Might convert this into an office," Josh said, and Marion thought she saw Carrie blanch.

"You won't want to spend a lot of time down here," Carrie said. "There's no natural light."

"Maybe not," Josh said, and grinned. "But it'll be the perfect place for hiding the bodies, eh, Marion?"

"Josh!" Marion said, swatting at his arm. "You and your twisted sense of humour."

Carrie showed them a thin, tolerant smile again. "So," she said. "What do you think?"

"I think it's a done deal," said Josh. "Right, Marion?"

Marion turned, and was a little disconcerted to find Wayne and the two children stood close at her back, peering past her into the gloom of the basement.

"Yes, well, we certainly can't argue about the price."

TWO WEEKS AFTER they moved in, Josh discovered the hole. He started talking almost immediately about turning the basement into an office. Unnerved at this idea, but not certain why, Marion suggested he convert one of the spare bedrooms.

62

"You can use the box room. At least, until we need it for, you know...other things."

Marion knew Josh understood *other things* meant babies, but neither of them dared say it out-loud until it became a reality. They had both agreed a family was the next step after buying their own home. Marion was already spending time on-line looking up baby names and window-shopping for cots and cute little clothes, usually when Josh was in the shower.

Josh insisted though he was going to convert the basement. Marion suspected he wanted somewhere all of his own, his shed, his man-place, somewhere she wouldn't go, somewhere he could play computer games which she wouldn't allow him to do anywhere else in the house because the constant noise of gunfire and explosions irritated her. He had started clearing out the junk Carrie and Wayne left behind, when he discovered the hole in the dead centre of the basement floor. It had been covered, he said, by a heavy wardrobe laid out flat on the floor which he'd had to take apart to move. The hole was perfectly cylindrical, and only about a foot in diameter. When Josh pointed a torchlight into it, they saw no bottom.

"Wow!" he said. "I wonder how deep it goes."

He seemed fascinated, but Marion had felt an immediate sense of anger and betrayal. "So that's it then! This is why she didn't want us coming down here at the viewing. I knew there must be something wrong for them to be selling at such a low price. I told you we should've had a full survey done, but oh no – you said we could spend the money fixing anything we found wrong. Well how much is this going to cost us, Josh?"

"Marion," Josh said, looking taken aback by her outburst. "It's just a hole."

AT WORK, DURING what they all called the three o'clock lull when the phones went quiet and her workmate Farrah popped out to buy cakes—most of which she ate herself—Marion liked to check for messages sent to her account on the Soulm8s dating site. She knew she should have closed her account after meeting Josh, but she'd found that when she felt low it gave her a little boost to know men were still interested in her. Farrah was always saying how glamorous she looked, coming into work, it seemed a shame not to get some reward for her efforts. She couldn't remember the last time Josh had paid her a complement.

There were the usual messages from lonely scaffolders and divorced dads, dull attempts to start conversations. *I like the cinema too*, one man

63

had messaged her. His profile picture had an intense stare. *Maybe we could catch a film together sometime.*

Marion mouthed the word 'No' and continued scrolling through the messages.

Coffee?

Hey, beautiful.

She had no intention of acting on any of the messages. She certainly wouldn't respond to any of them. But she enjoyed reading through them and looking at the men's profiles, imagining what it would be like to go on a date with them. It was addictive, the interest. There was the only word for it. Addictive.

ON THE WAY home that evening Marion took a diversion through the inner city. Carrie and Wayne—the previous occupants of 28 Arcadia Street —had left in one of the kitchen drawers a scrap of paper with a forwarding address written on it. Marion came across the scrap of paper that morning when she was looking for the spare house keys, and decided she was going to drive by Carrie and Wayne's new place. She didn't plan to call in. No, no. Not yet anyway. All she wanted was a look. Something about the whole situation still didn't add up for her, and she hoped by getting a look at where Carrie and Wayne had moved to all would become clear.

This proved not to be the case.

It wasn't the most desirable part of the city, but Marion imagined the property was cheap. Her car's navigation system, into which she had punched Carrie and Wayne's new postcode, led her to a tower block. It had to be fifteen stories or more. It made sense a flat in this building was all Carrie and Wayne could afford after selling 28 Arcadia Street at such a loss, but why had they done it? What was the urgency? The whole point of buying a home was to get on the property ladder, and the generally accepted idea was you went up the ladder, not down. At least not until you retired and decided to downsize. Otherwise you kept going up.

It was the hole in the basement, Marion was sure of it. That was why they'd moved, and that was why they'd covered it up. The hole had to be affecting the house's foundations or something. It had to be some kind of a hazard. Carrie and Wayne must have discovered it then decided to get the hell out, pass the house on to someone else and let them deal with it. She pictured Carrie, pale and put upon, snapping at her husband to put his phone away. And the children with their waxy expressions and hands they couldn't still. They were an odd family for sure.

64

WHEN SHE ARRIVED home, she found lights and the TV on in the living room, plus a half-dozen empty beer cans on the coffee table. Her husband was nowhere to be seen. And in the kitchen she saw no attempt had been made to start dinner.

Standing at the foot of the stairs she called, "Josh? You up there?"

No answer.

"Josh? Where are you, honey-bun?"

Nothing.

She sniffed. There was a trace of something pungent, slightly discernible. She knew what it meant.

So Josh was with his deadbeat brother—the marijuana enthusiast. Most likely they had both smoked a couple of joints with those beers, before opening the windows in an attempt to get rid of the smell before she got home. Well, they had failed. There was only one place they could be now. In the basement.

Marion disliked Josh when he was stoned. It made him greedy and selfish. He would get the munchies and eat his way through entire packets of biscuits or anything else sweet he could get his hands on. It was as if he couldn't be satisfied. He'd sit and munch and munch. It was unpleasant to watch. Unattractive.

"Josh, honey?"

She peered into the basement's gloom. With the light entering from the hallway behind her, Marion could make out the two figures sat cross-legged on the floor with their backs to her. Neither turned to acknowledge her. Josh held a torch which he directed into the hole in the floor. Marion moved slowly down the steps.

"Josh?"

Still no change. She saw now she'd been correct. It was Benjamin who squatted next to Josh. He was the only person they knew who wore oversized American ice-hockey shirts. Benny-the-B he liked to call himself, as if he was some kind of gangster, and Marion liked to extend this into Benny-the-Bug. Sometimes she called him The Roach.

She stamped her feet on the concrete floor as she walked towards them, but they continued staring into the hole.

"Josh?" she said, then: "JOSH!"

That did it. Both he and Benjamin jumped and twisted to face her.

"J-Jesus, Marion, what're you trying to do to us? We nearly fell in."

"You wouldn't fit down there, dummy."

"Scared us half to death creeping up."

"I've been calling you for the past ten minutes. What're you doing sitting down here in the dark?"

"I was showing Benny the hole."

Marion tried to avoid looking at the hole, though she found her eyes were drawn to it. The way Josh's torchlight illuminated its smooth interior both intrigued and unnerved her.

"What the hell do you want to show him that for?"

"It's fascinating," Benjamin said. "Take a look."

"Don't be ridiculous. You're both stoned."

"He is," Josh said, pointing at his brother and letting out a childish giggle.

"He is," Benjamin retaliated, also giggling.

Marion shook her head.

"You both are. You should have been getting dinner ready, but instead you're sat down here gazing into this stupid hole. What are you looking for exactly?"

"There's something down there," Benjamin said, though Josh made belated attempts to silence him.

"What? You mean like rats or something?"

"Not rats."

"What then?"

"Something good. We don't know what it is yet. Take the weight off, G. Have a look."

Marion sometimes felt like slapping Benjamin for the silly way he talked.

She began to walk away when Josh took hold of one of her hands, caressing the back of it with his thumb. "Seriously," he said. "It's a good thing. Sit down and have a look. You'll see for yourself."

Huffing, and shaking her head, making a show of her unwillingness but curious nonetheless, Marion sat down on the floor next to Josh. She looked into the hole.

"Well," she said. "There's nothing."

"Wait," Josh said. "Keep watching."

Marion went on staring into the hole. Once, she thought she saw something moving and her heart picked up, but then she realised it was only the torchlight had shifted. Still, it had given her a little thrill. The idea that there *might* be something down there. The possibility of it.

She went on looking. There was nothing there really. She knew there was nothing there. But the more she looked the more she found she couldn't stop. It took some effort for her to drag her eyes away. Reluctantly, she stood.

"Well," she said. "One of us better get dinner on. I suppose I don't need to ask if you're hungry."

JOSH TOSSED AND TURNED beside her in bed. She couldn't sleep herself, thinking about the hole and what might be inside it. When Josh got up, she didn't need to ask where he was going.

"One last look," he said. Marion listened to his feet padding down the stairs.

Though she was tempted to get up herself, she realised she had work the next day. It took all her willpower to remain in bed. It was hours before she fell asleep, and Josh still hadn't returned.

A week later, Marion didn't question her husband when he took the mattress off the bed in the spare room and dragged it down into the basement. That same night, she slept there beside him, both of them gazing into the hole by torchlight until they fell asleep. In the morning, waking in the dark basement, Marion would look again. She'd look for as long as she dared, then get ready for work in a rush with no time for a shower or breakfast. A few times she called in sick to work so she could stay with Josh in the basement and stare into the hole. The thing was; she never saw anything. And Josh never saw anything. He kept insisting there was something down there in the hole and if they kept looking, one day they would see it.

IT WAS THE look on her colleague Farrah's face when Marion arrived for work one morning that finally brought her to her senses. Farrah stared, a cookie raised halfway to her mouth, a look on her face of disgust and disbelief. Marion took herself off to the toilets and in the mirror she looked at herself, really looked at herself, for the first time in weeks. She had lost weight. Her face looked pale and drawn, her skin had a yellowish tint, and there were bags under her eyes. The eyes themselves were glazed and bloodshot. Her hair was greasy and the roots were showing. She'd meant to book an appointment at *Nikki's*, but she hadn't found the time. The worse thing was her clothes. Her blouse looked as if she'd slept in it, had a ketchup stain on the collar, and it didn't match the skirt she wore. The tights were ill-matched as well, and on her feet were the trainers she used to go jogging in. What the hell had she done to herself?

"Something needs to change," she muttered as she went about trying to put things right as best she could. "I'm going to tell Josh. We need to stop. This is...something needs to change."

But she knew she'd never get through to Josh. She pictured him, with his slack, unresponsive face, his eyes trained on the hole in their basement floor. When was the last time they'd made love? When was the last time they'd had dinner together? When was the last time they'd spoken more than two words to each other? All he wanted to do these days was stare into the hole.

There had to be someone else who she could talk to. Someone who could help her. She wracked her brain.

WHEN CARRIE OPENED the door, she had the same pale, put-upon look as she had months ago when she showed Marion and Josh around 28 Arcadia Street, but now there was something else in the mix: a look of resignation and defeat.

"Yes?" she said, blinking at Marion, whom she clearly didn't recognise.

"Don't you remember me? My name's Marion Swann. My husband Josh and I bought your house at 28 Arcadia Street." Feeling vengeful, Marion added, "The one with the *hole*."

"Oh," Carrie said. "I wondered how long it'd be until you came knocking."

"You knew about the hole then?" Marion said.

Carrie shrugged. "How could I not?"

"Guess you didn't feel like mentioning it to us."

"Well," Carrie cast her eyes downwards. "I was kind of hoping you wouldn't find it."

"That's why you moved isn't it? That's why you wanted a quick sale."

Carrie looked up again and nodded. "We had to get away. It had them, you see."

"Had them?"

"The girls. And Wayne–it got him too. And I was starting to...we had to get away from it. I wanted us to get our lives back."

"And did you? Did you get your lives back?"

Carrie drew a deep breath. "You'd better come in."

The inside of the flat was cramped and smelled of wet washing. As Carrie led the way along the hall, Marion glanced into the rooms they passed. The living room was small and unoccupied. In the tiny kitchen, crockery was piled up by the sink. The two bedrooms had boxes stacked in

68

them.

"Still not fully unpacked then?"

"Huh? Oh, we've been kind of...uh...busy."

"Don't worry, we haven't fully unpacked either. It takes time. Where's the family? They out?"

Carrie turned and shook her head. "I'll show you," she said.

There was a door at the end of the hall. When Carrie opened the door, Marion's first reaction was one of horror.

She's murdered them, she thought. *She's murdered them and now she'll murder me.*

She had begun to back up, when one of the girls lifted her head and glanced at her. The girl lay on her back on the floor of what appeared to be some kind of storage room. She was almost as long as the room itself, and crammed in beside her were her sister and her father. Neither of the other two acknowledged Marion. They didn't even move. Wayne looked chubbier than he had the first time Marion had seen him, and he had the beginnings of a beard. His attention, and that of the two girls, was held by something directly above them, something on the ceiling of the little room. Though Marion already had an idea of what she'd see, she stepped forward at Carrie's invitation, ducked her head inside the room and looked to see what Wayne and his daughters were staring at.

In the ceiling, a little to the left of the room's single light fitting, there was a wide, circular hole. Marion felt a familiar jitter of excitement when she looked into it and had to wrench her eyes away.

"There's... there's one here too?"

"They're everywhere," Carrie said.

"But what's the fascination? There's nothing there. There's nothing inside."

"There might be."

"There isn't. There—"

"I was about to join them. I don't suppose you want to..?"

Join them? So it had Carrie too now? It *had* her.

Before Marion could respond, Carrie knelt and lay down on the floor of the little room beside her husband. She lay on her back like the others, gazing up into the ceiling hole. Marion had an odd sensation that Carrie had departed. That all that remained of her now was this still and unresponsive shell on the floor.

Appalled, Marion turned to leave. But then she stopped. It couldn't hurt if she had a look could it? Only a few minutes. Where's the harm?

Maybe there was something here. Maybe this hole had something inside it. She was tired of sitting in her basement at home, waiting for something. Always looking. Always waiting. And never seeing anything. Perhaps here, in this hole, there would be *something*.

Still unsure, she crouched and squeezed in beside Carrie's two daughters. It felt comforting to lie there with the four of them. She let out her breath.

And together, they looked.

Wolvers Hill

"**N**EXT LEFT," FERGUS said.

Bisma glanced across at him. He held the road map only inches from his face and squinted at it.

"Are you sure?"

He didn't look at her. He hadn't looked at her for the past fifty miles, and had only spoken to give directions.

"One hundred per cent."

Bisma rolled her shoulders. Her back ached. "Maybe we should pull over and look at the map together. It's going to be dark soon. I'm tired. I don't want to get lost again."

He gave her a sideways glance. "Don't you trust me?"

"Of course I do, but—"

"Next left," he said, his voice blunt with irritation.

"This one?"

"Next left, didn't I say? Next left. You're gonna miss it."

"Okay, okay," Bisma said under her breath. The left turnoff was a narrow entrance between two fields. She probably wouldn't have noticed there was a turnoff had Fergus not alerted her to it. Something about it didn't feel right to her, but she took it anyway, not wanting another argument. The narrow road was overhung by trees on either side, which created a tunnel effect, and the sudden switch from sunlight to shade gave her an added sense of uncertainty but she said nothing. Deep down, she knew it was a matter of pride for Fergus. He could no longer drive but navigating gave him a feeling that he was contributing. She understood that it was difficult for him having to live with his worsening eyesight. First he'd had to sell his accountancy business, then been forced to give up his driving license, and now he had to rely on her to be the breadwinner and to drive him wherever he wanted to go. None of this was easy for a man like Fergus. She knew he felt like he was losing his manhood along with his sight, but as much as she tried to understand there were times when she struggled to control her irritation with him.

Light rain patterned the windscreen. She turned the wipers on. Shifting her gaze from the road, she noticed on the right-hand side the grave-looking entrance to an estate. A rusting iron gate hung between two

71

stone balusters, both of which were topped with a small statue of what looked like a dragon. Beyond she glimpsed a dirt track leading into the grounds of the estate.

"That looks gloomy. I wonder who lives there."

"What's that?"

"Never mind," she said, realising he probably hadn't seen the estate entrance. He'd hadn't been able to see anything in his peripheries for years, and now also had growing blind spots in his vision. His GP said that in five years he would be completely blind. Bisma still felt bad that her first thought on hearing this news was that he'd no longer be able to see her. She'd always known she was an attractive-looking woman, some people even said she was beautiful, and soon her own husband wouldn't be able to appreciate that. Though she never voiced this concern with Fergus, he must have sensed something because one day when she was brushing her hair in the mirror, getting ready for work, he'd told her how beautiful she was and how soon he'd only be able to appreciate her inner beauty. This had surprised her, as he usually didn't like to talk about his chrolodermia. It also worried her, and she hadn't been able to stop thinking about it all day. Eventually, she realised why. Though people had been telling her how pretty she was from a young age, of her inner beauty she was less confident.

The sun set somewhere behind the trees on the left, and the road they were driving grew darker still. The misty rain added to the murk. Bisma had to squint to see the unmarked road. She had an unpleasant thought which she immediately pushed away, that they had taken a wrong turn and Fergus had somehow steered them into his own darkening world.

"I don't recognise any of this," she said.

"It's been ten years since we were last here, Bis."

"Maybe we should turn back."

"I knew you didn't trust me."

"Look, don't start Fergus, okay?" She was always surprised by how sharp her voice could suddenly become. "I told you this trip was a bad idea."

"Why was it a bad idea?"

"Because..."

"Say it."

"I..."

"Because we're not the same people we were ten years ago? Is that it? Because we're not as *happy* as we were back then and coming back to Somerset now will only highlight that?"

She was stunned at how accurately he'd summed up the thoughts that had been turning in her mind ever since they'd left London. Had she communicated this somehow, or had he been thinking along the same lines?

"Fergus, I just don't see the point in going back to the same place, the same hotel. The last time we came here we'd only just met. We barely left the hotel room, remember? We hadn't even meant to come here, we were just driving. We were still in that honeymoon period. You never get that back, but what we have now is something more..."

She trailed off, seeing him reach forward to turn on the radio. She knew it was his way of shutting her out. He jabbed at the buttons but all he found was static.

"I'm not saying we're not happy anymore, Fergus. I'm not. I do wish you hadn't kept quiet about your condition for so long though."

"Can't find a damn thing," he muttered, keeping his gaze lowered. He continued stabbing one finger at the radio buttons. "What's wrong with this? There's no signal."

Bisma let out a long sigh. She knew it was useless trying to talk to him in his current mood. She felt weary thinking of the days ahead, holed up in some hotel having to pretend she was enjoying herself whilst all the time knowing that one careless word could uncork the resentments bubbling in their relationship. She drew in her breath and tried for a more positive tone when she said, "What's the name of this road we're on, Ferg?"

Leaving the radio to its hiss of static, Fergus sat back in his chair and picked up the map again. He held it close to his face for what seemed a long time. When she reached up and switched on the dashboard light, he tutted and threw her a dark look. "Wolvers Hill."

"Are you sure this road is going to take us up to the Mendips? Ferg?"

"Maybe you should have married a Muslim like your father wanted. He could have found you another dentist to chat about the different types of handpieces with. You could've had an arranged marriage."

"Fergus, don't..."

He leant forward to toy with the radio buttons again, but before he could touch it a sudden sound broke through the static. It sounded like a kind of snarl, followed by laughter and it gave Bisma such a start that she lost control for a second and the car swerved toward the right side of the road. There followed what sounded like a scream, broken by bursts of static, which continued until Fergus jerked forward and hit the off button.

Bisma switched her gaze to her husband. She could tell by his expression that he'd also been given a fright. "What on Earth was that?"

"I don't know. Interference."

"Interference? It sounded like...I'm turning the car around."

"What?"

"I don't like this road. It gives me the creeps."

"What're you talking about?"

"We're not getting anywhere, Fergus. I can't just keep driving forever. We're getting low on petrol. Look—the warning light's on."

"Well, I did say we should stop at the Services before we left the motorway."

"That's before I knew you'd have me driving around in circles for an hour."

"That was my fault, was it?"

"Of course it was, Fergus, you're navigating."

He fell silent, turning his head to the side, away from her. Bisma slowed the car in order to turn around, but as she did she noticed a figure walking along the right-hand side of the road ahead of them.

"There's a man," she said to Fergus, although the figure was just a dark blur against the trees and she couldn't tell if it was a man or a woman. She slowed the car. "We can ask if he knows where the hotel is. Check we're going in the right direction."

Had it been up to her, she would have simply turned the car around and gone back to the main road, but she saw an opportunity for Fergus to redeem himself. He was already winding his side window down as she brought the car up alongside the pedestrian. The man had been headed in the same direction they'd been driving, his back to them. He wore a long dark coat and his shoulder-length hair might've been grey or blond. Though it wasn't fully dark yet, Bisma decided to switch the car headlights on. They lit the face of the walking man as he turned when Fergus called out, "Excuse me."

At once, Bisma felt a lurch in her chest and she jammed her foot down on the accelerator. For a moment, she struggled to regain control of the car as it swerved to left and right in the road. She could feel her heart pounding. All she could see in her mind's eye was the man's face. Once she had control of the car again, she began to take deep breaths to steady her breathing. She was aware that Fergus stared at her.

"Bis...what the hell?"

She shot him a glance. "You didn't...?"

"I thought we were gonna ask for directions."

"Fergus, you...you didn't see?" But of course he hadn't. Most likely he couldn't see a thing in this gloom.

"What's got into you?"

"I...his face."

"What?"

"You didn't...?" But now she began to doubt what she'd seen. Perhaps she'd just imagined it. It was this road, and those weird noises on the radio. She was spooked, that's all.

She took a deep breath. "Do you want to go back?"

He turned on the dashboard light again, and his eyes examined her. She knew that he saw how white her knuckles were as she gripped the steering wheel.

"Let's just keep driving."

"How long is this bloody road? It just goes on and on."

His voice was subdued now. "There'll be a turn-off soon. You'll see. Shall I try the radio again?"

"God, no."

He reached one arm out and stroked his hand on the back of her neck. "It's all right, Bis. We're close now."

She looked at him, showing him her uncertainty.

They continued along the road. The car's headlights cut eerie funnels of light from the suddenly full dark. Bisma couldn't help but imagine forms and faces in the patches of illumination ahead of them. Seeing something on the left side of the road she eased her foot off the accelerator.

"What is it?" Fergus said when he noticed the car slowing.

"Another estate entrance." The car headlights picked out the iron gate, and the stone balusters topped with leering dragons. "It looks exactly the same as the one I saw earlier. Only before it was on the other side of the road."

"What're you saying?" Fergus said.

"Nothing. Just that it looks the same. Could we have got turned around somehow?"

"That's impossible."

"I'm going to...don't be offended, Ferg, okay. I'm going to pull over and we're both going to take a look at the map. Okay? I just want to check we're on the right road."

She glanced across at him and he shrugged. Taking this for agreement, she slowed the car and pulled up at the side of the road. Saying nothing,

Fergus handed her the map. She studied the map for a long time, checking the index a number of times whilst he sat in silence.

"Ferg," she said at last. "There's no Wolvers Hill on this map."

"What? Of course there is."

"There isn't."

"I'll show you."

"Fergus, you can't *see*," she said. "Why don't you just admit that you can't see? We should have got SatNav or something. Now we don't know where the hell we are." When she finished talking, she found she was breathing hard, struggling to keep her anger in check. Fergus only stared at her.

"I'll show you," he said again, in a small voice, holding out his hand. She thrust the road map at him.

"It was here. Wolvers Hill. It was here."

"For God's sake, Ferg."

"I'm telling you it was here."

Something heavy bumped against the rear of the car and Bisma let out a scream.

"What...?" Fergus said, twisting in his seat, but she was already starting the car. She performed a tight U-turn in the road then accelerated back the way they had come.

"What're you doing?" Fergus said. When she didn't answer, keeping her eyes fixed on the road ahead, he fell silent. They passed the entrance to the estate again, now on their right, but Bisma kept driving. By the time she realised there was something in the road ahead of them it was too late. There was a thump against the front of the car and she saw something roll across the windscreen and she screamed again. Fergus began yelling at her to stop, but instead she was pressing down on the accelerator. She was aware of the car pulling to the left as they rounded a bend, she saw the needle on the speedometer inching past 60 but still she didn't slow down. Eventually, Fergus' yelling brought her to her senses and she eased her foot off the accelerator. She looked at him. He sat twisted at the waist, facing her. He didn't look himself. His eyes were wide and manic, his face more lined than she'd known it to be previously. She remembered how much she'd enjoyed letting him take charge when they first met, how she was attracted by his surety and his confidence which offset her concerns about him being more than a decade older. *Throw a few things in a bag*, he'd said that day when she'd come home from the dental hospital after finding out that she'd failed her mid-year presentation. *You need to get out of*

London for a while. Then he had just driven with no destination in mind, and it was exciting for her. She always gave so much thought to everything she did, but just to ride in the car with him and not know where they were going was such a thrill. By sundown they were blasting through a landscape of green hills with the top down, both of them looking at each other and laughing. She could remember how her hair had fluttered around her face. She could remember how the whole sky had turned a dreamy-orange colour as the sun dipped below the horizon and she'd felt like she was a million miles from the stresses of London.

This was different. This was just a dark road with no end in sight.

"You have to go back," Fergus was saying.

"What?"

"You hit something, Bis. You need to go back and see what it was."

"Are you serious? I'm not going back there."

"You have to. What if it was a person?"

"It's not my fault. What were they doing in the middle of the bloody road?" Before he could answer, she leant forward in her seat and said, "Bloody hell. There it is again."

She hit the brake and both she and Fergus were jolted forward in their seats. Then she reversed the car a short way along the road until they were parked alongside the estate entrance. The glow of the headlights reached far enough to show her the rusty gate and the balusters topped with stone dragons. The dragons' heads were positioned in such a way that they appeared to be looking directly at the car. Directly at Bisma in fact.

"What're we doing?" Fergus said. "What is it?"

"Look."

"You know I'm nightblind."

Bisma felt a twinge of remorse. "It's that same estate entrance. The same gate. We've passed it four bloody times now."

"It can't be."

Bisma noticed that there was a dark square fixed to one of the balusters. She flipped open the glove compartment and routed inside until she found a torch. She directed the torchlight out of the window.

"What're you doing?" Fergus said.

"There's a name."

"What does it say?"

She took in deep breath and let it out slowly. "Wolvers Hill Estate."

He could have gloated. He could have said I told you so. Instead he remained silent. Eventually he said, "What do I hear?"

77

"Hear?"

She watched as he lowered his side window a few inches then moved one ear closer to the gap. Bisma listened intently aswell. For a short time there was only silence. Then she heard it. An odd sound. Animalistic, but human at the same time. It sounded like someone yelling in anger or perhaps despair. There were no words, just a kind of *Ra! Ra! Ra!* Another sound answered the first, a strange repeated call, low and guttural, and hearing that sound coming out of the dark made the hairs on Bisma's forearm bristle. She decided she'd heard enough, and reached forward to start the car. But when she turned the key in the ignition nothing happened. The fuel warning light still blinked. The gage pointed at 0.

"I don't believe it. I don't believe it. We're out of petrol."

"That can't be," Fergus said. "This car can go forty miles with the warning light on."

"It's been on since we started on this road, Ferg."

"Oh Jesus."

Hearing the dread in his voice was too much for her. "Shit!" she said, hitting the driving wheel with her palms. She began to weep, rocking back and forth in her seat. Words bubbled out of her aswell as tears. "I shouldn't be the one driving, Ferg. You were always the driver. You were always in charge. It should be you sitting here, not me. You wouldn't have let this happen. I can't do it, Ferg, I can't."

"Shush," he said, reaching across and drawing her closer to him. He put both his arms around her and held her. "It's okay. We're fine, aren't we? We're doing ok. None of this is your fault."

"The thought of everything getting darker and darker for you, Ferg. I just can't take it. It breaks my heart."

"Hey," he said. He kissed her forehead. "Let me worry about that."

A bang on the roof of the car brought them to their senses and they both jerked upright in their seats.

"What was that?" Bisma said.

"Nothing. Nothing. It was a bird or...something fell from a tree maybe."

"It didn't sound like a bird." Bisma pointed the torch light out of all the car's windows, but she saw nothing.

"I'll get out and take a look."

"Don't be an idiot," she said. "You're blind."

Catching the hurt look on his face, she felt ashamed. "I...I'm sorry. I wasn't thinking."

He settled in his seat again.

"Turn off the headlights," he said after a pause. "You'll drain the battery."

Bisma flipped the switch to turn off the headlights. Feeling that it drew attention to her, she turned her torch off also, plunging them into darkness. She strained to see in the blackness beyond the car window. She realised she shook, a quiver that ran the length of her body.

"I know you're still angry about the accident," Fergus said.

Bisma laughed under her breath. "Are we really going to have this conversation now?"

"Lots of drivers hit cyclists. Plenty of drivers without my condition. We have a weird blind spot to people on bikes. All of us in cars."

"A literal blind spot in your case."

"I'm just saying, it could have happened to anyone."

Bisma shook her head in the dark. "You shouldn't have been driving, Ferg. You should have told me about your chrolodermia a lot sooner."

"Would you have still married me?"

She said nothing.

"I'll understand if you wanna separate."

"What?"

"You're only thirty-five. You could meet someone else. Who wants to be stuck with an old blind man for the rest of their life?"

She was quiet a moment. Then she said, "I do love you."

"Enough?"

"I...I don't know."

"Well," he said. "It seems to me we've got two options. We can sit here and wait for daybreak, or we can walk up to that estate and see if there's anyone home."

Bisma turned her head towards where the estate entrance was, although she could no longer see it in the dark. "After what we just heard out there?"

"That was just an animal. Fox or something. You'd be surprised at the noises they make."

"I don't think it was a fox, Ferg."

"Well, I'm getting out. I'm tired of sitting down. It can't be very far to the estate house. Worth a try, I reckon. You coming?"

"You know you can't go alone."

She heard the clunk as he unfastened his seatbelt, then the sound of him springing the passenger side door open and her heart lurched suddenly. *Don't go out there!* she wanted to tell him. *This road we're on...there's something wrong. Don't you feel that?* But for some reason the words died inside her. She switched on the torch then pointed it through the windscreen, searching for him. He stood in front of the car with his arms folded, waiting. The sight of all the blackness surrounding him made her want to cry.

"You coming?" he said again.

She didn't want to go, but she didn't want to stay alone in the car either. She unfastened her seatbelt and climbed out. Pointing the torchlight toward the gate, she took his arm and led him towards the entrance. The gate hung at an angle on one hinge and was stuck half-open in the dirt. She avoided directing the light at the dragon statues, fixing it instead on the dirt track that led inside the grounds. There was a large stone in the path and she stumbled over it, letting go of Fergus' arm and dropping the torch. Luckily, it was undamaged. Grabbing it from the dirt, she pointed the light ahead. Fergus had walked on a little way without her. The darkness appeared to be swamping him from all sides, consuming him almost. She hurried to catch up.

"Fergus! Ferg!"

"It can't be that far," she heard him say. He walked too fast, leaving her behind. "Bis...where are you? I can't see you."

"I'm here. Wait. Wait."

"I can't see."

"Fergus! My darling...wait."

He was gone then, beyond the reach of her torchlight and she felt a thread of panic. She heard a weird shriek from somewhere distant, and the thought passed through her head to return to the car. She could go back to the car, lock all the doors and wait until morning. But then she thought of Fergus, that day she'd failed her presentation, saying *Throw a few things in a bag. You need to get out of London for a while.*

So she ran on, following Fergus into that darkness which had taken him, pointing the beam of her torch in all directions, calling his name.
Then...there...*there*...her light found him. He had strayed off the track and crouched in an area of long grass to one side of it. She ran to him and helped him to his feet. She was alarmed to see that he was weeping.

"Fergus what...what happened?"

He wiped the tears from his face with his fingers. "I'm sorry...I got scared. There were sounds...shrieks. I felt something touch me. I'm sure I did. I couldn't see...nothing. I couldn't *see*, Bis."

Bisma could feel her panic threatening to unravel again. Taking a deep breath, and gripping his hand in her own, she led Fergus back to the dirt track. She moved the torch from side to side so that the light arced across the track and into the grass on either side of it. Then she began moving quickly forward, tugging Fergus by the hand.

"Where are we?" Fergus said, sounding calmer, more like himself now. "All I see is black."

"I'll guide you," she said. "Stay with me. I'm here."

Combustible

SETTING FIRE TO Evie's baby blanket was the final straw for Serena; she threw me out of the flat that same evening. It wasn't as if I'd meant to do it. I just got over-excited bouncing my baby girl on my knee, forgot myself for a moment, and the next thing I knew the blanket went up in flames with a whoosh. I got it away from Evie straight away and stamped out the fire—no harm done—but Serena said I was a danger to them both.

"Where am I supposed to go?" I said when Serena tossed me my drawstring bag at the front door.

"I don't know." It hurt to see the fear in her face. I doubted I'd be getting any more chances after this. It was clear that, right then, all she wanted was to close the door and be rid of me. "Why don't you go and stay with Ritchie for a while?"

"Ritchie? I..."

"He gave you a key, didn't he? And he's certainly got the space."

"Yes, but the thing with Ritchie is...it's complicated. You know that."

"I don't care, Gene. Just go. Maybe you'll get lucky and find he's not even home."

"But..."

"Go see what you can set alight at his place."

With that, she closed the door.

I wandered the neighbourhood for a while, thinking that perhaps if I gave it a couple of hours before going back to the flat Serena would have a cooler head and might even let me back in. We lived on the outskirts of the city, out by the ring road, and the streets tended to empty after dark. There was nothing going on, just the wind stirring leaves into little eddies by the curb. When I got tired of walking, I sat down at a bus stop where a gaggle of pre-teen girls—all bad hair and braces—harassed a boy of similar age. The boy was playing it cool, responding to the attentions of these spotty shouting females with mutters and flicks of his fringe. I admired him for that. Girls used to avoid me when I was that age; everyone at school did, ever since that incident in the cloakroom. "Here comes the arsonist," the other kids used to shout when they saw me.

Ritchie was the one girls used to fawn over. Everybody loved Ritchie.

As if to spite me, one of the bus-stop girls' mobile phones started playing a song by The Dicemen, and that was it for me. I saw the bus coming and stuck out my arm. I didn't care where it was headed; anything to get away before those excitable pre-teens started proclaiming their love for The Dicemen and saying how hot and sexy the lead singer was. The bus rolled down into the city centre, where I got off, thinking to have a lager in one of the bars along Park Street before heading home to see if Serena would let me back in; but the streets were just as depressing down here. Music boomed out of one bar, but inside I saw only a few people sat alone. At the entrance to another, a small crowd had gathered around two bald men in checked shirts who were shouting and throwing punches at each other.

"Leave it, Dazzer," came a shrill female cry. "It's not worth it."

Without much thought, I boarded another bus; this one headed over to Westleaze, the leafy part of town. Maybe Serena had been right, and I'd be lucky and find Ritchie was out on tour or something. I could get my head down at his place for a few days, let the dust settle with Serena before I tried to worm my way back in. This seemed like a better idea than going back home tonight whilst the smell of that singed baby blanket was still in the air.

Ritchie's house—or one of them anyway—was a big, detached place overlooking the park on Braysdown Hill. He'd given me a set of keys the last time Serena threw me out, slung an arm around my shoulders, and told me I could crash at his place whenever I liked.

"Gotta look after my baby brother, ain't I?" he'd said, being half-cut at the time. That was the funny thing with Ritchie—no matter how much I resented him, or however much we fought, he was always generous. He stopped by the flat from time to time, always loaded down with expensive toys for Evie, things he'd picked up on his travels.

Hopping off the bus and walking the few streets to Braysdown Hill, I still hoped to find Ritchie's place in darkness; but before I'd even arrived, I heard the thud of beats from two separate PA systems competing with each other from opposite ends of the house. Reaching the gates, I saw that the upper floor windows were all lit up, and I could see people milling around inside. Why had none of the neighbours called the police? Most-likely because Ritchie had either charmed them or invited them over.

It has always annoyed me the way people forgive Ritchie his selfish behaviour: the girlfriends he cheated on, the friends he let down, the neighbours he kept awake all night with his loud music—none of them would say a bad word against him. All he had to do was smile and toss them a cheesy complement—*Hey, Mrs M, you're looking sexy today*—and all would be forgiven. Sometimes, I wanted to shake those people and shout into their faces: *Can't you see? Can't you see what he is?*

After scaling the fence, I rooted in my jacket pocket for the keys. At the back of the house there was an extension built by the previous owner. The granny flat, Ritchie called it. It was separate from the main house: just one room with an en-suit bathroom. I'd slept there the previous time, and since I was in no mood to join Ritchie's party, I headed there now.

The keys got me through two doors. Once inside, I felt the tension in my body slacken. Though the room was in darkness, it felt immediately familiar. From above came the *thud, thud, thud,* of music as well as the murmur of voices, which was strangely soothing. A kingsize bed occupied the centre of the room. I tossed my bag down on the bed then crossed the room to turn on a lamp. I was wondering whether to crawl under the duvet or take a shower first, when I was startled by a woman who sat up from the pillows and blinked at me.

"Hey," she said, pushing her hair back from her face and rubbing her eyes.

"Wha...? Hey."

"Guess I fell asleep." She squinted at me. "Oh, you're someone else."

My sudden presence seemed not to disconcert her in the least. Her looks were Asian, but she spoke with an Americanised twang. She was small, pale, pretty, with dark-eyes and fine hair tinted red and cut to look uneven and punkish. She was possibly in her early twenties, but she could have been younger. When she threw back the duvet to get up, I saw that she was fully dressed, even wearing knee-length boots and a corduroy jacket.

"You a friend of Ritchie's?" I said.

"Eun," she said, sliding off the bed and holding out her tiny hand to me. "You know what that means? It means charitable."

She laughed then, and I wasn't sure why but I guessed it was her way of telling me that she wasn't overly choosy about who she slept with.

"You a friend of Ritchie's?" I said again.

She grinned, nodding towards the wall behind me. "Oh, yes. I try to fuck him many times."

Turning, I saw on the wall at my back a large, framed black and white photograph of Ritchie. He was on stage somewhere, near-silhouetted

84

against the lights. He'd been caught star-jumping over the heads of the front rows whilst dozens of hands reached up towards him.

"That's new." I showed Eun a pained smile. Shot a finger out towards her. "You're a The Dicemen fan, then?"

"Everyone in Japan go crazy for The Dicemen. Everyone want to fuck Ritchie Burrel."

I laughed under my breath. "You sure? Everyone?"

Perched on the edge of the bed, she nodded enthusiastically.

"I'm, well, I'm his brother, you know. My name's Gene."

Her mouth fell open. "No. No way. You lie to me. You not his brother."

"I am. Honestly. My parents named me after Gene Clark. You know, from The Byrds? Isn't that ironic? I got the rock star name, but he's the one who actually *became* a rock star."

She said nothing, just sat gazing at me in wonder. A ripple of discomfort went through me. Ritchie had told me about women like this. *They collect rock star fucks the way you used to collect stamps when we were kids. 'Course, I don't mind being someone's Two Penny Blue.* And I, at the time, thought: *You? A Two Penny Blue? More like whatever Christmas stamp they printed up last year. Colourful but ultimately worthless. A passing trend.*

My entire stamp collection went up in flames when I was twelve.

"Listen," I said to Eun. "I don't know what your plans are, but I was hoping to crash here for a few days. Are you sleeping here, or were you just taking a breather from the party?"

She tilted her head from side to side and smiled in a way that I found unsettling. I felt like prey.

"You cute, Gene. You wanna fuck?"

"Er...what?"

"You wanna fuck? I tell everyone at home I fuck Ritchie Burrel brother. You want fuck me?"

After glancing around the room, as if I thought there was someone else here, my brother maybe, stood in a corner with his arms folded, shaking his head and chuckling to himself, waiting to see how I'd react. *Now, what're you going to do, baby brother?* I could imagine him saying. Whenever he'd recounted stories of life on the road with The Dicemen, and the groupies they encountered, I'd always told him it sounded sleazy. I viewed my life with Serena and Evie as much more worthwhile. Sure, I didn't have the money and the fame and the adoration, but I had something solid, something real. *Those groupies are people remember,* I would tell Ritchie.

85

Probably damaged or just naive. Someone's daughter either way. And he would throw back his head and laugh.

I considered Eun and took a deep breath. "Okay."

I guess a tiny part of me has always wanted a taste of Ritchie's life, just for a moment.

"I fuck good." She shrugged off her jacket and unzipped her boots. "I fuck you good, Ritchie brother."

Thinking I should make conversation, if only to cover my own awkwardness, I pointed at her jacket which she'd thrown on the floor near my feet. "Richie had a jacket like that when we were kids, you know. His had a big black collar. It was from the 70s. Retro. He saved up to buy it, collecting glasses in the local pub. And it looked so good on him. I stole it from his wardrobe once and wore it all day long. I wanted to know how it felt, see? To be that cool. Only, it didn't feel right. I felt self-conscious in it. I thought Richie would be angry at me when I got home again, but he just laughed when he saw me. He laughed like me wearing his jacket was the funniest thing he'd ever seen."

Eun just stared at me with a keen expression. I wasn't sure if she'd understood what I'd said or not. I was even less sure why I was telling her about the jacket. Perhaps, something about this situation reminded me, made me feel the same way as I had then, dressing up in my brother's clothes.

I kicked off my shoes before squatting beside her on the bed. "He's not that amazing is he? I mean, he's just a singer."

"He so talented. The way he dance. He so sexy. A sexy, sexy man."

She dipped her head and sniggered with one hand over her mouth. I couldn't help but laugh, too. The things she said sounded more learned than natural, as if she'd taught herself English watching porno movies, making her seem as cartoonish and fraudulent as the actors in those. What about the real Eun, the one underneath this act? What had her life been like back in Japan? What was her family like? Maybe she had siblings who were all high-flyers whilst she travelled the world trying to have sex with famous people; doing her best to become a line in a song, a note in a biography, anything to let the world know she was here, too. She existed. She fumbled to unbutton her blouse and got down on her knees in front of me. When her fingers went for my fly, I brushed them away.

"Wait a minute. Want to see something cool?"

Eun sat back on her heels and gazed up at me. She nodded. "You do cool stuff like your brother?"

"Way cooler than that. Ritchie's not the only talented one in our family."

I held out one hand, palm upwards.

Eun stared at it. Her eyes shone in anticipation.

I concentrated as hard as I could. What I attempted was a difficult thing to do on demand. It usually happened when I got emotional—angry or excited or joyful. That was when I had to remind myself—*watch out, it'll happen*. The amount of times I had scorched the sheets when in bed with Serena, the amount of times I'd had to rush out the next day and buy new ones to hide what I'd done. Or when we rowed, I had to remind myself to keep my hands balled into fists; and Serena sometimes looked at them as if she thought I was going to hit her.

Sensing that Eun was losing interest, I picked an emotion. Anger. I thought about the time I'd come home and found Ritchie and Serena alone together in the flat. They were fully dressed, sat in the living room on opposite sofas, drinking wine and chatting, but I knew something had gone on. I could feel a weird tension in the air. I could almost smell it.

"Hey, baby brother," Ritchie said when he saw me, and I knew it from his voice, from his expression, from the too-casual way he sprawled on the sofa. I could see it in Serena's smile when she looked up. I could see it in her eyes.

Eun fell back on her haunches as a small blue flame leapt up in the centre of my palm. She made a small grunting noise, clawed at the floor, then staggered to her feet. I held out my hand towards her, grinning, but she reared away.

"What you *do*?"

"It's a talent of mine. I can make fire in my hand. See?"

Serena's fears from earlier bloomed again in Eun's eyes. I closed my hand into a fist, smothering the flame.

"Cool, huh?"

For a long moment, Eun only stared at me.

"Sure. Sure," she said. "Very cool."

She hurried around to the opposite side of the bed, clutching at her jacket and pulling it on. She hunted around for her boots and pulled these on also.

"You didn't like it?"

"Oh yeah," she said in a clipped voice. "Very cool. Very cool. I got to go. I late."

"Late for what? It's almost midnight."

87

"I late. I got to go. It very nice to meet you, Ritchie brother. Very nice."

"You don't want to...I mean, weren't we going to..."

She shook her head. "No, no. I got to go. I late. I late."

"Okay." I shrugged. I glanced down at my hand, opening out my fist again. "It doesn't hurt, you know. There's kind of a...cold sensation. Isn't that weird? A cold sensation from a flame. I can control it, though, mostly. You don't have to worry about that. I just have to remember. Keep my fists closed when I think it might happen. It doesn't happen that often to be honest with you."

Eun was fully-dressed again. When she opened the door, music from above burst into the room. I heard a woman shrieking laughter.

"Goodbye, Ritchie brother." Something in her voice said more than her words, a kind of plea I'd heard before. *Please don't follow me. Just stay right there.*

"Gene. My name's Gene. Like Gene Clark from The Byrds."

The door closed. She was already gone.

I fell back on the bed, and my thoughts returned to that day I'd come home and found Serena and Ritchie alone together. I'd never challenged either of them, never raised my suspicions. Like I said, with Ritchie, you just forgave. I felt a cold prickle in the palm of my right hand, but I kept my fist clenched. Laughing under my breath and rolling my head from side to side on the mattress, I realised how stupid I'd been to try and impress Eun with my little talent. But all that talk about Ritchie, about how wonderful he is...I'd just wanted someone to think about me in that way, just for a nano-second.

A crash from above brought me to my senses.

Someone shouted.

The music stopped.

After a few minutes, I heard voices outside in the driveway. People were leaving. I waited a further half hour or so, then got up off the bed and opened the door in the left-hand wall. Beyond it was a set of stairs connecting the extension to the main house. I climbed the stairs to the ground floor hallway. Bottles, wine glasses and cigarette ends littered the floor. The rooms leading off the hallway were in a similar state. The front door stood wide open, letting in the wind, which stirred the cigarette ash on the carpet.

"Ritchie?"

I climbed the stairs to the first floor and looked in the bedrooms. I saw further disarray, but no sign of my brother. Then, at a noise, I turned. The door to one of the bathrooms stood ajar. Inside, a shirtless Ritchie stood bent towards the mirror above the sink with his hands on the taps. Blood from a cut on one side of his forehead trickled down along his cheekbone. My hand reached out to open the door, and I was about to call out to him when I realised that he was crying. His head fell down towards his hands as the sobs raked him. He drew a deep breath, righted himself, faced his reflection again, and said in a deep, authoritarian voice not his own, "Come on, Ritch. Pull yourself together, man. Come on, you weasel-wank."

He took a credit card and a small, clear bag of white powder from his trouser pocket, cut two lines on the edge of the sink and swiftly snorted them. Seeing him turning towards the door, I ducked back towards the staircase and acted as if I'd just arrived there.

"Hey. Hey. Hey, baby brother." He opened out his arms as if to embrace me though I backed away from him. "Come and join the party."

"Party's over, Ritchie. Everyone's left."

"What brings you here? Looking for work? Want me to get you some work with the road crew again? We've got a new tour coming up."

"No thanks."

"Why aren't you at home with that adorable little family of yours?" Was there mockery in his tone? I wasn't sure. I hadn't detected any. As much as I resented the life he had, perhaps he felt the same way towards me. Maybe that's what sleeping with Serena had been about, Ritchie trying to sample my existence in the same way I'd tried to sample his with Eun. Something cruel snaked across his expression.

Plucking a cigarette from his back pocket, he stuck it in his mouth and tottered towards me in a fit of giggles. "Hey, baby brother—got a light?"

Bastard. Feeling a prickle in my left palm, I closed my hand into a fist. Noticing this, Ritchie narrowed his eyes.

"I know you slept with Serena." I hadn't planned to say it.

Ritchie huffed. "What the fuck are you talking about?"

"That day you dropped by...what was it? Two years ago...?"

"Two fucking years, man?"

"I walked in and found you and Serena talking. I knew something had gone on."

Ritchie sucked on the unlit cigarette, took it from his mouth, and gazed at it as if he couldn't figure out what the problem was.

"You're out of your mind, Gene-o."

"Just admit it."

"I never kiss and tell."

I slammed him against the wall, trapping him there, my face close to his. His eyes were pinned, the black of the pupil almost eclipsing the surrounding blue.

"Just fucking tell me."

He grinned and rolled his eyes as if trying to remember. Blood oozed down the side of his face. "Okay. Okay, I admit it. I tried it on with her..."

"You son-of-a-bitch."

"Hey." He sharpened his gaze. "That's our mother you're talking about."

"So you did sleep with her."

"*Mum?*"

"Serena, you moron."

Ritchie raised his hands defensively. "I tried it on. That's all. I'm sorry. I don't know why. That's just what I do, Gene. I just have to...It didn't mean anything. Honest. And Serena was having none of it anyway."

"What? She didn't...?"

He pursed his lips and dampened his voice. "Do you know what she said? Do you know what she fucking *said* to me? She said she just didn't fancy me. Can you believe that? Didn't fucking fancy *me*."

Releasing him, I fell back, laughing. "Because she *has* to fancy you, right?"

"Right? *Right*? I mean..." He threw out his arms as if to say: *just look at me*. All I saw was a man who looked in need of sleep, and a good meal, and maybe some medical attention for that head wound. I tried to make out whether he was joking or not. I couldn't tell, but I suspected he wasn't.

"Unbelievable." I shook my head.

"You don't blame me, do you? You don't hate me for *that*?"

"Why wouldn't I?"

"Oh, jeez...listen...I've just got to work what I've got, man. It's just front, Gene. That's all I've got: front. All this...it's all an act. It's wearing me out being Ritchie-fucking-Burrel. Do you know how much I'd give to have your god-damned shitty life just for a fucking day?"

"Fuck you."

"I'm serious. You don't know how lucky you are. You've got Evie and..."

"Fuck off."

"And you got the *real* talent."

"Now what're you talking about?"

"That." He pointed at my left hand, still curled in a fist. "What you can do. Why didn't I get a talent like that?"

90

"It's not a talent, Ritchie. It's a fucking curse. It makes people...it terrifies them."

He grinned. "Jimi Hendrix terrified people. Kurt Cobain...Jim-fucking-Morrison terrified people. Back in the 60s, he wandered out on stage drunk as hell and shoved his cock in people's faces. If I did that today, the entire front row'd be snapping away with their camera phones. You can't shock people now. They've seen it all before. They'd think it's fake, just done for publicity. But *that*...what you can do. That's *real*. That comes from some place deep inside you. The same place Hendrix's music came from. The place Kurt Cobain was singing from. *Fire.* Coming out of your fucking palms. That'd get people's attention."

"Bullshit. Know what? Serena threw me out because I set Evie's baby blanket on fire. My own daughter...I nearly..."

He was silent a moment, contemplating the wall at my side. "Think she'll take you back? She usually does, right?"

"Maybe not this time."

"You do it on purpose?"

"Of course I fucking didn't."

"Either way, maybe you should just take the hint."

"Hint? What hint?"

He sighed. "Find a place of your own, man."

"A place of my own? What kind of place would that be? I don't have your cash, Ritchie. And anyway, I couldn't stand not to see Evie every day. Not to tuck her in at night. I couldn't."

He fell silent again, gazing away. After a few minutes, he eased himself away from the wall. "Want to see my art collection?"

"What?"

"Art. It's where all the rockers are putting their money nowadays. Some guy from Metallica started it, I think. Modern art collections. It's supposed to be a great investment or some shit. Wanna see mine?"

I shrugged. "If you like."

He led me to the room at the end of the hall. Inside, the floor was bare except for an L-shaped sofa in the middle of the room and a few bottles and glasses from the party. My attention was first drawn to the lush green curtains hung over the room's one window, and I remembered something Serena had said when we'd visited this house once, something to do with money and taste not being mutually exclusive.

The walls of the room were lined with paintings. A large one took up most of the back wall: big splashes of black paint on a white background.

91

One of the smaller paintings just had the word CUNT written on it in red lettering, whilst another had doll's limbs and bits of text cut from a newspaper stuck in random patterns.

"What do you think?" Ritchie said.

"I..."

"Be honest."

"Honestly...?"

"Yeah?"

"I...I think every single one of these paintings is fucking dreadful."

Instead of getting angry, Ritchie laughed so hard he bent double.

Regaining control, he dabbed at his eyes with the back of his hand. "Dude, they're worth a fortune."

"Doesn't stop them being awful."

He examined the paintings one by one.

"*Jesus*," he said in a harsh breath as if he'd seen something that made him shiver. "You're right."

"I'd much rather be at home in my poky little flat than living here surrounded by this shit." Had I meant to be cruel?

Ever since childhood, Ritchie and I could spend days firing barbed comments at each other in the name of brotherly love. Nine times out of ten, this verbal sparring would end in fisticuffs. Perhaps that was what I was looking for; some kind of explosion; some kind of outlet.

He shoved me sideways.

"Hey...what...what're you doing?"

"I lied about Serena. I did sleep with her. She fucking loved it."

"What?"

He shoved me harder. "She loved it all five times, said I was a sex-god."

I didn't believe him, but my anger swelled. "Bullshit."

"Compared to you, that is."

"You're lying."

"You and your tiny little dick. And what about Evie? Do the math, Gene. That's my kid, not yours."

True or not, I was furious. "You fucking arsehole. You fuck..."

He stood smug, the unlit cigarette hanging off his lip.

I socked him in the jaw.

It felt good.

He came back at me, and we grappled.

I pushed him against that CUNT painting, knocking it from the hook. It slid down the wall and smacked against the floor.

Ritchie kicked it across the room then flew at me.

I ducked his right fist, but his left swing connected with the side of my head. The pain brought tears to my eyes.

The familiar cold-feeling seared both my palms.

Ritchie head-butted me, and I toppled towards the window. I grabbed hold of the curtains to stop myself crashing against the pane.

As I let go of the curtains, a quick line of fire shot along the hem.

"Oh shit." My anger turned to panic.

Ritchie nodded his approval at the flames.

"Do something"

I searched for a fire extinguisher, something to smother the flames, but all he had were those ridiculous paintings.

I yanked the curtains free to stamp out the flames, but Ritchie shoved me away.

Smoke filled the room.

Ritchie flung the curtains onto the sofa.

"What the hell are you doing?"

He restrained me until the entire sofa blazed. It went up quick.

We had to get out of the thick smoke.

I dragged Ritchie into the hallway, both of us coughing and spluttering.

"Where're the fire extinguishers?"

"*Fire*. That's what I'm talking about. *Fiiiiiiiiiii-er*."

"You crazy bastard, this whole place is gonna burn."

Ritchie whooped.

Smoke poured from the room, coiling after us.

We ran, reaching the fence.

Plumes of grey smoke billowed from the first-floor windows against a black sky.

How quickly the flames took hold.

Had this happened at home, my family would have nowhere to run. Why hadn't I seen it before? I was a genuine threat to my loved ones.

The mix of black despair and self-hatred I'd first felt years ago when I set fire to the cloak room at school returned.

My legs gave out, and I collapsed onto Ritchie's overgrown lawn.

I didn't want him to see my tears.

I was alone, and I'd always be alone. That was the price of my *talent*.

It had never impressed anyone. It filled them with fear. It made them want to run, to get away from me, just like Eun had run, like Serena—in a sense—was running.

93

Ritchie's expensive life popped and collapsed inside the house.

The corner window exploded.

Ritchie whooped again. "Yes. Now, that's what I call a bonfire."

Unbelievable.

Blood from his head wound gleamed through a mask of soot on his face. The unlit cigarette hung off his bottom lip, broken.

"You crazy bastard." My jaw ached. "What did you do that for?"

"You did it." He clapped his hands like a kid at a fireworks show. "You burned my house down, bro."

"You made me."

He shrugged.

Sirens in the distance.

"Me and Serena. It was only that once, you know."

"Fucking liar." I wiped at the tears and the grime on my face with the back of my hand. "She doesn't fancy you."

"You gonna go back there?"

I drew a deep breath. My throat hurt. "No. I can't do that. I can't risk it. If something like this happened at home, I'd never forgive myself."

"Thought you'd see sense."

"*Sense?*"

"You just needed to see what you're capable of."

"What do you mean?" I winced as a section of the roof collapsed with a crash and a great expulsion of smoke and cinders. The glass shattered in the rest of the windows along the top floor and flames licked around the frames. How could so much fire and smoke and devastation come from me? "You didn't...I mean...all this wasn't just to make a point was it? You wouldn't. You...?"

"You can still see them. I know you love that little girl."

The fire engines pulled up outside the gate.

"We all do."

Collectable

*I*SN'T THIS JUST *typical*, Dylan thought, flopping down on the sofa and casting his eyes around for the TV remote control. Kristi had been nagging him to get ready from the moment she arrived home from work that evening, now here he was, showered and dressed and waiting for *her*.

Always the same. I should have learnt my lesson by now.

Unable to see the remote control, he picked up one of his wife's magazines from the coffee table. *Hot Now!* was the title. The cover showed an attractive couple Dylan half recognised: the blond man was a premier league footballer, whilst the woman he had his arm around was a soap opera star; or else she was from one of those reality TV shows Kristi liked so much. A jagged line had been added to the picture to separate the couple, plus the headline: *What the hell were they THINKING?*

"Who cares?" Dylan muttered, shaking his head.

He began to flick through the magazine. The first few pages were devoted to blurry, unguarded holiday snaps of a pop singer whose music Dylan hated. LOVEHANDLES! Read the copy beside the pictures. CELLULITE!

"Christ almighty, Kristi. Why do you read this garbage?"

He began flicking faster through the magazine. There was a story about some film actress' failed relationships (WILL SUZI EVER FIND TRUE LOVE?), another detailing a former model's mental breakdown (CAN'T COPE WITH LIFE WITHOUT THE CATWALK), and various side panels concerning celebrity women who'd either lost or gained weight. Dylan was about to fling the magazine aside when he came across a small picture of someone whose name he actually knew. Tyler Reven's doleful, outlined eyes gazed out from the pages of the magazine. Reven was the singer and guitarist from a band called The Cherry Poppers. Dylan had loved The Cherry Poppers first album, *Suicide Ride,* a dark, sludgy mix of punk and metal with tortured lyrics and radio-friendly hooks. He'd been waiting years for the follow-up, something he would now never get to hear as Reven, in homage to his album's title, had shot himself full of heroin one night and driven his car at speed into a lamppost. DID DEATH ROCKER KILL HIMSELF? read the article. CHERRY POPPERS SINGER

IDENTIFIED BY DENTAL RECORDS AFTER HIGH SPEED CRASH. Dylan had just started reading, when Kristi entered the room.

"Okay, babe, I'm ready."

"About time," Dylan said, dropping the magazine back onto the coffee table and standing up. "I can't believe you're making me go to this thing when The Sirens are playing at the Stadium."

"You can catch The Sirens next time they get strapped for cash and decide to reform. Every year they do a tour, and every year it's their farewell tour. Besides, it'll be nice to catch up with Dee and Landon."

"Nice for you, maybe."

"Don't be like that. Sis' said Landon's got some new stuff he wants to show you that he thinks you'll appreciate."

Dylan let out an exasperated groan. But then his face lit up and he went to the bookshelf where his vinyl records were stacked and began fingering through them.

"Now what are you doing?" Kristi said. "We better get going. They said to be there around eight."

"I just want to—aha! Here it is! Good job I looked at that magazine of yours. I might have forgotten otherwise." Pulling a record out from the stack, he waved it at Kristi. "I bet Landon doesn't have anything that can top this."

"What are you talking about? What is that?"

"This," Dylan said, holding the record close to her face. "Is a pink vinyl copy of The Cherry Poppers first single *Die! Die! Die!* They released it on an independent label before they signed their big deal. There were only a thousand of these made." Seeing Kristi roll her eyes, he flipped the record around and pointed to a black scrawl on the back of the sleeve, "And check this out! It's signed by Tyler Reven himself."

Dylan was disappointed to see that he hadn't managed to convey his enthusiasm for the record to his wife, but what could you expect from someone who read *Hot Now!* magazine.

"How much did you pay for that?"

Dylan drew back, offended. "This is highly collectable. Especially now he's dead."

"How much?"

"Only a couple of hundred."

"Bloody hell, Dylan."

"What? What's the problem? Your sister doesn't get all pissy about the stuff Landon collects. In fact, she encourages it."

"Landon has a *job*, Dylan. A very good job in fact. He's got the money to pay for all that junk. And, anyway, he knows what he's buying. The things he collects are like investments to him."

"*This* is an investment." Dylan waved the record in his wife's face. "I bet Landon hasn't got anything as collectable as this record is right now. Now Reven's gone and topped himself, I could sell this on for twice what I originally paid."

Kristi let out a long sigh. "Well do it then because we're short on the rent this month. Or shall I?" She snatched the record from him, then turned and marched out of the room.

"Hey! Be careful with that – that's mint condition. If you scratch it, it's worthless. Kristi. Come on..."

"You coming or not?"

DYLAN COULDN'T HELP but feel conspicuous as he drove his old Volkswagen through the gates and up the driveway to the house where his sister-in-law and her husband lived. No matter how many times he came here, he was always struck by how big the house was. It had eight bedrooms, four of which were on-suite, and downstairs there was even a small movie theatre where he and Landon had once watched all the *Star Captain* films back to back.

"Sheesh. Your sister really landed on her feet, eh?"

Kristi threw up her hands. "Every time. You say that every single time."

"Well she did."

"It's nice one of us did."

Before he could respond to this, Kristi popped open the passenger side door and climbed out of the car. She was tottering on her heels towards the front door before he'd even had a chance to undo his seatbelt.

"Wait up!" Dylan said, grabbing his copy of The Cherry Poppers' *Die! Die! Die!* from the back seat. He couldn't wait to see Landon's face when he showed it to him.

Kristi had already reached the front door. She pressed hard on the doorbell. It was a chilly night, and without a jacket she shivered.

"Dee was always a bit of a vampire through, wasn't she," Dylan said as they waited.

Kristi's mouth fell open. "That's my sister you're talking about."

"Admit it, though, she was. How many men did she go through before she landed old moneybags? It must've been quite a few."

"She's done very well for herself."

"Yes. She has. But she did kind of fuck her way-eeeellll hello," Dylan said, seeing the door open in front of him. Kristi shot him a black look.

Landon stood holding the door. He was tall and tanned and completely bald. He had a penchant for wearing turtleneck sweaters that Dylan always thought made his head look like an egg sitting in an egg cup. At that moment, the egg was grinning.

"Welcome! Hi Sis'. Hi Dylan."

Landon thought of himself as a character. Every time they met, he would act out the same gag. He would give Kristi a kiss on each cheek, then he would pretend he was about to do the same thing to Dylan but at the last moment he would rear back and say, "Oops! Sorry! Getting carried away!" In private, Dylan had suggested to his wife that this might be Landon's way of edging up to his latent homosexuality. Kristi would only shake her head and say, "Jesus Christ, now you think he's in love with you. It's just a joke. Maybe you're the one with *issues*."

After watching Landon go through his routine, Dylan laughed through gritted teeth and shook the man's hand.

"What's that you've got there?" Landon said, noticing the record Dylan held in his other hand. "Brought something to razzle-dazzle me with?"

"You're not going to believe this," Dylan said, although the sarcasm in Landon's last remark had taken some of the wind out of his sails. He held up the record for Landon to see. Kristi sighed and pushed past them both, entering the house and calling to her sister.

"Very nice," Landon said, examining the record. He slipped the vinyl from its sleeve. "Mint condition, I suppose."

"And not only that," Dylan said. "Turn it over."

Landon flipped the record. "Signed as well. Have you had it checked out, though? Is it genuine?"

"Of course. That there is the handwriting of Mr Tyler Reven. Now he's dead, this thing's worth a fortune."

Landon raised one corner of his mouth in a glum smile. He handed the record back to Dylan.

"Nice, eh?" Dylan said as he followed Landon into the house.

"It's okay."

"Okay? There were only a thousand of these printed."

Landon shrugged. "Real collectors aren't interested in limited editions these days, Dylan. *We're* more keen on one-off's."

"One off's? You mean like white-label stuff?"

Landon let out a humouring little laugh and shook his head. It was one of his many mannerisms that frequently made Dylan want to punch him. "No, no, no. I'm talking about real one-offs. One of a kind stuff. What's the point in buying something nine-hundred and ninety-nine other collectors have, when you could get your hands on something truly unique? After dinner, I'll show you a little item I picked up that'll make that bit of plastic of yours look like something you found in a bin at Oxfam."

"You wouldn't find this in..." Dylan began, but Landon had already walked on ahead of him. Dylan hurried to catch up.

"Ah," Landon said, as he and Dylan entered the kitchen. "There she is. My treasure. My prize."

Dee and Kristi stood in a confidant's huddle by the breakfast bar. Both had a glass of white wine in one hand, and both looked around as if they weren't sure which of them Landon was referring to. As he went on, it became clear.

"Doesn't she look beautiful all bronzed."

Dee moved forward to give Dylan a kiss on each cheek. "We just got back from Dubai."

"Dubai? Wow."

"Yes. Landon's joined an exclusive group of dealers and collectors who meet their every year."

"Very exclusive, very select" Landon said, looking at Dylan and winking. "I just made my first purchase through some dealers I was introduced to there."

"Plus, we stayed on an extra week to celebrate," Dee said. "It was our second wedding anniversary."

"Congratulations," Dylan said. He thought that his sister-in law looked more haggard than she had the last time they met, and he wondered how long before Landon set his sights on a younger model. Landon, Dylan suspected, could have any woman he wanted. Even Kristi giggled and flicked her hair more than usual around him, though Dylan knew it was the money and the house and the holidays that made her act this way rather than the man himself. At least, he hoped it was. Landon had, on more than one occasion, made a jocular comment about adding Kristi to his harem. This joke always made Kristi and Dee laugh; but the sly glance Landon would give Dylan when he said it, and the way he always licked his lips afterwards made Dylan uncomfortable.

"Landon bought me this ring," Dee said, holding out her hand to Dylan. Something sparkled under the pendant lights.

"Lovely."

"And you should see what I got him. It was..."

"Ah-ah!" Landon interrupted. "We'll save that for after dinner."

Leaving the women, Landon led Dylan into the dining room where the table was already laid out. The lights had been dimmed, and a real fire blazed in the hearth. Dylan drifted towards a bookshelf crammed with vinyl records which lined one wall. He began pulling records out a random.

"So," Landon said. "Any work lined up? Dee tells me you're still a man of leisure, as they say."

Man of leisure! Yeah, right, Dylan thought. *With all the running around Kristi has me doing.* "Not lately. Still hoping the band's going to take off."

"Ah yes, that's right. You're a bass player, aren't you? What was your outfit called again?"

"We're just called *The* now."

"The?"

"Yes, it's like a statement, you know. *The.* Like there's no real name, we just want people to focus on the music. Like: you tell us what our name is. Right? Why put a label on us? What are we? The...what? The audience decides."

"Oh," Landon said. "I see. Got any shows lined up?"

"We're working on getting some." Dylan was still pulling records from the shelf. "Oh man, haven't heard this in ages."

Landon moved closer to see what Dylan was looking at. "Oh yes. Most of those were recalled. They printed the songs in the wrong order on the sleeve. See?"

Dylan pulled out another record. "This an original? 1966 pressing?"

"Of course."

"Dammit, I'd kill to have that in my collection."

"Take it if you want. I've got another twelve of those. Three of them signed by Barrett himself."

"Thanks, but I couldn't." Dylan slotted the record back into place. He didn't want any handouts from Landon.

He moved through the records until he came across the first album by The Cherry Poppers. The sleeve was signed by each member of the band, of course. Slotted in next to this were a number of the band's early twelve inches, and a few picture discs. For a moment, Dylan felt a little flutter of concern, but then he smiled to himself when he didn't come across a copy of *Die! Die! Die!*

"I didn't know you were such a fan."

"Fan?"

"Of The Cherry Poppers."

"Oh, yes indeed. They were a great band. They have a special place in my heart. Didn't you know that Dee and I met at one of their concerts? It was when they played the Academy. Dee and I had our first kiss to *Corpse in the River*."

"I did not know that." Dylan was thinking that perhaps Landon's earlier dismissal of his signed copy of *Die! Die! Die!* was simply his way of covering up his envy. The man was a fan of the band, yet he didn't have a copy of that record in his collection. He had to be stewing about it, secretly. Had to be. Dylan knew that he would be, if he were in Landon's position. He couldn't help but smile to himself again.

Landon went on talking. "Oh yes. Great gig. I had backstage passes and everything. I was looking forward to meeting Reven. I idolised him a bit. But he took off right after they finished playing, and we only got to meet the others."

"That's a shame. Reven was quite a frontman, wasn't he?"

"He was that," Landon said, he frowned and turned to a drinks cabinet. "Definitely one of a kind. Now then, what can I get you? Please tell me you're not still drinking snakebite."

"Mind if I light up a J?"

"Be my guest."

DINNER CONVERSATION MOSTLY concerned itself with the trip to Dubai. Then, just when Dylan thought he'd run out of ways to say "That all sounds wonderful" and after Kristi had kicked him three times under the table for yawning, Landon stood up and said, "Well, I think it's time."

"Time?"

"To show you the new addition to my collection. You're going to turn green, Dylan, I promise you. You're going to hate me so very much."

"Ha, ha. Never," Dylan said. In truth, he'd forgotten that Landon had promised to show him his latest acquisition. The joint he'd smoked earlier coupled with the holiday talk, and the pictures that had been passed around plus all the wine he'd drunk, had dulled his mind.

"This way," Landon said.

"Oh, you're in for a treat," Dee said as Dylan stood from his chair.

Landon led Dylan along the hallway to a door by the stairs which Dylan hadn't noticed before.

101

"What's this?" Dylan said, watching Landon fiddle with a set of keys. He felt groggy and had to steady himself against the stair banister.

"Basement." Landon unlocked the door and opened it. Reaching inside, he flicked on a light and Dylan saw stairs leading down.

"You're going to wet yourself with jealousy," Landon said, with undisguised glee in his voice.

As he followed Landon, Dylan's attention was drawn to the various items hung on the wall of the staircase. There was a white Les Paul guitar with a signature on it Dylan couldn't make out however much he squinted at it. There was a single drumstick mounted on a white background inside a picture frame. Then lower down there was a battered fedora hanging on a hook.

"Oh, man...is that...from that movie, right?"

"Yes. Those things are from my early days as a collector. They're all fairly worthless now."

At the bottom of the stairs was another door, which Landon eventually unlocked after spending some time searching through his set of keys again.

"Down here's where I keep all my really collectable items," Landon said over his shoulder to Dylan. Once the door was opened, the smell from inside the cellar hit Dylan right away. It was the thick, damp smell found in most cellars, but mixed with this was a more human odour of sweat and shit. It made Dylan think of gym changing rooms and public toilets. Noticing when Dylan covered his mouth with one hand, Landon said:

"Excuse the smell. It can get a bit ripe down here. But it'll be worth it, I promise."

Landon leaned around the wall. There was the click of a light switch, and a burr of fluorescent lights flickering to life before the cellar was illuminated. Landon turned and looked at Dylan as he led the way inside. He had a wide grin on his face.

Dylan stepped down into the attic, then halted. He blinked. The fog in mind cleared.

"What the...?"

The attic space had been split in two by a set of floor to ceiling bars which spanned the room from wall to wall. There was a narrow walkway on the doorway side of the bars, where Landon and Dylan were standing. The larger portion of the space was on the other side of the bars. This space had been set out as a kind of room. There was a stacked bookshelf along one wall, then in one corner was what looked to be a toilet cubicle with a sink next to it. On the opposite side from this was a single bed, and it was this that had stopped Dylan in his tracks. Sat on the bed, bent forward with his forearms resting on his thighs, was a man. The man had raised his head when the two entered, but had otherwise remained still. He had long hair with peroxide streaks that hung forward and obscured his face, but Dylan recognised him. He took a few tottering steps forwards towards the bars. Landon watched him, beaming with pride.

"That's..."

"Cool, huh?" Landon said.

The man behind the bars lifted his head a fraction more to look back at Dylan, and his fringe parted to reveal his face. He had the same expression of weary resignation as the gorillas Dylan had seen at the zoo when he was a child. That look that said they had long ago set aside all struggle and accepted captivity. A dead expression. Empty.

Dylan turned to Landon. "This is a joke, right?"

"I don't joke about my collection, Dylan. This is the real thing."

"But it's..."

"That's right. You might have the record upstairs with the signature on it, but I've got the hand that signed that signature. And the mouth that sung those words. I shouldn't really be showing you this, but you understand, right? We're both collectors. Besides, even if you did go to the police there are all kinds of security measures in place to ensure maximum deniability. My new dealers are very experienced with these kinds of items. They have it all covered."

"It's not an item, Landon, it's a person. It's..."

"Beats a bit of coloured vinyl any day, eh?"

"But he's...he's supposed to be dead."

"Oh, the crash was faked. Hell of a thing to pull off. That wasn't him they pulled out of there, it was some other chump. A stand-in. It was all a set-up."

"But...his dental records. The identified him with dental records. I read it just...just today. I read it."

"Oh, that kind of thing is easily falsified. All you need do is bribe a few people here and there. You wouldn't believe how much planning goes into acquiring something like this. And the money! Do you know how much I paid for this? Then there was the cost of all the renovations down here. Silly money. But actually, I didn't pay. Dee got it for me as an anniversary present."

"But he's got a wife. And a baby. You can't just keep him locked away down here. He's..."

"His wife? Ha! That junkie bitch? She was in on the whole thing. She helped stage his death. Can you believe that? She's going to inherit *millions*. The marriage wasn't working out, I believe. She'd been casting around for a collector to take him off her hands for months." Landon lowered his voice, though there was only Reven to overhear, and it occurred to Dylan that if Landon was worried about that he might have lowered his voice a lot sooner. "Do you know – and this is all between you and me of course – that I met a couple of collectors over in Dubai who're in possession of some very interesting items. There's an oil trader I met who's had a certain female blues singer hidden somewhere in the Blue Ridge mountains for over forty years. And then there was a software guy from Japan who actually claimed to have...well...choked on his own vomit indeed. Ha ha."

"You mean...?"

"Twenty-seven years of age seems to be the preferred vintage. But I shouldn't be telling you all this."

Dylan's mouth worked, but he had no words. He allowed Landon to turn him back towards the stairs, then stood in silence as Landon switched off the lights inside the cellar, then closed and locked the door. In his mind's eye he could still see Tyler Reven sat there on the edge of that little bed. A man he'd once watched perform on stage with so much anger and passion, a man whose music he'd been listening to since he was a teenager, reduced to sitting alone in the prison Landon had constructed for him with that resigned expression on his face. He paused to turn back, to say something – he had to. Didn't he? - but he heard Landon whisper in his ear, "Security measures. All in place. Maximum deniability. They'll ruin you. Make you look like a clown. A mad man. What would Kristi say?" And he felt Landon's hand on his arm, and he was ushered back upstairs to the dining room, where Kristi and her sister where talking about some TV actress' baby.

"So ugly," Kristi said, then fell silent when she saw the expression on Dylan's face.

"Honey-bun," Dylan said. "I think we'd better go."

The Six O'clock Ghost

A TERRIBLE THING happened yesterday. The woman from the top floor, the one who was always working late, fell down the stairs in the dark on her way out and now she's dead.

It was Agata who told me after I arrived for work today. She said the woman fell down one flight and slammed her head against the wall at the turn of the staircase. How awful. It must have been quite a tumble. She died of a brain haemorrhage, Agata said. She wanted to know if I'd noticed anything unusual, since the woman's office was on one of my corridors. I told her I always start work at the top of the building then work my way down, so I would've been on the ground floor by the time the woman left. She'd been at her desk though, as usual, when I went into her office to empty the bins.

"When was that?"

"That would've been around five-thirty."

"Did she say anything to you?" Agata wanted to know.

"No," I told her. "She never did. Never so much as a hello or a thank you."

Of course, there'd been that one time when I'd politely asked if I could vacuum her office and the woman had snapped at me and said, "Of course not, I need to concentrate. I have work to do, you know." I could've told her that I too had work to do, but people like her don't like being spoken to in that way by people like me. In their minds, they're at the top and I'm somewhere close to the bottom. I'd had to go all the way back up to the top floor at the end of my shift to vacuum her office, even though I don't like going back into the main building after Ken, the security guard, has turned off all the lights in the corridors. But she was still there and it was almost seven o'clock so I left because I wanted to get home in time to watch my soap operas. Then the next day I was told there'd been a complaint. One of the top floor offices hadn't been vacuumed. So, from that day on I had to go back up in the dark to the top floor just to vacuum her office after she left which meant I always missed the start of *The Young and In Love*.

But I didn't mention any of that to Agata. What for?

"No," I said. "She never said a word, and never took her eyes away from that computer screen."

"I've been telling them for years that stairway's dangerous," Agata said. "The door at the top opens the wrong way – *into* the stairwell. Something like this was bound to happen. How awful. Jessie, you must've been the last person to see her alive."

"I suppose."

When Joan arrived and heard the news, she gasped and put her hand to her mouth. "Heavens to Betsy," she said. "They're dropping like flies in this place. What was the name of that chap who died last year? You know the one. Thought he was the absolute bee's knees until he got sick. He was always at the water cooler, filling up that funny little bottle he kept on his desk. You'd see him walking around sipping on it. I reckon he had some kind of oral fixation. He was like a baby, sucking on a teat."

"It's good for you to drink water," Agata said.

"Well it didn't do him much good, did it?" Joan said. She pointed a finger at me. "You know who I mean, don't you?"

"Mr. Jenkins," I said. "From floor two."

"Aye. Another one of yours, Mouse."

Joan called me Mouse because she said I sounded like one when I talked. "Squeak, squeak," she said to me sometimes. "What's that little Mouse? Speak up." She liked telling people about this one time when she says I almost gave her a heart attack because she looked around and I had just appeared behind her. "A big girl like her should stomp around," she would say, "but she doesn't, she creeps. You don't hear a thing until she's right there breathing down your neck. Oh, my heart's never been the same. I get little flutters every now and again and I can't breath. That's because of her."

Only Agata seemed to notice how red in the face I got when Joan said things like this. "Just ignore her," she said once. "She's old."

"Did they ever find out what he died of, that Mr. Jenkins?" Joan asked.

I shrugged. Then I put my back to the others and started preparing my kart. It was true what Joan said. Mr. Jenkins had a little water bottle which he kept on his desk and he was always filling it up and slurping on it. I would see it sat there half-full when I was dusting around his desk. He was a jogger. He had jogged past me once, years ago, as I was signing-in at the reception desk at the start of my shift. I had almost bumped into him as I stepped away from the desk, and as he ducked around me he shouted to Ken: "Warning—this vehicle is reversing!" I knew it was a joke about my

106

size. Ken had looked like he wanted to laugh, but since I was facing him he'd pressed his lips together in a line, shrugged, and shown me this face like he didn't know what Mr. Jenkins was talking about.

"Something strange is going on in this place," I heard Joan say. "People dying. Something's not right."

It crossed my mind then to tell her and Agata about this thing I call the six o'clock ghost. But then I realised they'd only laugh at me. Anyway, I'm not sure the six o'clock ghost is a real thing or if it's just a feeling I get after most of the people have left the building. Even though I know I'm alone on my corridor I get this sort of prickly feeling, as if there's someone else there, watching me. The feeling gets so strong that I can't think about anything else. Sometimes I daren't raise my eyes from whatever job I'm doing in case I catch a glimpse of something. One time I was cleaning the sinks in the toilet and I happened to glance up into the mirror and just for a split second I thought I saw someone stood behind me. It was a woman, I think. Most likely, I imagined it.

I told Agata I didn't want to clean the top floor corridor today, in view of what had happened. Just the thought of having to go into that dead woman's office was making my stomach churn. Agata said that was okay, she'd do it for me if I cleaned her ground floor toilets. I think she just wanted a nose around up there, but I was grateful.

The next day when I arrived for work another odd thing happened. Not odd like a woman falling down the stairs and smashing her head in on the wall, but it did upset me a little bit, I don't know why. I was just entering the lobby, when someone called my name. Looking up, I saw a man stood by the lifts with his arm around a young woman. He was grinning at me.

"Jessie," he said. "Jessie Cain, right?"

"I...uh...?"

"Don't you remember me? It's Conrad. We were at school together."

Truth is I had recognised him; I just hadn't known what to say. He seemed genuinely pleased to see me as if we were ex-comrades when in fact we hadn't even been in the same class at school and had only known each other in passing. We did have one thing in common. At school, we were both bullied.

At senior school I was the person no one wanted to know. Even those I thought of as friends, and sought out at break-times so as not to stand alone, would eventually scatter like startled pigeons when they saw me coming. What it was about me that made me so untouchable I had no idea. Maybe it was the way I spoke. *Squeak, squeak. What's that little Mouse?* I was bullied relentlessly by my classmates. They called me fat, they called me ugly, they told me I was stupid and that I stank. I took it all, everything they could dish out, without a word of retaliation. Maybe I thought it was all I deserved.

Conrad was picked on because his clothes were cheap, or maybe because he had red hair, or because of his name. Who knows? They didn't really need a reason. I realised on seeing him again that I'd admired Conrad back in our school days because he fought back. Often, walking the school corridors, I would come across him in a tangle with another boy, or boys. Fighting. Always fighting.

"You don't work here too, do you?" he said.

"Yes," I said. "I'm a cleaner."

His smile faded for a second. I looked at the girl on his arm, a plump freckled thing, nothing special to look at but you could see she was good-natured.

"I remember you were always good at art. Do you still draw?"

I shrugged. "What's the point?"

He nodded, still smiling, but his eyes said something else. Looking at him standing there in his shirt and tie, with his arm around that sweet freckled girl, I thought: *Those fights you rarely won back in school, you've won them now.*

Me? I haven't even started.

It was this thought, I think, that upset me.

I NEVER WANTED to be a cleaner. No one, I think, wants to be a cleaner. Who likes leaving their job smelling of bleach and toilet cleaner? When I was a child I wanted to be Beatrix Potter. I used to draw pictures of rabbits and mice and ducks wearing little hats and bow ties, and I'd make up stories about them. In my school report, the art teacher, Miss Miller, wrote that I had 'flair'. She used to show my drawings off to the class. But somewhere along the way I lost faith in myself. There was always that chorus of voices in my head telling me I was fat and ugly and stupid and that no one would ever be interested in anything I did. That's how I ended up here, emptying bins and hoovering floors and scrubbing toilets. Sometimes when I'm lying in bed at night, I imagine this other life, the life I should have had, a life that got taken away from me by those bullies at school, the ones who go on and live their lives and have success and always get what they want and always win.

Agata says I should stop blaming others for my lot in life and go out and get what I want before it's too late.

Only, I don't think I want that anymore. I don't want to be Beatrix Potter. It's lost its appeal. I can only think of one thing I want these days. Sometimes I feel it cursing through my body like electricity. It's anger. It's a need. It's what I want: revenge.

AS IT TURNED out, all that talk of Joan's about her poor heart was true as she was dead of a heart attack before the year was out. They found her body out by the bins behind the main block. It gave me a chill going out there on those dark nights. I imagined someone hiding there, lurking, waiting to leap out. I wondered if Joan had met the six o'clock ghost. Agata said it was probably the job that killed her. She said a woman of Joan's age shouldn't have been working, but apparently she loved to spend money on the bingo and her pension couldn't cover it so she had no choice.

"She should've been taking it easy at her age," Agata said. "And now look."

I felt sad for Joan, but part of me was glad that I'd never have to suffer her teasing anymore. She reminded me of the girls at school who used to make a whispering noise in imitation of me whenever I spoke. I don't like to admit it, but sometimes when I'm alone I say the names of those girls under my breath and wish that they are dead too. I'd imagine the places where they now worked, bright offices where they were team-leaders or managers or consultants, and I'd imagine the six o'clock ghost moving through those bright corridors, searching for them. One by one it would find them. And with a little push, or a bit of bleach, or a surprise when they were least expecting it, they would get what was coming to them.

THERE'S SO MUCH that I'd like to tell, it's almost bursting out of me, but I know I can't tell anyone; although sometimes I imagine telling Conrad. I'd find him at his desk when I arrived for work and I'd ask if I could speak to him out in the lobby. He would stand up dutifully and follow me out though the double doors. There by the lifts, in a whisper, I'd tell him everything. About Joan, and Mr. Jenkins, and the woman who fell down stairs, and all the others I hadn't yet found. About the six o'clock ghost.

I imagine how he'd look concerned at first, but after a while he'd smile. He'd smile and I'd smile. Our smiles would just get bigger and bigger as we stood there in a huddle, and we'd cover our mouths with our hands and laugh.

109

"Oh my God, Jessie," he'd say, giggling.

"That's right," I'd say. "It's our turn."

The Garden of Lost Things

LIZ HAD BEEN unpacking books and photograph albums from a box and placing them on the shelves David had erected in the living room, when she heard her husband calling to her from the garden. Wanting to be done with the box, she lifted the last few items from it and set them on the floor. She saw, though, that a few of the photographs had slipped out of the albums and lay scattered at the bottom of the box. As she retrieved them, she saw that one was of Carol as a baby. Carol sat in her pushchair, wrapped up in a too big winter coat and bobble hat. She stared directly into the camera with big dark eyes. Her face wore that questioning, confounded look so typical of babies. It should have been cute or comical, but all Liz saw in her daughter's expression was accusation. Squeezing her eyes shut, she slipped the photo into one of the albums then got to her feet. She felt a twinge in her back and heard her knees crack.

"Lizzie! Liz!"

"What is it, dear?"

Entering the kitchen, she saw him by the patio doors. He was holding something up in his hands. At first she thought...but no, that photo of baby Carol had put odd ideas into her mind. It was a doll of some kind, that's all.

"What've you got there?"

"Buried treasure."

"What?"

"I started digging, and I found this."

They hadn't even finished unpacking yet, and already he'd started on his pond. Koi carp, that's what he wanted to put into it. He'd been talking about it ever since their first viewing of the bungalow.

"Nice big garden," he'd said. "Maybe I can finally build that pond I've always wanted. Get some Koi carp."

"Why not?" Liz had said, not thinking for a moment that he was serious. They'd been married for over forty years and throughout that time he'd come up with various plans and schemes which he'd never carried out. This Koi carp thing was just the latest one. "You'll need something to keep you busy now that you're retired."

He still held the doll out towards her. Its body was black from the earth, and it had soil embedded into its eye sockets, nostrils and along the line of its lips.

"What do you want me to do with that?" she said. "Just throw it away."

"It looks old. Maybe it's worth something."

He began brushing the soil from the doll's face when Liz reached out a hand and stopped him. She took the doll and examined it. It wasn't a doll at all but a monkey. Its head and body were soft, but its face was made from hard plastic. Its eyes were closed into slits and it had white tears painted onto its cheeks as if it were crying.

"It's Bam-Bam," she heard herself say.

"Bam-Bam?"

She glanced up into David's face. "I...I had a toy just like this when I was a child. I called him Bam-Bam. He was a monkey. Exactly like this one. I took him everywhere with me. Then one day I left him on a train. I must've cried for a week. I couldn't believe I'd lost Bam-Bam."

"Well," David said, smiling. "Looks like you've found him again."

"Oh, this isn't...this couldn't be the same one. They made hundreds of these things. What a coincidence though. I had this exact toy."

"I think it *is* Bam-Bam," David said. Liz detected a hint of mockery in his tone. "I think he missed you, and I think he's finally found his way back to you."

"Shut up, you old fool."

"Don't I get a kiss for digging him out of the ground?"

"You get back to your pond," she said. "You'd better finish it now that you've started."

SHE THREW THE monkey in the kitchen bin, but David must have retrieved it, cleaned it up and left it out in the sun to dry. She was preparing for bed in the new, still-unfamiliar bedroom when he presented it to her again. It now looked so much like the lost Bam-Bam that the moment she set eyes on it she was dizzied by a swirl of childhood memories. She turned away, flapping a hand.

"I don't want that dirty old thing. Get it away from me."

David laughed. "Are you talking about me or the monkey?"

"Which one do you think I'm talking about?"

"He's not dirty anymore. I gave him a wash."

"What on Earth did you do that for?"

"It's Bam-Bam. He's come back to you. Go on, give him a cuddle."

112

"You really are a silly old sod," she said. "Bam-Bam's lost. I left him on a train." Drawing a deep breath, she let it out slowly. She shook her head. "I always was careless." Looking into the mirror above her vanity table, she was surprised—as she sometimes was—by her own reflection. The face looking back at her was so creased and lined, like a silk shirt put through the washing machine, how could it be hers? And that shock of white hair— who did that belong to? She'd been a redhead once, a fiery redhead, until her hair turned grey almost overnight and then as she aged became thin and brittle and white. *Crone*, she thought. *Who could love such and ugly old crone?* Shifting her gaze, she caught her husband's eye. He dropped his head, pretending to examine the monkey's features instead.

"You're not still beating yourself up are you, Liz?"

"I just wish I wasn't such a flake."

"You're not a flake," he said. "We all lose things from time to time."

"Not like me. I've been absent-minded since the day I was born. I used to imagine that there was a room somewhere full of all the things I'd lost during my life. My own personal lost property office. It would be full to the brim with all the things I've dropped or mislaid or forgot somewhere. Just my things. It would be overflowing with them."

He was silent a moment, turning the monkey over in his hands. Liz was suddenly afraid of what he might say next.

"Well, I suppose it's true that you are always losing things," he said, and her heart dropped. Then he raised his head and she saw that he was grinning. "Remember your virginity?"

Liz smiled, despite herself. "I didn't lose that. You took that from me. You charmed it right out from under me."

He lay down on the bed, clutching the monkey to his chest.

"No, you were under me, remember?"

"Either way, that one's on you."

"And what about me?" he said. "I've lost stuff. My heart, for one thing."

"Ha! See— that's it! That's the stuff you used on me. I was only a girl then, but it's been forty-six years. Don't think you can work that smarm on me anymore."

"Come to bed," he said.

"I'll come to bed when you get rid of that monkey. I've already got one antique cluttering up the place. I don't need another, thank you."

He tossed the monkey on to a chair in the corner of the room. "Come to bed. Please."

NEXT, IT WAS her grandmother's watch. The one with the peacock inscribed on the casing and a little butterfly on the dial itself. It was sitting on top of a mound of earth David had dug up from the hole he was making in the centre of the lawn. She'd been taking him a cup of tea when she saw it sat there, half-buried.

"What's this? More treasure?"

She wiped dirt from the watch face with her thumb, blinked at it, and then her mouth fell open. The hand in which she held the cup went slack, and David's tea spilled onto the grass.

David looked up, squinting against the bright sunshine.

"My cuppa! What's the matter, love? Don't tell me that's some more of your lost property."

"It's my grandmother's watch. Or one just like it."

He laughed. "Pull the other one."

"It is, David. It's the watch my mother gave me. She'd got it from her mother. I wanted to hand it down to Carol, but then the one time I wore it—when we went to that charity dinner, remember?—I lost it. It must have dropped right off my wrist. The clasp always was a bit loose. I never forgave myself. It was supposed to have gone to Carol."

"Well," David said in an off-hand tone. He cleared his throat. "It could never have gone to Carol anyway."

Liz turned the watch over in her hands. "It looks exactly the same. Isn't that strange?"

"Has to be worth a few quid."

"But, David—first Bam-Bam, and now this. Don't you think that's strange? And this wasn't some mass produced toy like that monkey. There can't have been too many of these made. It's...it doesn't make sense."

"Well," he said. "You used to think there was a lost property office full of all your stuff, but in actual fact there isn't. There's a garden. *This* garden."

"That's crazy."

"I'm going to keep digging. To see what else is down here."

Liz took a deep breath. Her chest felt suddenly heavy. "I wish you wouldn't."

SHE REFUSED TO accept it.

She refused to accept that all the things she had ever lost during her life could be somehow buried in the garden behind their new cottage. It was coincidence, that's all. Some kind of crazy coincidence. Even when David pulled from the ground a sheepskin flying jacket exactly like the one she'd

114

owned years ago in her thirties, and worn every day for two years, the one everyone told her she looked so good in until she forgot it one day in a café and by the time she remembered and rushed back it had gone.

"It's your old jacket, Liz," David said, shaking off the dirt and holding it up by the shoulders.

"No, it's not."

"It's exactly like the one you used to wear."

"It's not. It's not mine."

"You know what I think?" David said. "Bam-bam, your grandmother's watch, this jacket. These aren't just things you lost. They're things you *loved* and lost. These are your most precious things I'm digging up here."

Liz turned away from him, putting a hand to her head. *Precious things? Oh God. Precious.*

"What's the matter, love? Getting a headache? Maybe it's the sun."

A sudden anger took hold of her. "These aren't my things," she snapped at him. "I told you. It's just coincidence. Someone buried a load of old junk in this garden, and now you're digging it up bit by bit."

"I wonder what else could be down here. What's the most precious thing you've ever lost, Liz?"

She wanted to rage at him. *Shut up! Just shut up!* How could he be so careless with his words? So insensitive? Or was he doing it on purpose?

When he glanced up to catch her eye, she looked away. When she returned her gaze to him, he was looking at her with an odd, wide-eyed expression. It was an expression that came over him whenever thoughts connected in his brain. His face would go slack and his eyes would bulge and he'd just stare. *Poor David*, she used to think whenever she saw this look on his face, *his thinking is always a step behind everyone else.*

"I'm going inside and I'm going to take a bath," she said.

"Alright, love." His voice was distant, subdued.

Lying in the hot bath water, she couldn't help but think about Carol. When she was a baby, Carol used to love bathtime. She'd sit up and splash at the water with her plump little hands, laughing every time. She never got bored. Then she'd cry whenever Liz lifted her out. Liz would wrap towels around her, so that only her face was visible. Those big watchful eyes. *Precious*, that had always been David's name for Carol. *Where's my little Precious*, he would say when he arrived home from work. *Look at her, my little Precious.*

Remembering this, Liz pushed her head under the water, drowning the tears that welled in her eyes.

What's the most precious thing you've ever lost, Liz?

He hadn't meant it.

He couldn't have meant it.

He could never have been so cruel, surely?

When she emerged from the bathroom, the house was dark and silent. Crossing to the window in the bedroom, intending to draw the curtains before turning on the light, she put a hand to her mouth as she looked out into the garden. David was still out there, digging by torchlight. And it looked as if he'd dug holes all over the lawn. There was hardly a blade of grass left. For a few moments, she could only stand there, making little moaning sounds under her breath. Her hand moved to open the window as she thought to open it and yell at him: *Just what the hell do you think you're doing?* But it was as she did this that she understood and her hand froze.

"Oh no. Oh God. He's not...he's..."

No. You can't. You stupid old sod. No.

Slipping her feet back into her slippers, she left the bedroom. In the hall she paused to thrown on her coat, then she went through the kitchen and out through the patio doors into the garden. The day had been warm, but the night had turned chilly. She shivered and pulled her coat tighter around herself. Her wet hair felt icy against the back of her neck. A full moon, bright and pale, was caught in the branches of the cherry tree at the furthest end of the lawn. She heard a child's voice in her mind, singing:

"I see the moon and the moon sees me.

The moon sees the somebody I'd like to see.

God bless the moon and God bless me.

God bless the somebody that I'd like to see."

Pushing the voice from her thoughts, she moved forward until she stood at the rim of the hole her husband stood in. He hadn't noticed her, hadn't paused in his digging. There were various objects scattered around the edge of the hole, some of which glittered in the moonlight, some of which were half-buried in the loose soil David had thrown up from the hole, but she refused to look at them, refused to recognise them, refused to remember them. They had no right to be here, here in this garden. What were they doing here?

"David," she said. "Stop it."

She saw now that some of the holes he'd dug were quite deep, they had to be three feet, some of them. David was standing up to his thighs in one

116

of them, working tirelessly with the spade. His torch was perched on a mound of sod along the edge of the hole.

"David," she said again. "Did you hear me?"

Startled, he glanced up. "Love?"

"Just what the hell do you think you're doing? Look what you've done to our garden, you daft old bugger."

"Looking, love. Just got to keep looking."

"What for? Do you really think you'll find her, down there under the soil?"

He looked up again and this time his expression was marked with guilt. Then he shook his head and returned to digging again.

"She's not down there," Liz said. "She's gone. I lost her and I'm sorry, I've been sorry for thirty years. I only turned my back for a moment. I thought she was right there, but...I lost her and she's not coming back, so stop making our lawn look like no-man's land and get your silly arse back in the house."

"Liz," he said. "Bam-Bam was gone. The watch was gone. But I found them again. I found them right here in this dirt. I think everything you've ever lost is here. That's what I think. I don't know why, or how, but if I just keep digging, I'll find everything you ever lost. You said yourself—that watch, it wasn't mass produced. How could one be here, in our garden? And Bam-Bam. Don't you see? It's too much of a coincidence. I just have to keep digging and then somewhere, somewhere I'll find..."

"*David*," Liz said, her voice sharp with anger although part of her wanted to jump down into that hole with him, jump down and help him dig. She'd use her hands if she had to, claw at the earth, get it all up, get it all out, to see what was buried there. Tears hung at the rim of her eyes. Maybe if they did find something she wouldn't have to feel guilty any more. She wouldn't wake up remembering. Wouldn't see her daughter's face every time she closed her eyes. Wouldn't dread the day of her daughter's birthday every year, wouldn't have to see the anguish on her husband's face when he said, *She'd be thirty now. A grown woman. She'd be thirty-one now. Thirty-two now, thirty-three now.* Every year he would say the same, and every year she would think that she couldn't stand it anymore, the guilt, the pain, the sorrow.

"Get out of that hole, right now, get inside that house and get yourself cleaned up. Then you're going to get in bed with me. Then tomorrow we're going to fill in all these holes, every last one, and we're going to forget about all this nonsense. Is that clear?"

He stopped shovelling dirt out of the hole, and stood with his head bowed. Then he lifted his head and met her eyes.

"I don't blame you," he said. "I want you to know I don't blame you. It could've happened to anyone. You're not a flake, you weren't born absent-minded. You're just..."

Liz closed her eyes for a long moment, letting the tears spill down across her cheeks. When she opened them again, she saw her husband still stood thigh-deep in the hole. He looked so pathetic, so forlorn, and for some reason so heroic at the same time that she had to smile.

"Get out of there, you daft old bugger," she said, reaching out a hand to help him. "Before I start filling it in with you in it."

"I just miss her so much," David said. "I just thought...there might be a chance..."

"I know," Liz said, reaching out her hand to him. "I know."

Ghostlights

*H*ALF-FALLING THROUGH THE door as it opened, Leona scrambled towards the stairs calling her sister's name. "Izzy. Izzy."

The music was so loud Leona must have heard it the moment she entered the house, but it only registered when she reached the first floor landing. A drumbeat, flat and urgent, as if inciting Leona to hurry, resounded throughout the house. A quick synth line followed the beat *diddley-di diddley-di*. What was it? Something from the 80s. Something they used to listen to when they were teenagers. Though she couldn't make out the vocal, a snatch of lyric sprang into Leona's mind.

It won't be long until you do exactly what they want you to...

"Izzy." She screamed the name. "Izzy. Please. No." Then to herself, clawing at the floor as she ascended to the second floor landing: "Oh God."

SHE'D KNOWN SOMETHING was wrong since before they'd left the house that morning. Izzy had been more morose than usual at breakfast, gazing into space, leaving her tea and toast untouched, and not responding when Leona spoke. The previous evening they had argued after Leona caught Izzy using her laptop to look at audition notices on *backstage.com*. The row had ended with Izzy screaming, "It's what Mum wanted!" before tearing up the stairs and slamming her bedroom door.

"What is it?" Leona had said as they sat together at breakfast. "Are you tired? Aren't you feeling well today, Iz?"

Izzy only shook her head. "I can't do it," she said in a low voice. "I can't. It's just..."

Leona would have suggested her sister take the day off, but she was scared to leave her alone in this mood, and she didn't dare take another day sick herself this month. She'd already had a Stage One meeting with Mr Balding. After that, it was too easy to progress through the stages until you were on Stage Three which usually ended in dismissal.

"Come on. Get your coat on. We'll be late."

"Wait," Izzy had said when they reached the front door. "Let me go upstairs. Just for a minute."

"We're going to miss the bus."

"I need it, Leona."

"I thought we'd decided. We've put all that behind us."

"You decided."

"Yes, for both our sake."

"I can't face it. Being jammed into that cubicle all day. I can't. I need to move."

"No, Iz. You know you shouldn't. You don't know when to stop. That's the problem. Now hurry or we'll miss the bus." She could have added, as a counter to what Izzy had yelled at her the previous evening, *This is what Dad wants for us.* But she'd thought better of it.

Izzy's mood had deteriorated further after that. She sulked all the way to the bus stop then let Leona board first and find a seat so that she could choose not to sit with her. She sat alone near the front of the bus. When a heavy-set man boarded and sat down next to Izzy, boxing her in against the window, Leona watched her sister squirm.

I need to move.

When they arrived at work, Leona caught Mr Balding's eye and saw him checking his watch.

"Sorry," she said, though they were only a few minutes late. Izzy said nothing. She walked to her cubicle as if in a trance and slumped down in her chair without taking off her coat. Leona checked on her whenever she could through the morning, spinning her chair around to glance over towards Izzy's cubicle. It was around 11:30 when she looked and saw her sister gone. When Izzy hadn't returned by 11:45, Leona knew something wasn't right. She crossed the room to her sister's desk.

"Where's Izzy?" she asked the people in the neighbouring cubicles.

"Dunno," someone said. "She just grabbed her coat and left."

"She...?"

"That sister of yours is already on a warning." Mr Balding had appeared at Leona's back. She whirled to face him.

"I'm sorry."

"Something will have to be done." Some of the heads in the surrounding cubicles were turned towards them. He lowered his voice. "A month off work with depression and now this."

"I know. I'm sorry, sir."

Mr Balding opened his mouth to speak, but Leona cut him off.

"I have to go."

Out of breath, Leona reached the door to the attic space. She twisted the doorknob. It wouldn't budge.

"Izzy!"

The music coming from the other side of the door was almost like an affront, like a raised middle finger; that nagging electronic drumbeat, the snaking synth melody and the muffled vocal, doomy, portentous.

....exactly what they want you to...

Leona added a pounding of her own, her fist on the door.

"Iz. Let me in. Can you hear me? Open it."

She thought she heard laughter from inside the room. Delighted laughter, not aimed at her. She doubted her sister even knew she was there. A shadow moved through the crack of light at the foot of the door. The boards beneath Leona's feet quivered. It was happening. She could see it happening in her mind. She seized the doorknob again and wrenched on it. In her mind she saw her sister moving to the music, spinning, spinning, moving, moving, as lights began to appear all around her.

"Izzy!" she screamed in frustration at the door. "Stop dancing!"

THEY WERE BORN to it. That's what their mother had always told people. *My little mirror girls. They were born to be dancers. They could have made a career of it, but they got stubborn and wouldn't do it anymore. They wanted to rebel against me. That's all it was. They cut their nose off to spite their face. To spite me.*

Sometimes Leona felt angry when she recalled this. Sometimes she felt sorry for their mother. She thought of all the years their mother had spent tap dancing across stages as a child, a grin frozen on her face, or trying to shine in kiddie chorus lines, with desperate energy, willing the audience to love me love me love me until tendonitis brought an end to all her dreams. And what a joy it must have been for her to discover that her twin girls also loved dancing. She'd signed them up for ballet and tap lessons even before they started school, not knowing that what her girls loved more than anything was to be left alone in the attic and find some kind of freedom in music and movement.

But it wasn't rebellion that had made them stop. It was fear.

Because their mother didn't know what happened when they danced.

Their mother didn't know about the ghostlights.

After one last desperate plea to her sister, Leona turned, hurried down the stairs to the first floor, and began searching the bedrooms for something she might use to open the attic door. Something heavy would do it. Something she could use as a battering ram. In their mother's old room she froze and listened to her sister's footsteps thump across the floor above – two light steps, and then a heavy one. Thinking that she heard a shriek of joy, Leona was seized with panic again. On her mother's dresser she noticed the framed picture of herself and Izzy in their ballet costumes, aged seven. They looked like a reflection of each other. That was why their mother had called them her mirror girls. It wasn't only that they looked alike, but sometimes when they danced it was as if they shared one mind and their bodies would synchronise. This, their mother decided one day when they were children, would be the basis of their 'act'. One girl would stand inside a frame and pretend to be the other girl's reflection. Leona was unsurprised when she learned that it was she who was to play the reflection. Their mother had always favoured Izzy. Izzy controlled her pirouette's better. Izzy mastered the back-flap. Izzy had snake hips. Izzy had a natural charisma. Leona had never resented Izzy for this, since Izzy appeared as wearied by their mother as she was, more so in fact since Izzy was the favourite. Together they would mock their mother. "Head up, smile," Izzy would shout, in imitation of their mother, as she watched Leona dance. "For Godsake, girl, do it like your sister! Head up and smile!"

Except that day, when her mother told them about 'the act' and how Izzy was to be the real girl and Leona the reflection, she'd felt the first flicker of resentment.

"But I don't want to be the reflection. I want to be the real girl."

"I don't want to be the reflection either," Izzy had said.

"Honestly, you two," their mother had said. "It doesn't matter. You'll both be stars."

NOTHING IN THE room suggested itself as a battering ram, and the thump of feet from above seemed to have picked up pace. Leona knew she was running out of time. She ran to her own room, and after a quick fruitless search, went on to Izzy's.

"Something," she muttered to herself. "Something must—"

On the floor next to Izzy's wardrobe stood a large bronze dancing girl sculpture their father had brought back from Egypt. It was perfect.

Leona had often wondered if it was their mother's obsession with turning her daughters into stars that had driven their father away. When he first bought the house he'd confessed to Leona that he planned to turn the attic into a storage space for his antiques, the ones he hadn't room for in his shop, but their mother had other ideas. The attic space ran the length of the house, and the floor had already been reinforced with plywood boards by the previous owner. It would make the perfect dance studio, their mother said. Then, before their father had a chance to object, she had fitted one wall with mirrors, and had a ballet barre attached to the opposite wall. It was in the attic that Leona and Izzy were now to spend their time when they were not at school, working on 'the act'. When their mother got tired and went downstairs for a rest, the girls would eject her Tchaikovsky or Ravel CDs from the boombox and slip in Depeche Mode or Donna Summer. It was then that they truly began to enjoy the space, forgetting the rules and constrictions of ballet and tap, and simply letting themselves move to the music.

It was during one such break from their mother's tyranny that Leona, aged twelve, had first noticed the ghostlights.

A song with a particularly fast beat had played on the boombox, Leona couldn't remember which song, and the twins got carried away trying to keep up with the music. Leona would later come to recognise these moments when the music and the dancing seemed to become everything. Her thoughts would stop and she would feel an overwhelming sense of joy. This is how it had been that day. In the midst of the dance, she had happened to catch her reflection in the mirror and seen a dozen or so tiny orbs of lights in the space over her head. As soon as she stopped dancing, the lights began to disappear, but when she looked at Izzy, who was still moving, spinning and leaping with her eyes closed and her mouth open as if in the throes of ecstasy, she saw the same set of lights above her sister. Only, as Izzy continued to dance, more lights had begun to appear around her. Leona had watched, dumbstruck, for a few moments, as the beat picked up and Izzy laughed and moved in time. When she did the lights appeared more rapidly, suddenly there were maybe fifty lights, the next moment double that. The lights began to blend together until Izzy was almost entirely surrounded by white light. When the lights clumped together, Leona found herself looking into a portal on the other side of which she imagined she saw indistinct and elongated figures beckoning and reaching out. Reaching out towards her twin. It was only there for a moment, but on sight of this, she had found her voice.

"Izzy!"

Too lost in the music, Izzy kept dancing.

Knowing she had to stop her sister somehow, Leona, in her desperation, had kicked the boombox halfway across the room. The plug came free of the wall and the music died.

Leona watched as the lights around her sister began to separate and then vanish, the little orbs winking out one by one.

"What?" Izzy said, looking from Leona's face to the boombox. "What did you do that for?" She scrunched up her face when Leona spoke. Leona still didn't know why she said what she did. It was a feeling she'd had, that was all.

"They were about to take you."

THE DANCING GIRL sculpture was heavier than Leona had imagined it would be. As she struggled with it up with attic stairs, feeling the tension in her calves, she thought of their father. It was he who had bought the statue, and it was he who had given it to Leona as a reward for helping him in the shop one summer when she was fifteen. In truth, she'd only volunteered in order to escape their mother, whose dance instruction in the attic took on a new urgency when she discovered she had breast cancer. Leona was scared too, scared of the things she and Izzy had nicknamed the ghostlights. Izzy hadn't been quick enough to escape their mother's clutches, and had spent every day of that summer up in the attic with her. The sisters had always been inseparable, but that summer – though she missed her sister–Leona had a strange sense of liberty, a sense of herself as an individual rather than half a pair for the first time in her life.

Leona didn't know if it was their mother, or Izzy, who had taken the dancing girl statue and put it in Izzy's room, but she remembered when she had brought it home and her mother had scoffed and said that she should give it to Izzy, because it was Izzy who deserved it, and it was Izzy who was going to be a star. Whoever moved it in the end, it had been in Izzy's room for years and Leona had forgotten that it had ever been hers.

It was their father, too, who had got Izzy and herself jobs in the customer services department at Bridwell Insurance shortly after the cancer came back and their mother died in her bed after making Leona and Izzy promise that they would not give up on her dreams. After the funeral, their father had let them keep the house, but he insisted that they learn to support themselves 'now that all your mother's theatrical nonsense can be put to bed'. They'd only worked at Bridwell for a year, and Izzy already

124

said the job was killing her. Though Leona wouldn't admit it, she knew what her sister meant. Their father may as well have fitted them both with straightjackets. Sat in her cubicle, the wire of the headset attaching her to her computer as if by umbilical, she ached to be free. She ached to move. Her fingers drummed patterns on the desk, and colleagues sat nearby would sometimes complain about the tapping of her feet under the desk. Was this how Izzy felt? She knew it was only a question of time before either she or her sister cracked. Sometimes she pictured them both leaping simultaneously from their chairs and doing a mirror dance around the cubicles like actors in a musical, or animals that had broken free from their cages.

THE SONG IZZY danced to was coming to an end. The vocal and synth line had dropped away to a succession of frantic beats and pulses that carried the music along to its climax. Leona could definitely also hear her sister laughing, and it was this sound that filled her with renewed urgency. Reaching the top of the stairs, she rushed forward and slammed the foot of the statue against the door frame above the knob. The door shuddered but did not open. Leona took a few steps back and brought the statue forward again with another crash. Still the door did not give. The music carried on. Izzy's footsteps continued to shake the floorboards. Leona paused to think. Sweat had broken out on her brow and the statue felt heavy and slippery in her grasp. As she brought it against the door a third time, she had to leap back as the statue fell from her grasp and crashed to the floor. She clutched her breath, and was about to attempt to pick up the statue again, when she noticed that the screws fixing the latch set onto the door had fallen out and the there was now a narrow gap between the door and the frame.

"Izzy," Leona shouted.

The music inside the attic was fading out now. Instead of trying to pick up the statue again, Leona threw her weight against the door instead and was surprised when the door gave easily. As she toppled into the room, she thought she saw white lights blinking out in front of her, but when she righted herself she was relieved to see her twin stood on the other side of the room, looking back at her. Her sister's hair was thrown forward around her face, damp strands sticking to her forehead and cheeks. Her eyes were full of panic and fear.

"Izzy, what were you doing? What happened?"

As she took a step forward, Leona realised that what she was looking at was not her sister at all, but her own reflection in the mirrors along the opposite wall. That flushed face and those panic-stricken eyes were hers, not Izzy's. Momentum carried her forward so that she stood in the centre of the room, spotlit by a beam of sunlight from the room's only window. Dust motes floated through the beam of light, like negatives of those lights that had sometimes surrounded her and her sister when they danced.

"Izzy?" she said, twirling on the spot. Then again, her tone growing frantic, "Izzy?"

Dropping to the floor, Leona grabbed the boombox and hit the play button. The song, Izzy's song, started again.

"Don't worry," she said under her breath. "Don't worry, I'm coming too."

Getting up, chocking back a sob, Leona started to dance. Her eyes checked the mirror. Nothing. She would have to let go. She would have to lose herself. She tried, closing her eyes and focusing on the music, on the beat, moving her body in time with it. She checked the mirror again. Still nothing. *Come on, come on.* She moved. She moved. She tried to forget herself, but the image of Mr Balding kept returning to her mind and she kept picturing her empty cubicle at work, and her father in his shop. Forget that. Forget that. Just dance. Dance dance dance.

She played the song over and over and danced until her whole body ached, but she couldn't quite let herself go and when, after what seemed like hours, no lights appeared around her head she collapsed and lay full length across the floor, staring up at the ceiling, panting and soaked with sweat.

"Izzy?"

She groaned as she picked herself up. Crawling on hands and knees to the boombox, she jabbed a finger at the play button and started the song playing again.

Hear

WHEN THE NEWS broke, a sense of shock was shared the world over. No one could believe Zachery Flynn had killed himself.

His death was front page news for days after a security guard at his L.A. mansion discovered the body. People shook their heads and wondered aloud how someone who appeared to have everything—looks, money, fame, talent—could wake up one day and decide they no longer wanted to live.

Vikki, Elle, Nadine and I met for ice cream the following Saturday and all of us shed a few tears, even though the Flynn Brothers posters had long since come down from our bedroom walls and their CDs only came out for a nostalgic blast every once in a while so we could all sing along and tease each other about how well we knew the songs.

The only person unsurprised, apparently, by Zachery Flynn's death was my mother. "It was that song," she told me. "What must it have been like to go on stage and sing that song every night?"

I knew the song she meant. To the astonishment of my fifteen year old self, she had broken down and cried the first time I played her 'Emily, Hear My Plea', Flynn's biggest solo hit released after the breakup of his boy band. My embarrassment at the sudden display of emotion became even more acute when Mum—apparently unable to control herself—sobbed, "Help them. We have to help them." I thought she was reacting to the song's lyrics which were a soppy paean to some girl Flynn claimed to have glimpsed in the front row at one of his concerts.

From the lip of the stage, I asked your name, and you cried out 'Emily', the song went. *Emily, didn't you know, every song that night was for you? Only for you. Emily. Oh Emily. But after the show you were gone. I'll never see your face again—oh Emily, Emily, lost in the crowd.*

A year previously, in the grip of my Flynn Brothers obsession, I would have been acutely jealous of this *Emily*, whoever she was. I would have wanted to scratch her eyes out. But something had changed. When 'Emily, Hear My Plea' was released, although I rushed out to buy it like loads of other girls my age, I cringed when I first heard the lyrics. It was clear the listener was supposed to picture themselves as this Emily; or imagine that they might be the next one to capture Zachery Flynn's heart from the front row. At fifteen I was too old for this kind of syrupy nonsense, so I was a little ashamed of my mother—a grown woman—for reacting to it in the way she did.

"There probably is no Emily," I told her, in my best *get-a-grip* tone of voice. "It's probably all made up."

Mum looked up, dabbing at her cheeks with the cuff of her sweater. She stared at me for a long moment then said, "It's not the words, Kathleen, it's the music. Listen to the music."

The backing track was another reason I hadn't liked the song. The Flynn Brother's songs had been mostly upbeat; but this song was slow and melancholy. It had a plaintive, almost dirge-like quality that sounded strange to my ears. In truth, the song disturbed me in some way I couldn't quite put my finger on. But it was just a pop song. I couldn't understand what my mother was getting so upset about.

"Listen," she said. "Can't you here that? It's like—" But whatever it was she heard, she couldn't find the right words to express it.

Later, she denied that she had ever cried over a Zachery Flynn song. She also swore on my grandmother's grave that she had never once said, *Help them.* "I had something on my mind that day," she would say if I teased her about it. "I was thinking about something else, that's all."

'Emily, Hear My Plea' became a huge hit for Zachery Flynn, bigger than anything he'd recorded with the Flynn Brothers. For a few months you couldn't escape it. It was everywhere, constantly on the radio, blasting out of PA systems at the mall, and every time I heard it I felt restless and hopeless at the same time like the song was trying to tell me something beyond Flynn's banal lyrics. There was a general feeling in the air that summer, like something was wrong, like a house was on fire a few streets away with people screaming from the windows for help but no one was doing anything about it. That's the only way I can describe that feeling. It used to keep me awake at night, tossing and turning in bed, and I wasn't the only one. Mum and I used to find ourselves sat at the kitchen table some nights at three o'clock in the morning, drinking herbal tea and gazing at each other as if someone had asked a question to which we didn't know the answer. It was that summer too that my friends and I decided we were done with Zachery Flynn if 'Emily, Hear My Plea' was any indication of the kind of music we could expect from his solo career. We had all come to hate that song and the anxious way it made us feel. Besides, other things had caught our interest, namely the boys we liked at school—real boys that were within our reach—but also Joey Pearce from the *Lost Cause* movie franchise. He had an air of danger about him which we now preferred to Zachery Flynn and the Flynn Brothers' squeaky clean please-and-thankyou American apple-pie niceness. His was the poster that now adorned our bedroom walls.

Still, Zachery Flynn and his music had been a fixture of my early teens, so I was sad when I heard that he'd taken his own life. What bothered me most was his suicide note. It was leaked to the press a few weeks after his death, and apparently it said: LIGHT YEARS AWAY. WE COULDN'T HAVE HELPED THEM ANYWAY. His family, his friends, journalists and fans the world over were confused by this. No one had the first idea what it was supposed to mean. The tabloids suggested the note was evidence of Zachery Flynn's deteriorating state of mind, or perhaps substance addictions, but when I heard about it I got a chill down my back. I remembered my mother crying and saying *help them* when I played her 'Emily, Hear My Plea', and I felt certain Zachery's suicide note was somehow linked to that song. I dug the CD single out from under my bed and played it, and though I was again struck by the dumbness of the lyrics, I felt a familiar unease inspired by the backing track. It was that *house-on-fire-a-few-streets-away* feeling all over again. It made me believe that someone was reaching out to me and asking for my help. *Help them, we have to help them* I again remembered my mother saying when I played it for her. Curious, I checked the CD booklet to see who had written the song. *Words by Zachery Flynn*, it said. No surprise there. *Music supplied by NASA.*

NASA? What the hell did that mean? I of course knew all about Zachery Flynn's fascination with outer space. He spent much of the magazine interviews my friends and I had poured over in our early teens talking about it. At the time we found it boring. We wanted to know what music he liked, where he bought his clothes, whether or not he had a girlfriend. I can remember Nadine saying one day when we were sat in my room, "I do wish Zachery wouldn't keep going on about *space* all the time." We all called the Flynn brothers by their first names, as if we knew them personally. "I know," Elle said, "It's *all* he ever talks about."

So NASA somehow supplied the music to 'Emily, Hear My Plea'? Though shocked, I was intrigued and wanted to find out more.

This became a bit of an obsession for me in the years to come. I had a boyfriend for a while—Billy Dickson—but he eventually got fed-up with me talking about 'Emily, Hear My Plea'. He would pull a face or pretend to

129

shove a finger down his throat whenever I mentioned Zachery Flynn's name.

"It's just a stupid song," he said one day. "And the music's really creepy."

"What do you mean *creepy*?" I knew exactly what he meant, but I wanted to hear him say it.

"It sounds like some kind of..." He had to think for half a minute. "Cry for help, or something."

"A cry for help?" There it was again. House on fire. My mother saying *help them we have to help them.*

"Didn't the singer kill himself?"

"Yeah."

"Well, there you go then. A cry for help."

"But it's not in the lyrics, is it? The lyrics are silly. It's the music. Zachery Flynn didn't write the music. The music came from NASA."

"NASA? Are you joking?"

I had to dig the CD out from under my bed again, just to show him that I was telling the truth. *Music supplied by NASA.* Billy said it was probably a misprint. NASA, he said, weren't in the business of writing soppy ballads for ex-boy band members.

Eventually, Billy stopped replying to my texts and then someone told me he'd starting seeing Nadine. After that he was neither Billy nor Dickson (as his male friends called him) to me, he was just *Dick*. Then Nadine, to the envy of us all, moved on to Rob Northwood—the most handsome boy in sixth form, and Billy came crawling back.

"Hello, *Dick*," I said when I discovered him standing on my doorstep one day. "What could you possibly want?"

"Kathleen," he said. "There's something I want to show you. Remember that song you were obsessed with?"

"Emily, Hear My Plea?"

"Yeah. Well, I found something online. I wanted to show it to you."

I knew this was some kind of rouse to get back into my good books, with a view to us getting back together, but I was intrigued enough to allow Billy inside. I led him up to my bedroom, and he immediately went to the computer and fired up Internet Explorer.

"It took me hours to find this."

"*Aw*," I said, in a kittenish tone, folding my hands at my breast and pretending to be moved.

"Turn the speakers on," he said.

Still playing it cool, I did as he asked. He found the webpage he was looking for and started some WAV file playing. A weird Theremin-type sound started coming out of the speakers.

"What's this, Billy? Whale song?"

"These," he said, "are sounds picked up on a NASA space probe a few years ago. Radio waves. But it's this one in particular I wanted you to hear. Listen to it."

"I am listening to it."

"Can't you hear that?"

"What am I supposed to be hearing? Sounds like—"

Billy must have seen the shock on my face as he broke out in a grin.

"Oh my God," I said. "Play it again, play it again."

"I'm thinking this might get me to at least second base," Billy said, and I batted my hand at him, too transfixed by what I was hearing to fully react. What he'd played for me was the music for 'Emily, Hear My Plea'. It was a weird, stretched-out version that repeated over and over, but basically the song was there. Zachery Flynn had used sounds picked up on a space probe as the basis for his biggest hit. I couldn't believe it.

"So what d'you say?" Billy said, still grinning but raising his eyebrows suggestively at the same time so I could be in no doubt of what he was referring to.

"No thanks," I said. "Your just Nadine's sloppy seconds now. Piss off, will you?"

He went off in a huff, and after he left I sat and played that WAV file over and over. Just like 'Emily, Hear My Plea' it made me feel sad and restless, like there was some kind of urgent crisis I needed to attend to, a house on fire, a person trapped down a well, a child in need, an overturned ship. *Something*. I didn't know what it was the music was trying to tell me, but it communicated that sense of crisis and desperation perfectly. It was some kind of plea, but not the silly love-struck plea Zachery Flynn had turned it into. This was life and death. A call. S.O.S. It told—not in words, but in sound, in feeling—what we had all known it to tell, from the very first time we'd heard it: that somewhere somebody needed our help.

I imagined Zachery Flynn hearing this music every night on stage, having to sing those banal lyrics he'd penned over the top whilst whoever had created the original sounds picked up by the NASA space probe waited and waited and waited for some kind of response.

And I tried to imagine how that would've made him feel.

You Will Never Lose Me

I'M REMEMBERING AGAIN. Remembering—if that's the word for it. The memories swamp me as I settle down to sleep. A ratty blanket with clumps of soil stuck to it was all I could find to wrap myself in. After discovering naught but ruins for miles, I was glad to come across something which still had four walls. But this shack can't keep out the cold. It seeps up through the floor slats, and whistles through knotholes in the wall. My bones ache with it. I shiver as the images flood my mind. This time, I let them come. Let them swim over me. Swim, that's it. Swim. Swimming.

Swimming in the ocean. The sun hangs overhead, a dazzle of light. I can feel the warmth of it on my face. Cold currents snake through the warm water, moving against and around my naked body. There's a feeling of well-being, of pleasure, tinged with fear as I'm rocked by waves. All of it, I savour. I duck below and push for the floor, keeping my eyes open, seeing through a greenish haze the quavering patches of sunlight on the many coloured stones.

Sitting on a park bench. Blue sky overhead. Low sunlight, pale and hazy. The grass heavy with dew. A child beside me, laughing every time I switch my head around and say in mock-seriousness: *Whadda ya want?* We're alone in the park. All this blue sky and all this green grass, it's ours. For the moment it's ours. *Whadda ya want?* I say, and the child laughs. Head thrown back, laughing. Laughing.

I sit alone at a table. Before me there's a basket of some soft brown-black fruit. I take one of the fruits and peel it before placing it, whole, into my mouth. The sweetness of it seems to fill my whole being.

These memories don't belong to me. They're his. The old man's. He had a gift. Something unnatural. He unloaded his memories into me as he sank to his knees, his blood muddying the dust between his feet. His wavering hands reached out when I stepped away to clean my blade and cemented themselves onto each side of my head. I tried to pull away but couldn't; the old fool locked onto me so tightly. I could see the grime embedded in the lines of his face. The grease in his beard. His eyes were wild, but there was something deep in them, something determined. That's when he did it. That's when he put these memories in me. They were the only weapons he had. Knives of recollection. Blades of joy. Stabbing them into my head. Right before he died.

I'D BEEN HEADING east. I don't know why. But in the morning, escaping that shack, I decide to head south instead. I let the compass show the way. The compass was his too. I patted him down after his eyes went dull and discovered it amongst his rags. The gold is tarnished, and the hoop where it might once have hung on a chain or a string around the neck is broken. But it still works. There are words engraved on the back. They gave me a weird little chill the first time I read them.

Why south? Maybe it's that memory of his, the one where he's swimming in the ocean. It's put something in me, some kind of a yearning. I want to taste the salt water on my lips. I want to feel those cold currents. I don't just want to remember it, I want to feel it, really feel it. Feel something other than this numbing cold and the grit in my mouth.

There's a road just discernible under a thin blanket of ash. In one of the old man's memories he's walking through a field of freshly fallen snow, and that's what this reminds me of. Only, where the snow gave him a feeling of vitality and newness, this ash only makes me feel heavy and soiled. I soon start to detest the way it sticks to my boots, forming clumps along the sole, so that I have to keep stopping to knock it free.

The road is lined with the scorched skeletons of trees. The sky looks like dirt smeared on a windowpane. None of this seemed strange to me before. It's all I've ever known. That is, until the old man filled my head with sunshine and laughter and the blue of the sea.

I carry his memories like splinters beneath the skin.

I wonder if that world he remembers is still out there somewhere. There's nothing else for it. I suppose I'll just keep walking.

IT'S NOT BLUE like he remembers it. It's grey, turning towards black, though there are rainbows in the oily film on its surface. Hunks of brownish foam slosh about in the shallows. There are dead things in the shallows too and in the debris strewn across the entirety of the beach.

After all the miles, after all the days, after all the scratching around for food and shelter and warmth, seeing this actually makes me weep. I thought I'd cried myself dry as a kid, but no. I can't help but laugh, remembering how much I'd wanted to taste saltwater, really taste it, and here it is spilling down my cheeks. Then I shake my head, and cry some more.

I have to put my back to the ocean. Where now?

Some nights, huddled against the wind, I study that inscription on the back of the compass, tracing the outline of the letters with my finger before I let his memories in.

And I realise what an evil thing it was he did to me.

And how perfect his revenge.

Under Iron

"**W**HAT THE HELL'S going on in here?"

Confusion and concern had got Christie out from under her duvet, but now—seeing that her son was not in bed but standing on top of it, facing the wall—she felt a rising anger which she struggled to contain. After everything they'd been through over the past year: the court case, the funeral, then the incident at the river where the boy had almost drowned, she'd thought life was at last returning to normal. When she turned on the light, Lucas had appeared to be attempting to reach or stretch towards the air duct high on the wall near the ceiling, but seeing his mother stood in the doorway, hands on hips, he shot her a guilty look and dived for his pillows, yanking the Star Wars duvet his father had bought him up over his head as if he thought he could still pretend he'd been sleeping.

"*Lucas!*" Christie said, hearing the contained emotion in her own voice. "What were you doing? Who were you talking to?"

Lucas didn't move. He didn't make a sound. Christie strode to the bed and pulled back the duvet. The boy blinked up at her. He looked so much like his father—the same soft curls, the same wide dark eyes—that for a moment she was taken aback. He'd even mastered the same *butter-wouldn't-melt* expression his father had used whenever she'd confronted him over his many indiscretions.

"I asked you a question. Who were you talking to?"

"No one, Mummy."

"I heard you talking, Lucas. You woke me up. Who were you talking to?"

He didn't answer, but shifted his eyes towards the air vent high on the wall. Christie followed his gaze.

"Mummy," Lucas said, "When can I see Dad again?"

"Lucas, for God's sake...?" Christie let out a long breath and pressed the heels of her hands into her eyes. "We've been through this."

"But he wants to see me. He misses me."

He peered into her face now, but Christie turned away, pursing her lips and squeezing her eyes closed. She took a deep breath before she faced him again, making every effort to speak in a calm voice.

"Lucas, Dad's not around anymore. You remember the funeral, don't you? When we went to say goodbye to him? Right?"

"But where is he?"

Her lips worked soundlessly. It would've been easy to tell Lucas his father was in heaven, but she'd made a pact with herself not to fill his head with ideas she didn't herself believe. She still resented having all that religious nonsense forced on her as a child; she wasn't going to do the same to her son. She bent forward to cover him with the duvet and stroked a hand through his hair.

"Do you know what time it is, buddy-boy?"

"But, Mummy...?"

"Back to sleep. You've got school tomorrow."

"Dad misses me. He told me."

"He told you? When?"

He pursed his lips, his expression resolute, defiant. Tears welled in his eyes. But he didn't answer.

"I'm sorry, baby. Dad won't be picking you up at the weekend anymore. Dad's gone."

"He's not gone! He's not!"

"Sleep," she said, in as firm a voice as she could muster. She could sense that a tantrum wasn't far away, and she'd learnt that the only way to deal with those was to turn her back on them. She did so at once and switched out the light; then felt her way in the dark back to her own bed. The digital clock on the nightstand read 03:41.

Lying in bed, she listened for sounds from Lucas' bedroom but the only noise she heard was the bleep of her alarm clock waking her up at 06:30.

THE NEXT DAY was cold, silent and grey; the kind of day that made Christie wonder why she'd returned to England. Winter in L.A. was a warm rainy season—you wouldn't even call it winter, not really. This was winter: frost on the windows and a numbing cold throughout the flat which made her ears and nose prickle. She couldn't afford to put the heating on; at least not too often. Not until the tussle over Jules' estate had been resolved. And why shouldn't she get everything? Legally, she was still his wife. She'd been there, supporting him, encouraging him, long before he signed his first record deal. She'd given birth to his son. Eighteen excruciating hours of labour during which she'd begged for an epidural which they wouldn't allow because of her history. Why shouldn't she get it all?

136

Sometimes she wondered if the only reason she'd left America was to make it harder for Jules to see his son. Or maybe she just hadn't liked the thought of Lucas being around all those groupies and drug dealers and record company sycophants Jules had come to think of as his friends. And maybe she hadn't wanted to be around those people either.

Not that it mattered now, of course.

Lucas began playing up as they left the house; all because he wanted to wear some shoes his father had bought him. They were hideous things: gold high-top trainers Jules had brought back from America just before he died. They had wings that went around the back of the foot and LED lights along the sole, and were about as far from acceptable school footwear as it was possible to get. Lucas insisted that his father had bought them specifically for him to wear to school so he could be the coolest kid in class. Christie thought this was probably true. It was the kind of thing Jules would have said, having no idea of the day-to-day reality of raising a child. Halfway along their fifteen minute walk to school, Lucas went rigid and refused to walk any further, so Christie had to carry him the rest of the way. Before they reached the school gates he started asking for sweets.

"I don't have sweeties, Lucas."

"You always have sweeties in your bag."

"How would you know that?"

A pause. "Dad told me."

"Dad...? Jesus Christ, not again. Lucas, how many times do we have to go through this?"

"You have sweeties in your bag, I know you do."

"Not today. Anyway, only good boys get sweets."

"Can I have sweeties after school?"

"No."

This brought on another bought of hysterics. When she finally deposited him at his classroom door, she was exhausted and furious. Beads of sweat had broken out under her brow, turning to icy rivulets at her temples.

Giving Lucas a quick kiss on the top of his head, she ushered him towards his waiting teacher and said, "No sweeties for you after school today, bud." Before he could reply, she turned and walked away.

Despite the million and one things she had to do, she didn't feel like returning home and spending the day alone so instead found herself catching a bus into the city. She walked along a lonely stretch of river where prostitutes and drug dealers sometimes plied their trade, though not today. It was too cold a day for soliciting. She walked until she reached the spot where a wide cast-iron bridge crossed the river. She'd heard that people were now calling it Jules' bridge. Someone—she couldn't remember who—had told her that people travelled from all over the world to see it. At the time she'd laughed. How absurd was that? They came to scratch their name into the brickwork beneath the bridge, or some dedication to Jules, or a lyric from one of his songs. *You and me, baby, under iron, under iron.* Christie imagined how disappointed those people must be when they saw the bridge. It wasn't even ugly enough to be interesting; it was nondescript. An old rusting iron bridge. That had been Jules' talent though. He could take something dull and make poetry out of it.

As she neared, she saw a group of teenagers huddled together in the half-dark under the bridge. All wore loose clothing and had shoulder-length hair so she couldn't tell if they were boys or girls. They shot sideways glances at her as she approached, their eyes hidden behind strands of greasy fringe. She could sense their animosity towards her when she stopped just inside the shadow of the bridge and leant against the wall. She wondered how they'd react if she told them how Jules' song 'Under Iron' was actually written about her.

You and me, baby, under iron, under iron.

Yeah, that's me he's singing about. We used to come here years ago to score drugs and shoot up. Here's where we'd do it. Right under this bridge. That's what the song's about. About us. About me.

Most likely, they wouldn't believe her; and even if they did it would only disappoint them. She knew what she looked like to them: some frazzled early-thirties mother, a pale thing, sleep-deprived, as disappointing as the bridge they'd come from who-knows-where to see all because some guy with a guitar had written a song and made it sound like a sanctuary for the lost. She'd invaded their temple, made it more mundane just by being here. Out of the corner of her eye she saw the group throw a few last disdainful glances her way, then shuffle off in the other direction. She was glad. She wanted to be alone here, although she was still unsure why she'd come.

It was colder in the shade of the bridge. She could hear water dripping. A shopping trolley lay half-submerged in the shallow river. Squinting her eyes against the gloom, she saw that what she'd been told was true. The brickwork was covered in scratchings and graffiti.

JULES STARR RIP.

STARR-MAN LIVE FOREVER UNDER IRON.

There were even a few unlit candles clustered together on the pathway by her feet like a little shrine together with what looked like a small bust someone had made which was presumably supposed to look like Jules but didn't. Not at all.

GRACIAS POR LA MUSICA.

JULES STARR. VIVRE ETERNELLEMENT.

Jesus Christ.

Christie snorted. Jules Starr hadn't even been his real name. Overcome with scorn, she routed in her handbag and found a nail-file which she then used to scratch out an epitaph of her own. *SIMON KINNEY*, she wrote, *I'M SORRY*. Almost at once, she felt a pang of guilt and scratched out SIMON KINNEY. She left the I'M SORRY. Turning to leave, she sensed that there was someone else there with her under the bridge. Peering into the half-dark, she thought she saw a shape move away from the wall and then someone approaching. It was a tall, thin imposing man in a leather trenchcoat. Under the coat he wore a hooded sweatshirt with the hood raised to cover most of his face.

Oh fuck! Christie hitched her handbag higher onto her shoulder. She felt a jolt of panic, sure she was about to get mugged or worse. What had she even come here for anyway? She wondered if she could still make a run for it but the man had quickly blocked her escape route. She heard him say her name under his breath. She glared at him, trying to make out his face inside the shadow of the hood. Fear flashed through her again when she saw a skeletal grin but then she realised it was only one of those bicycle masks people wore nowadays. He pulled down the mask and she saw that it was Lou. Loopy Lou, people knew him as—a moniker she'd always suspected he'd chosen himself to sound dangerous; just as Jules had picked Starr as his surname in the hope that people would see him as one. She found herself thinking about men and their identities, how it was all just smoke and mirrors.

"Christie," Lou said again. Despite his aura of menace, he spoke in little exhales of breath, the words barely there. "Fancy meeting you here. Why you not answering your phone, girl?"

"I...I've been busy." Compared to his voice, hers sounded loud and jarring.

"What you doing here? Looking for something?" He gave a wheezy laugh.

"No. No. I—"

"You sure? I got brown, coke, crystals."

139

Feeling a familiar pang, Christie shook her head rigorously.

"Something to smoke? You know what I've got, some of that acapulco gold. That's some strong shit. You tried it?"

"No. I don't. I can't."

He grinned, showing teeth stained brown and black. "No matter if you ain't got the funds, girl. I can take payment off you the way I sometimes did in the old days. Remember?"

Christie felt her stomach heave as he looked her up and down, his grin widening.

"You're not quite what you were back then," he said. "But I'm a reasonable guy."

Something flashed through Christie's mind. She remembered being pressed against the wall here under the bridge, the gritty feel of the brickwork beneath her palms and against her knees. Lou behind her, hands gripping her at the waist. His mouth somewhere close to her ear, making little sounds of pleasure that seemed born more from the power he had over her than from what he was actually doing. She pictured Jules stood nearby, waiting, pretending not to notice, his eyes fixed on the opposite bank. It wasn't difficult, not really, that's what she would tell Jules afterwards: just a few moments discomfort and a lingering sense of shame easily washed away with whatever they'd been looking to score. It was nothing really. She could do it again. She could...

"I'm a mother now, Lou."

He gazed at her for a long moment, fixing her to the spot with his eyes. The grin fell away and his expression changed. His eyes narrowed to slits.

"Why you didn't told me Jules had just come out of rehab?"

"What? I...I had no idea."

"You told me he was a burnout."

"He was the last time I saw him. He *was*."

"That bombita you had me deliver...that was what done it for him. You know that, right?"

"It was no one's fault, Lou. Nobody forced him."

"Nobody needed to. If I get busted for this..."

Glancing down, Christie saw that a knife had appeared in Lou's hand. A small steak knife, like the one she had in her own kitchen drawer.

"No one's going to know anything, Lou. It was an accident. Right? Right? I'm a mother now. I have a son. Lucas."

He was staring hard into her eyes. "My thinking is: you planned it all."

"I never, Lou. I promise you, I never." Then, looking imploringly into his face, she said again: "I'm a mother, Lou."

Lou sucked air through his teeth. "Having me tell him that packet was from an old friend. It killed him, Christie. *You* killed him."

Tears sprang up in Christie's eyes. She shook her head, pleading: "No. No, I didn't."

"If this comes back to me..."

Lou raised the knife and made a sudden slicing gesture across her throat with it. She made a startled sound, grabbing at her neck. For a second she thought he'd actually cut her. But it was just a warning. He took a step back, the knife vanishing into his coat again. She shook with relief and fell against the wall as he turned and strode away. She let the tears come freely then. After a few moments she caught her breath and jerked her head up, again sensing a presence with her under the bridge. Had Lou returned? Stepping away from the wall, she glanced around but saw no one. She had spooked herself. But no, she felt something in the air: a terrible anger. Something dark. A hatred, a fury that sent shivers up her arms. There was somebody here. Somebody. Somewhere. A presence she recognised.

Jules' bridge. Jules' place.

"I said I'm sorry and I am!" she barked at no one. Was she losing her mind? She could still feel that vicious anger, closing in on her. "I had to do something," she cried out desperately, feeling like a cornered animal. Her eyes darted about the gloom, looking for someone, something, some source for the black emotions she could feel directed at her. There was no one. Just shadows. Ripples moved along the surface of the river. Christie turned and fled back the way she'd come. She didn't stop running until she was able to leave the riverbank and cross an industrial estate where at least there were a few people milling around. She stopped and leant against a wall, gasping for breath, dabbing one cuff of her coat at the cold sweat on her brow. Glancing at her watch, she saw that she had no time to linger. It was time to pick Lucas up from school. *No sweeties for you today,* she thought, remembering what she had told him that morning.

And none for me either.

PUSHING OPEN THE door of the church hall, Christie saw that a heavy rain was falling. She lingered under the shelter of the door, taking deep breaths. The room where the NA meetings were held always felt airless and stale. The longer she spent in there, the more she felt she was being suffocated. It was always a relief to step outside into the fresh air.

She waited in the doorway and watched the others from the group exit the building and hurry away into the night. Some nodded to Christie or said goodbye before they went on their way. The last to leave was a woman named Sandra. Sandra was somewhere in her late twenties, but years of heroin abuse had left her with a drawn, waxy complexion that made her look older.

"Christ," Sandra said, halting in the doorway when she saw the rain. Then, seeing she wasn't alone, she smiled and said, "Christie, right?"

Christie nodded then gestured at the downpour. "Don't think it's going to let up any time soon."

"Ciggie?" Sandra said, holding out a pack.

Christie smiled and shook her head. "Don't tempt me."

"You're one of those that had to give up everything, huh?" Sandra said. She popped a cigarette into her mouth and lit it. "How'd you do it?"

"For my son, I suppose."

"Yeah?"

"I fucked up."

"Tell me."

"We...we were having a picnic one day by the river, and some guy I didn't even know offered me a cigarette which turned out to be a joint. I smoked it anyway, got hazy for a few minutes, and my son fell in the water and almost drowned. Well, he jumped in actually. After that I decided to stop everything. Cigarettes. Booze. The lot."

Christie was always surprised at how frank she could be talking to people like Sandra, people who understood, people who'd been through similar experiences.

Sandra nodded. She let out a long exhale of smoke which hung in the cold air for a few seconds. "I had a daughter. Savannah. She was beautiful. They took her away from me. She ended up getting adopted. I'm not allowed to know where she is. They said she might look for me when she's eighteen, but I don't think she will. She's gone, you know? I think about her every day, wondering how she's doing."

"I'm sorry."

"So why'd he jump in the river? Your son, I mean?"

Christie glanced away. "His dad had just died."

"Huh?"

142

"He said he wanted to be with his dad." Christie held back from telling Sandra how Lucas had said he'd actually seen his dad, under the surface of the river beckoning to him. Despite the spirit of openness, she didn't want anyone thinking her son had mental health issues.

"Wow. That is some dark shit."

"I know."

Sandra exhaled another cloud of smoke, which Christie watched dissipate. "You ever feel like you just want to go and score something? Just to take away all the guilt and the pain. Just for a little while?"

"I...all the time."

"It doesn't go away, does it?"

"Nope."

"One day at a time and all that shit."

"Exactly."

They both fell silent then, watching a car turn into the church car park.

"Here come the sex addicts," Sandra said.

As they watched, a chubby middle-aged man climbed out of the car, trotted across the car park and hurried up the steps towards the entrance. He was balding on top and wore glasses. He reminded Christie of one of her schoolteachers, Mr Yates, a genial sort, the only one of her teachers she'd actually liked.

"Evening, ladies," the man said as he passed.

Christie waited until the man was inside before saying to Sandra. "Sex addicts? You're kidding, right?"

"Oh no. No joke. They go in right after us. The SA's. It sure ain't the way we all thought we'd be spending our Friday evenings, I know that."

"But he's not...I mean...he doesn't look the type."

"Oh none of them do. Believe me."

They both laughed.

Christie glanced at her watch. "Well, going to have to make a dash for it. Got to collect my boy. See you next week, yeah?"

"You betcha," Sandra said in a tone that made Christie suspect she wouldn't in fact see Sandra next week, or ever again; and as she walked away she wondered if maybe she should go back and talk to her some more. But exiting the car park, she saw her bus coming and ran to catch it.

SHE WAS DRENCHED by the time she reached her mother's house, her hair hanging in wet strands around her face. As soon as her mother

143

opened the door, she began looking Christie over. *Here comes the examination*, Christie thought.

"You look a state, Christie."

"Raining," Christie said, in a sharp tone, "I can't help that."

She stepped into the brightly lit hallway, where she continued to find herself under scrutiny. Christie knew that her mother was looking to see if the pupils of her eyes were dilated, or pinned; or for signs of a nosebleed or white power around her nostrils. Though her coat was wet, she kept it on. Underneath she wore a short-sleeved blouse—an open invitation to her mother to check her arms for signs of tracks. She wasn't prepared for that, not today. She understood that her mother's inspections were something she'd have to endure for a while—in the NA meetings they talked a lot about rebuilding trust with loved ones—but she couldn't help but feel angry every time she had to endure one. She would cast her eyes over the crucifixes and framed pictures of Jesus and the Holy Virgin on the walls, and she would think: *We all have our little addictions, mother.* On a couple of occasions, she'd come close to saying it out loud but had so far managed to stay silent.

"Where's Lucas?"

"He fell asleep watching TV. I'm worried about him, Christie."

"Worried?"

"He's been behaving oddly again. Some of the things he says..."

"What do you mean?"

Christie walked ahead of her mother into the lounge where she saw Lucas fast asleep on the sofa covered with a blanket. She was always amazed how just the sight of him could lift her spirits. The television showed a soap opera. Her mother liked to watch TV on mute with subtitles. The silence of the room felt oppressive to Christie. In here too there was more of what Jules used to call her mother's 'Jesus knick-knacks', including a cast iron figure of the man himself hanging off the cross which was fixed on the wall above the TV. She didn't like bringing Lucas here to be surrounded by all this stuff, but currently she had no other option.

Unable to resist a growing urge to lash out, she said, "I hope you're not filling Lucas' head with all your Catholic guilt-trip nonsense, mother."

The barb hit its mark. Her mother said nothing, just turned her head to the side as if she'd been slapped. It was ridiculous really, overly theatrical. A reaction not just to Christie's comment, but to all the suffering heaped on suffering that Christie had inflicted on her mother over the years. Christie could have laughed, but instead she felt a twist of guilt just as she was supposed to. She tried to think of something to say, some kind of apology.

"You know I applied for that Open University course. I'm going to do my A-levels then I'm thinking I might do a degree."

"That's nice, dear."

"I thought you'd be pleased. I'm trying to make a better future for us. Me and Lucas."

"I am pleased. It's just that I know you. You can't stick at anything."

"I can *try*," Christie said, a trace of anger showing in her voice. Hadn't her mother been the one who always talked about her getting an education?

"Take your coat off," her mother said. "Sit down. I'll make some tea."

"No," Christie said. "Don't bother. We need to get going."

Christie began trying to rouse Lucas whilst her mother stood over them and watched.

"I need to talk to you before you go, Christie."

"About what?"

"Lucas, of course. I left him watching cartoons earlier while I made dinner, then when I came back he was lying on the floor in that corner over there talking into the air vent."

"What? What air vent?"

Her mother pointed towards the wall beneath the window. There was an air vent there just above the skirting board. Christie couldn't remember noticing it before.

"Talking into it?"

"Last week it was the mirror in the downstairs loo. He..." Her mother pursed her lips. "He said he was talking to his father."

Christie laughed under her breath and shook her head. "It's just his way of coping, Mum. He misses Jules. He'll get over it."

"I'm telling you it isn't right. Look what happened at the river that time. He almost..."

"That won't happen again."

"You should take him to a child psychologist, Christie."

"Mother, for God's sake."

"He says his father wants him. He kept saying he's going to go and live with his father. Haven't you explained to him that Jules is...?"

"Of course I have. We all went to the funeral, didn't we?"

"But wasn't Jules trying to get custody of Lucas just before he died?"

"What does that have to do with anything?"

145

"He wanted the boy, Christie."

"So?"

Her mother said nothing. An anguished expression came over her face. She wrung her hands together at her breast and cast her eyes around the room as if she thought there was someone else present listening in on them. There wasn't of course, unless you counted Jesus.

"Look Mum, Jules is dead and Lucas knows that. I've *explained* it all. I've told him his father's gone, okay, and he will never see him again."

Her mother shifted her eyes and met Christie's gaze. "Then why does he keep saying that he *is* seeing him again?"

THE FOLLOWING MORNING as she got Lucas ready for school, he began asking if he could wear the gold trainers again. His stubbornness and insistence made her so furious that she took then and threw them into the dustbin whilst he watched. He cried all the way to school.

"I hate you!" he kept saying. "I want Dad."

They were standing outside the school gates when Christie lost her temper again and yelled at Lucas, "You're Dad's dead, Lucas!"

A few of the other parents, hurrying their children in through the school gates, shot a glance at her, making her feel so guilty that she fell on her knees and hugged Lucas whilst he cried.

When she got home she found a letter waiting for her. It was from the Open University. Her application to study A-Levels had been declined.

"Fuck."

OF ALL PEOPLE, it was the man from the group who met in the church hall after her NA meetings. The one who reminded her so much of her kindly schoolteacher, Mr Yates. He approached her in the church carpark the following Friday and asked her if she was Narcotics Anonymous. She didn't see what business it was of his, but he caught her off-guard and she nodded. He then told her that, if she was interested, he had some W-12s. When she shook her head and shrugged, he explained to her that W-12s were opiate pills.

"Perfectly legal," he said. "They can't touch you for having these."

Christie looked at him for a long moment, wondering what kind of arsehole offered opiate pills to a recovering drug addict?

"How much?" she heard herself say.

He starting talking about how he could tell that she was a nice girl, and that she probably had bills to pay, so perhaps didn't have a lot of spare cash, but he could see that she needed something, something to give her a little lift. She knew exactly where his talk was going.

Christie could hear Jules' voice in her head, that voice he'd used whenever she refused to score drugs with him. That simpering voice of his. *I know you Christie. I know what you like.* It was similar to the voice the man was using now.

He was still talking. Christie interrupted him. "What do you want?"

The man thumbed over his shoulder at his car. "Just a handjob."

It wasn't too difficult a thing to do, not whilst she was doing it, although she couldn't get the face of Mr Yates, her old school teacher, out of her mind. She found she could shut off just like in the old days, but afterwards she remembered Lucas and felt so disgusted with herself that she stumbled to the edge of the carpark and vomited. The man gave her the pills anyway; three round grey pills in a little plastic baggie stamped with a yellow smiley face. They looked like screwheads. Without saying anything, the man then walked away towards the doors of the church hall. *Going in to confess his sins*, Christie thought. She had a powerful desire to take one of the little pills out from the baggie and slip it onto her tongue; but such was the feeling of self-disgust surging through her that the urge to just hurl them into the bushes was equally as strong. She would never find them again in the dark. Telling herself that someone else might find them in daylight, some kid maybe, she merely tossed them into her handbag instead. She would flush them down the toilet when she arrived home. It had been a momentary relapse that was all. She'd been doing well. She wasn't going to throw it all away now. And there was Lucas to think off. What if she got on a slippery slope with drugs again and he ended up getting taken away from her and adopted like Sandra's daughter? She couldn't bear the thought of that. It terrified her. If she lost him, it would kill her. She knew that much. After everything she'd done to keep custody of him—things she didn't even want to think about—she couldn't bear the idea of him calling someone else Mummy. She was his mother. She would always be his mother. "You're the best Mummy in the world," he used to say to her when they played together, before Jules turned his head with promises and presents. That was her drug now. Lucas was all she needed.

No, the pills were going straight down the toilet the moment she arrived home, disposed of properly and safely, and what had taken place between her and that arsehole Mr Yates-lookalike would be written off with all her other past mistakes.

147

She ran to catch the bus which would take her to her mother's house where she was initially glad to find her son awake and in good spirits until her mother took her to one side and said, "He's been talking to the mirror again. He told me today that his Dad has a plan. Take him to a child psychologist, Christie."

"He's mourning, that's all," Christie said. She felt more tired than she had ever felt in her life before.

Lucas appeared and yanked at her handbag.

"What are you after, little man?"

"Sweeties."

She shook her head. "I don't have any."

SHE KNEW THE moment she opened her eyes that something was wrong. The clock beside her bed read 10:52. She sat up. Lucas should have woken her a long time ago. She couldn't remember a Saturday morning when she'd slept past eight. Lucas was normally up early, excited at the thought of what they were going to do with the day, and calling out to her from his bedroom. Could it be that he'd simply been tired and had slept until almost eleven?

She got up, calling out to him before she even reached his room. Out of the corner of her eye, she noticed her handbag sat open in the hallway at the top of the stairs, and though it only registered distantly the sight of it added to her concern. In the doorway to Lucas' room, her breath caught in her throat and she halted, one hand shooting to her mouth to stifle a scream. Lucas lay unmoving across his bed, on top of the Star Wars duvet rather than under it. He was fully dressed in jeans and a hooded sweater, and was also wearing the gold trainers which he must have somehow rescued from the dustbin without her noticing. His eyes were open and fixed on the ceiling. With a shuddering breath, Chrissie took a few steps towards him then stopped again. She noticed something else lying on the duvet by his hand. It was the little baggie with the smiley face on it. She had meant to flush the pills down the toilet, but she'd forgotten all about them. They were gone now, the baggie empty.

"Lucas!" she screamed, hurrying to the bed now and falling across him. "Lucas!"

He didn't blink. His face and arms felt cold. She tried for some time to rouse him, shaking him and lightly slapping his face, but when she got no response she shook him harder and still didn't get a reaction.

He says his Dad has a plan.

148

"No! No!"

With a roar of anguish she hoisted herself up on the bed so that her face was level with the air vent on the wall above it. She began screaming into the vent. She screamed until her throat was ragged. *"Jules!"* she screamed, over and over again, pounding on the wall with her hand. *"Jules! Give him back! Give him back!"*

She didn't know how long she went on screaming. At some point the police arrived, then an ambulance.

A young woman with a kind face gave her a sedative as two men zipped something into a large black bag and carried it out of the room.

"I want my son," Christie said. "I want my son."

The kind-faced woman placed a hand on the top of her head and said, "I know." Another woman, it was a policewoman, took hold of her arm, and said, "You'll have to come with us."

Something's Knocking

HERE WAS NOTHING exceptional about the doorway. It was a regular doorway on an inner city backstreet which Richard used as a shortcut on his way to work. The sombre forest-green paint was cracked and flaking, and the door always stood open allowing a view of a dingy hallway at the end of which a staircase descended into gloom. The hallway's carpet, which might once have been red, was worn and stained, and the paper peeled from the walls.

No, it was not the doorway that caught Richard's attention – how could it? – but the posters affixed to the brickwork to the left of it. The posters always contained a few words, hand drawn in elaborate script, and an arrow which pointed towards the open door. The words on the posters changed daily. NORTH TOWER RUMPUS, the poster said one day. Another day it read: THROB OF A GLORIOUS EVENING, and the day after that: SWEET TONGUE CASCADE. Always underneath there was the same arrow pointing inside the open doorway, as if to imply that whatever was suggested by this nonsense could somehow be found inside.

Richard never saw anyone entering the doorway, but one evening after he'd been working late he saw a woman emerge. Stepping out into Richard's path, the woman at once put her head down and hurried away into the night, only throwing a single glance over her shoulder at the doorway, but Richard had time to notice that she wept. Then, further along the street, just before she turned a corner, the woman had halted and begun to laugh. For a moment she'd been bent double with laughter. Then she righted herself and continued on and all he heard after that was the fast-fading clip-clop of her heels.

His reasons for entering the door himself after work one Friday evening in July would remain a mystery to him for the rest of his life. Perhaps it was the tedious day he'd spent approving and declining mortgage applications. Sometimes he came close to declining perfectly reasonably applications just to introduce some chaos into his existence, but of course, he never did. Or perhaps it was the thought of another dinner with Janet, sawing at overcooked pork and listening to the usual tittle-tattle about their neighbours. He had grown to despise the box of Turkish delight she would always bring out after dinner and the way she'd smile as she placed it on the table as if presenting him with some luxurious treat, then she'd say in that semi-serious tone, *"Just one, remember,"* which always made him want to gobble the lot the moment her back was turned. Perhaps it was the thought of the weekend ahead, tending the garden and watching women over the hedge. Or perhaps it was the words that had been written on the poster that day. Could something about them have enticed him inside? THE RUNNY MORNING. He could not imagine what that meant.

The stairs groaned under his weight, and he thought of turning back, but then he saw a door at the foot of the staircase opening, and he was caught in the yellowish light leaking out. As his eyes adjusted, he saw that there was a tall, wiry young man holding open the door at the bottom of the stairs. The young man was dressed like a theatre usher in red jacket with gold piping, and bell boy cap. He showed Richard a welcoming smile. Beyond him, Richard thought he saw some kind of activity.

"Good evening, sir."

"Uh...er...hello. I...uh..."

"May I take your coat?"

"Well...I...uh...wasn't planning to..."

But the young man was already helping him off with his coat, so he had no choice but to step inside the door. He found himself in a small room with six or seven round tables set out in front of a little stage situated at the furthest end. Grey drapes covered the walls, and the only light apart from the stage lights came from single candles set upon the tables. Richard wrinkled his nose at the incense overlaying a more stale smell – damp and rot. Only one of the tables was occupied by an elderly couple who sat very still, apparently engrossed in what was being enacted before them. Onstage two men, who appeared to be dressed as fried eggs, pretended to paddle a canoe whilst a woman in black Lycra ran around the stage holding aloft a big yellow cardboard sun and shouting "Hot! Hot!" in a threatening manner over and over again.

The usher - or whatever he was supposed to be — spoke again, drawing Richard's attention away from the stage.

"Your name, sir?"

"I...uh...Richard. Richard Martin." Then he thought: *What am I telling him that for?*

The usher smiled in a humouring way and shook his head. "No, sir. Here you'll have a different name. You must choose one from the table. See?"

With a flourish of his hand, the usher indicated a square table stood behind him on which a number of handwritten labels were set out. The labels said things like RASMUS CHALKDUST, ALESSANDRO HEADHAWK, ESPERANZA FLORES, SYLVESTER TOTTY, VALENTINO SATIN, and LOLA HONEYBLAST.

"You want me to pick one of those?"

"Yes please, sir."

Richard blinked. In his confusion and anxiety, his vision had started to swim. He thought of Janet at home at the dinner table with potatoes that had boiled dry and beef gone tough in the oven. How was he ever going to explain this to her? For a moment he thought about turning on his heel and making a run for it.

"Sir?"

Flustered, he grabbed the label that said LOLA HONEYBLAST, then before he could correct his mistake the usher, who had nodded with approval, took the label from him, peeled off the back, and patted it onto his shirtfront.

"Excellent choice. Would Miss Lola care to take a seat?"

"Er...what?"

"Here perhaps?" The usher indicated a table near the front of the stage. Richard's only desire was to escape from that place, he had made a terrible mistake – he realised - in going there, but despite himself he sat down. On stage now the two fried eggs had abandoned their canoe and were chasing the woman carrying the cardboard sun around the stage with garden forks. The usher pressed a card into Richard's hand. When Richard looked at it he had to blink a number of times before words arose from the jumble filling his vision. He eventually realised that he was looking at a cocktails list. The names of the cocktails were as ridiculous as everything else here.

"Oh, I'll just have a beer, please."

A flicker of disapproval crossed the usher's face before he snatched the cocktails list from Richard's hand, gave a little bow and said, "Very well. Enjoy the show."

Richard could make no sense of what was happening on stage, so instead looked at the elderly couple seated to his left. In the same moment, the female half of the couple turned her head to meet his gaze and he saw that tears ran down her face. And she was smiling. Glancing away, he noticed a small card, about the size of a business card, sat on the tabletop. He picked it up. On one side was a single capitalised word: UNLOCK. On the reverse was printed a telephone number. And beneath this, written in cursive script: *Call us and tell us about your most secret dreams.*

He found himself thinking about the recurring dream he'd been having recently, the knocking dream, and at once he no longer wanted to be in that place. What was he doing there anyway? What would Janet say if she knew he visited such a place? He had to get home. His wife waited for him. Seeing the usher walking towards him with a bottle of beer on a tray, Richard stood so abruptly that the actors on stage paused to glance at him.

"Madam, your..." the usher began.

"I'm sorry, but I have to go."

"But, madam...?"

"No really. I have to be on my way. If I could just have my coat."

"Madam, you..."

Richard saw his coat hanging on a rack by the table of names, and went to retrieve it himself. Ignoring the usher, who was still calling after him, he made for the door, hurried up the groaning steps and along the hallway's tatty carpet until he was out of the door. The evening air felt fresh and bracing. At a fast walk, he continued on towards the multi-story carpark where he always left the Honda Crosstour which he'd overheard some of his colleagues at the bank laughingly refer to as *Ricky's Pussy Wagon*. He sometimes remembered this when he was driving and he would glance across at Janet sat pale and tense in the passenger seat and he would be filled with inexplicable rage.

By the time he arrived home, Janet had already gone to bed in the spare room. She'd left a single lamp on in the lounge and a plate of beef stew in the microwave. After eating, Richard prepared for bed himself. In the bathroom, he spent some time in front of the mirror, staring at his reflection as if it were a stranger looking back at him. Of course he'd never been what women called a *hunk* or a *stud-muffin*, but now what was he? An overweight, middle-aged man with bad skin, turkey neck, and a spreading bald patch. When did this happen? Spying Janet's make-up bag sat atop the medicine cabinet, he took it down and looked inside. Selecting a lipstick, he carefully rouged his lips. Next he found some eyeliner and applied that. *I'm not Richard anymore*, he thought when he was done. *I'm Lola Honeyblast.* He gazed at himself in the mirror and smiled until, hearing a footstep in the hallway, he came to his senses, grabbed a washcloth, and scrubbed his face clean.

He heard Janet's voice. "That you, Richard?"

"Yes, dear." He winced at the catch in his own voice. "Just me."

153

There was the sound of a door closing and then silence. As he undressed, Richard discovered the card from the theatre in his trouser pocket. He couldn't remember taking it. He studied the phone number written on it and the line of text: *Call us and tell us about your most secret dreams.*

No, no, no, no, no!

Tossing the card down on his bedside table, he finished undressing, climbed into bed and turned out the light. He lay staring into the near darkness, remembering the fried eggs chasing the cardboard sun around the stage of that little theatre, and wondering what kind of madness had made him enter that place to begin with.

THOUGH HE HAD no intention of ever entering through that green door again, he found himself once more overwhelmed by the tedium of his daily routine and each time he passed the open doorway on his way home it seemed to call to him. He studied the text on the posters pinned up beside the door and found himself wondering what bizarre scenes were being acted out on the stage in that candlelit basement. It wasn't long before he succumbed and was once more enticed inside. Again he was given a friendly greeting by the usher, and again the LOLA HONEYBLAST label was applied to his shirtfront without him having the time to choose an alternative.

Upon his second visit he was so unnerved by what was taking place on stage, he didn't stay long. In some nightmarish playlet, a naked man was being pursued around the stage by a woman in a giant butterfly costume. The woman, hoisted above the man on wires, flapped her huge wings and emitted hungry *cock-caws* whilst the man cowered and ran from her. It was too much for Richard. A week later, he returned again. This time, the poster outside read THE SONGBIRD'S REQUIEM. On stage, a woman stood trapped inside a giant birdcage and sang to a man sat in an armchair reading a newspaper. The man appeared not to be aware of the trapped woman. He went on reading his newspaper, even when the woman's singing turned to shrieks and she began to shake the bars of her cage. Whether she sang, or shrieked, or beat her fists against the bars of her cage the man took no notice. Eventually, the woman collapsed theatrically to the floor and the man still did not look up. He turned a page of his newspaper. For some reason the performance affected Richard so deeply that he left the theatre blinking tears from his eyes. Passing the usher, he was handed another of the business cards that had UNLOCK written on

154

one side and *Call us and tell us about your most secret dreams* and a phone number on the other. Absently, Richard slipped it into his trouser pocket, but he would discover it again that evening as he once more prepared for bed.

Crossing the bedroom, he looked out into the hallway, saw no one, and carefully closed the door. Then he took the phone from the bedside table and dialled the number on the card. He felt lightheaded. His heart beat fast in his chest. On the other end of the line, a phone rang a couple of times before there was the click of an answerphone picking up. A woman's voice said: "Unlock. Tell us about your most secret dreams. Spare no detail." There was a beep and Richard realised he was listening to the sound of his own breathing. He glanced towards the door thinking he'd heard a footstep in the hall again. But then he realised he could hear Janet's snoring through the connecting wall between the two bedrooms.

"I...uh...we're having dinner, my wife and I," he whispered into the phone. "In my dream I mean. It's the roast pork she always cooks on Sundays. We sit facing each other across the table. We're not speaking. My wife...she looks up at me and gives this dry smile. I hate it, that smile. I hate how pale and waxy she looks. Her hair full of grey. How her eyes look pained when she does that smile." He took a deep breath, and lowered his voice further, murmuring into the phone. "Then I start to hear this knocking sound. Just a low knocking sound at first. I look around the room and up at the ceiling, trying to work out where it might be coming from. My wife, she carries on eating as if she hasn't noticed anything. *What's that?* I say to her, but she doesn't reply. She just gives me that dry smile again. It's like camouflage, that smile. It's a lie. The knocking gets louder. I can't work out where it's coming from. It seems to be coming from everywhere at once. It gets louder, and my wife still doesn't seem to have noticed. *Can't you hear that?* I say to her. I have to shout because the knocking's so loud now. It's a loud booming sound. Boom! Boom! Boom! Why can't she hear it? She shows me that smile again. I can't stand it. Something's knocking. Knocking, knocking, knocking. Something. Somewhere. And only I can hear it. It's in the walls, it's in the floor, it's in the ceiling. I stand up from my chair and clutch my head in my hands. *Can't you hear that knocking?* I scream at my wife. *Can't you hear it?* But she just smiles, she...she just..."

A beep signalled that he was out of time and an automated voice said: "Thank you for calling."

Stunned, Richard set the phone down in its cradle. He was out of breath and breathing heavily. A line of sweat had broken out across his brow. He cast his eyes around the bedroom like a man who'd woken up in a strange place. Everything seemed unfamiliar suddenly. Why of Earth was the room so yellow? The wallpaper, the carpet, the curtains, the bedspread – it was all different shades of yellow. Why? And why hadn't he noticed it before? It was sickening.

He stared at the phone for a moment then looked at the wall behind which Janet lay snoring. He closed his eyes against a wash of guilt.

What have I done?

He still held the UNLOCK card in one hand. He tore it up into the smallest fragments, took it into the bathroom and flushed it down the toilet.

HE WAS DONE with it. The madness had to end. This time, he had no intention of stepping through that green door again and descending those rickety stairs to that bizarre little incense-infused theatre, but one Monday evening when he was passing he noticed that the poster outside read: SOMETHING'S KNOCKING.

What?

He halted in his stride and gazed at the poster, blinking.

What had they...?

What had he...?

He stormed down the steps, but his anger dissipated when he saw the young man in his usher uniform opening the door at the bottom and smiling at him.

"Miss Honeyblast. How lovely to see you again."

"Listen," Richard said. "This is...I'm not..."

"May I take your coat, Madam?"

"Look..." Richard said. His coat was removed from him. With little else to do, he surveyed the inside of the theatre. But for himself and the usher, there was no one else there. The stage was lit but unoccupied except for a dining table and two chairs.

"I suppose you want me to sit," Richard said, pointing at the table near the front which he had occupied on his previous visits.

"Wait," the usher said. "Your name!"

Reaching behind himself, the usher plucked a label from the table, peeled off the back and pressed it onto Richard's shirt front. LOLA

HONEYBLAST. As Richard made to move towards his table, the usher stopped him again.

"If I may."

The usher reached now into a cardboard box beneath the table, took out a purple dress hat similar to one Janet had worn to a wedding the previous year and placed it on to Richard's head. Next came a pearl necklace which he strung around Richard's neck, then a large flower brooch which he quickly and expertly affixed to the lapel of Richard's jacket. As Richard stood dumbfounded, the usher leaned back, crossed his arms, looked him up and down theatrically and smiling.

"Perfection."

"Shall I sit down?" Richard said.

"Of course," the usher said, with a wild gesticulation towards Richard's table. His voice rose. "The performance is about to begin. Would Madam like to see the cocktails list?"

"Oh, just bring me something. Anything. I know it's going to be something daft."

"Very well."

RICHARD SIPPED AT his drink. It was a mauve coloured liquid in a tall glass. There was a blot of cream at the bottom of the glass and a plastic toy shark with a buoy clenched in its teeth balanced on the rim, one pectoral fin sunk into the generous helping of ice. With every slurp at the straw, Richard got a different taste; sometimes bitter, sometimes sweet. If someone had asked him what it tasted like, he would have said: *Like life*. And he was quite pleased with himself for thinking of something so poetic and profound.

From somewhere came the blast of a trumpet and Richard sat up straight. A young woman, dressed like an old woman in grey wig, glasses, oversize cardigan and slippers, walked onto the stage carrying a plate with a large hunk of meat on it. She sat down at one end of the dining table set centre stage.

"No," Richard said to himself. He shook his head. "No. No. No."

Then a young man, also dressed old and also carrying a plate with a slab of meat on it, stepped out on stage.

"No," Richard said again. "That's not me. It's not. I...it doesn't even...it's..."

The man on stage took a seat opposite the woman, and the two took up their cutlery and in silence began to hack in an exaggerated way at the

157

meat. This went on for some minutes as Richard looked on in horror until from stage right came a dim knocking sound. The man on stage lifted his head and looked around, but the women went on hacking at her meat. A louder knocking came from stage right, then a louder one from somewhere beneath the stage. Then the knocking began from all three places at once, there was a crash of cymbals, the ringing of a gong, feet stomping, and the man leapt up from his seat.

"Can't you hear that, wife?" he shouted. Richard's mouth fell open. The wife on stage looked up at her husband and smiled – it was Janet's dry smile, just a movement of the mouth nothing more – and the man reached dramatically towards her as if he wanted to strangle her. But then he pulled away. The wife returned to cutting her meat. The cacophony of banging, stomping, cymbal crashes and ringing gongs increased in volume and fervour, and when the man on stage once more leapt up and clutched his head in his hands, Richard did the same. Then something happened that had never happened in Richard's dream. The man grabbed his wife from her seat and began to waltz about the stage with her. Their movements became increasingly exaggerated, as they collided with the table and knocked over chairs. The plates of meat fell to the floor with an awful thud as did the cutlery which was kicked about the boards by the dancing couple. Then the couple separated. First the man, and then the woman began to tear the clothes from their bodies. They flung the garments aside one by one until they were running naked about the stage, laughing and cavorting, trampling the meat and pushing the table over on its side. Then the man began grabbing up the woman's clothes from the floor of the stage, and the woman took up the man's clothes and they began to dress. When they both wore each other's clothes, the knocking became a rhythm and the couple became flamenco dancers, flailing their arms, twirling on the spot, and stomping about the stage.

Then the woman pulled away from the man and ran to one end of the stage. She pressed one wrist to her head and shouted out, "But haven't you got work tomorrow, dear?"

The man responded with a dastardly laugh. "No, because I burned the whole building and everyone in it to the ground! Come to me, my darling and be my Dolce Vita! Be a tiger tonight, my love! This ordinary life sickens me! Soon enough we will be in our graves!" Finally, they ran towards each other and embraced. They fell conjoined to the floor of the stage and began to roll around in the trampled meat as the curtain descended.

As silence fell, Richard came slowly to his senses. Behind him, someone was slow clapping. Feeling wetness on his cheeks, Richard raised his fingers to his face and touched the tears.

"What have they done?" he said, under his breath. "What have they done to my dream?"

Forgetting that he still wore the dress, hat, pearls, and flower brooch, he jerked to his feet, ran up the stairs, and staggered out into the street. He still wore the items placed on him by the theatre usher when he arrived home. Luckily, Janet was already in bed. The single lamp had been left on and there was a plate with a steak and broccoli on it covered over with congealed gravy in the microwave which Richard, overcome with revulsion, frizbee-ed out of the kitchen window.

Janet. He had to see Janet. He had to tell her about...about tonight.

Dashing upstairs, not stopping to take off any of the Lola Honeyblast regalia, he went at once to the spare bedroom and flung open the door.

"Jan—" he began, but the sight of Janet lain out on the bed like a corpse on a mortician's slab halted him. He looked at that pale, waxy face; a face that he had once loved. She was deeply asleep, and engaged in a loud rattling snore.

He began to withdraw from the room, but then he stopped. Next to the telephone on Janet's nightstand, he saw one of the UNLOCK cards. He caught his breath. How had it got there? Hadn't he torn his up and flushed it down the toilet, just to be rid of it? But no – he remembered now. He had brought one home before that, after his first visit to the theatre, and left it on his nightstand. He had not noticed its disappearance.

He found himself thinking about that one performance he'd witnessed, the one that had brought tears to his eyes. THE SONGBIRD'S REQUIEM, hadn't it been called? The woman trapped inside a birdcage singing and then shrieking and finally collapsing to the floor whilst a man in an armchair read a newspaper and ignored her.

"Janet," he said in a kind of desperate plea. Then again, just, "Janet."

Land of Youth

MATT HAD BEEN told the house would be easy to find.
"If in doubt," the young woman he'd spoken to at the post office back in Glendalough had said, "just follow the train tracks." The woman had been cheery when first approached—almost flirty in fact—but Matt saw her expression change when he asked about Tír na nÓg. "Going to visit Miss Candelaria, are you?" she said with a hint of wariness in her tone.

"Yes. I'm going to interview her. I have GPS on my phone. I just wanted to make sure I was headed in the right direction."

"GPS won't help you find that house," the woman said. "Just head west along the railway line. You'll see it."

Though dubious, Matt had resorted to doing exactly as the woman instructed after discovering she'd been right about the GPS. No matter. It was a pleasant walk, the day being fine and the views of the surrounding mountains quite stunning. But for the strap of his overnight bag cutting into his shoulder, he would have described it as idyllic. He passed the ruins of an old graveyard, at the far end of which was the medieval round tower he'd read about online when researching the area. Any other time, he would have been excited by these sights and by the thought of exploring the area further. The only thing he could focus on at the moment though was the knowledge that he was about to meet Ava Candelaria.

He'd interviewed a couple of big names since he started writing for *Action!* Magazine—and felt the requisite thrill at meeting stars in the flesh—but as far as he was concerned Ava Candelaria was his biggest coup yet. Though she was no longer considered a big name, in fact but for her early acting roles Hollywood had all but forgotten her, this was the woman who'd adorned his bedroom wall when he was a boy. In her *Starship XII* role as Queen Anelia, she had stared defiantly outwards with a sword clutched in both hands and one bare leg stretched out from under her skirts. He'd innocently pinned up the poster aged eleven or so but it had later become the focus for all his swirling pubescent lusts. He could scarcely believe he was actually going to meet her. Queen Anelia. He took deep breaths to calm his jitters as he walked along the edge of the train tracks. At one point a loud hoot startled him, and turning he saw the familiar yellow and red nose of a *Virgin* train approaching. The sight would hardly have been noteworthy back in London, but in these surroundings he was struck by how sleek and modern the train looked, like something bulleting towards him out of the future. Taking a step back, he stood and blinked at the train as it blasted by on its way to Dublin.

He crossed a wooden bridge over a stream, passed through a tunnel in the railway sidings, and shortly after this he saw the house. He knew at once that he was looking at Tír na nÓg, and a mixture of excitement and nerves stirred in his belly. It had been built on a rise a short distance from the train tracks, and was partially shielded from view by fern trees and hawthorn bushes. It was a circular three-story brick-built house which, but for its white-window frames, blended almost perfectly with the dark mountains it was set against. He felt another flutter in his stomach at the thought that Ava Candelaira—*the* Ava Candelaira—could right then have been watching him from one of the house's many windows.

The house had no grounds. The front door was reached via a set of granite steps which had almost vanished into the hillside. As Matt climbed the steps he took a tissue from his pocket and wiped the sweat from his brow. After this he quickly combed his fingers through his hair; then aware of how dry his lips were, he took a bottle from his bag and drank, swilling the water around his mouth before swallowing. Reaching the front door, he found that his courage almost failed him. Summoning strength from inside himself, he pressed the doorbell and heard it chiming inside the house.

Waiting, he reminded himself that even though he was about to meet Ava Candelaria, a lifelong ambition, he was a professional journalist working for a glossy magazine. The last thing he wanted was to come across as a snivelling fan-boy who'd spent his early teens masturbating over a *Starship XII* poster.

After a few minutes, he heard footsteps and the door was opened by a short, plump, woman in her mid-sixties who wore horn-rimmed glasses that gave her a schoolmarm-ish appearance and over the rim of which she peered at him. Her dark hair was threaded with grey and held loosely behind her head with a Spanish comb.

For a few moments the woman looked up at him, smiling.

"Matthew," she said then in a warm, delighted tone. It wasn't a query. She spoke as if he were already known to her.

"Matt. Please," he said, holding out his hand. He was just about to ask if Miss Candelaria was home when he saw the old woman's mouth tilt up in a sly smile, the same smile he'd seen her use in countless movies. This woman before him...*this* was Ava Candelaria. He realised that he'd foolishly expected her to look the same as she had on the *Starship XII* poster that had adorned his boyhood wall. Despite his obvious mistake, he couldn't help but feel an acute disappointment. "It's...it's a pleasure to meet you, Miss Candelaria," he spluttered out. "I'm a massive fan."

She took his offered hand and held on to it, gazing up into his face again. Her touch was light and papery. He couldn't help but notice the liver spots on the back of her hands.

Perhaps catching some change in his expression, she tilted her head to one side and smiled. Behind her glasses, her eyes twinkled with humour and mischief.

"It's such a let down, isn't it?" she said. "Don't worry, I feel the same way every time I look in the mirror." Watching him stuttering over a response, she released him at last and batted her hand in the air. "It's a cruel thing to be young and beautiful, really. One eventually has to watch oneself getting ugly and old." She looked closely at him again. Her smile broadened into something sardonic. "You'll see I'm right. One day."

Not knowing how to respond to this—did Ava Candelaria just imply that he was beautiful?—Matt heard himself say, "It...it's a lovely house you have. Really stunning."

"Yes, it's a very special place. I knew that as soon as I saw it. Built on top of an old fairy fort, or so they told me. There are quite a few around here." She smiled now with one side of her mouth, as if sharing a joke. "But the Irish will tell you all kinds of tales just to get you to buy something. There's a young couple from Japan—absolutely loaded—who're always offering to buy the house from me. They're collectors. *Starship XII* obsessives. They want to make babies in the house where Queen Anelia lived. You're laughing, but they're deadly serious. I told them they can have it after I'm dead. Until then, it's my house not some bit of memorabilia. I've lived here on and off since '86. Whenever I needed to get away from Hollywood, here I'd come. And I do love trains."

Matt glanced back towards the train tracks. "The noise doesn't bother you then?"

"Oh no, I love hearing them. The Dublin line loops around, you know. At some point it crosses over itself. I believe there was a collision some years ago. It's a wonder it doesn't happen more often. Sometimes the trains thunder through here so fast I wonder if they don't pass themselves on the way back. Imagine that."

162

Matt smiled. "And was it you who named the house?"

At this she laughed, her head falling back. "You've found me out, young Matthew. It was a hopeless gesture. Quite hopeless. I always loved the story of Oisin and Niamh. Are you familiar with it?"

"I can't say I am."

"In Irish folklore, Oisin was a man who fell in love with a woman from the Otherworld. That was Niamh. She whisked him off to Tír na nÓg, The Land of Youth, on her magical horse. But after a few years he was homesick for Ireland and wanted to leave. Niamh let him go, but told him never to touch the ground. When Oisin got back to Ireland he found that three hundred years had passed. The years caught up with him as soon as he got off his horse and he grew elderly and died of old age."

"Charming," Matt said.

"Terrifying," Ava said, and laughed. "But don't let me keep you standing there on the threshold. Come in, come in. Let's get this thing over with."

Turning, she led the way inside. The hallway was decorated with dark wood, expensive-looking rugs, and a few framed photographs on the wall. One of the pictures appeared to have been taken on the set of *Starship XII*. It showed a young Ava, smiling for the camera and wearing her Queen Anelia costume. She was being carried by General Zond, a towering lizard man and her mortal enemy in the film.

"Romain was a true gentleman," Ava said, when Matt paused to examine the photograph. "And so handsome. It was such a waste putting him in that awful costume. It was so hot under there too. Poor chap. He hated it."

"Really?"

"Oh yes. Every day of filming he would say he'd had enough and he was going to walk off set. I suppose they could have used anyone really."

A staircase led upwards on the right, but Ava gestured towards a doorway on the left.

"I thought we could do the interview in here."

"Of course."

He followed her as she entered the sunlit lounge. From the large bay window he could see the train tracks passing in front of the house and beyond those a distant line of mountains.

"Please call me Ava," she said. "We're not strangers, after all, and Candelaria's such an awful mouthful. It was only a stage name, you know, although I do have some Spanish in me from my father's side. He was from

163

the Basque country originally. My real surname is Garrastazu." She laughed. "Now that *is* a mouthful. Tea?"

"Sorry?"

She smiled. "Would you like some tea?"

"That would be perfect. Ah...did you say we're not strangers?"

She gazed at him for a long moment then laughed and shook her head. "Of course, you wouldn't remember."

"Remember? We've...we've met before? I think that's one thing I *would've* remembered."

"Never mind." She cast her eyes around the walls of the room. "It's this place. It's got me all confused." Before he could respond she went on. "So how many times have you seen *Starship XII*?"

He swallowed. "Ah...excuse me?"

"I know a fan-boy when I see one. I bet you had that poster too, didn't you? The one where I'm showing a bit of leg?" She repeated the pose for him, sticking one leg out to the side and even pretending to clutch an imaginary sword. "Oh dear," she said with a grin, righting herself. "All your teenage fantasies just went up in flames."

He felt a blush rising in his cheeks. How could she know—?

Before he could say anything, she laughed. "Don't worry, I'm just playing. You like a bit of foreplay, don't you? Earl Grey okay?"

"Earl Grey?"

"The tea."

"Ah..." He nodded then said quickly. "I love some of your other films too. *The Doomsday Event*—"

"Ha! Absolute trash. I spent most of that film running around half-naked. The director just wanted some nubile thing who could recite the lines. Though, what I wouldn't give to have that body now of course."

"And you got an Oscar nod for *In Absentia*."

Ava's face lit up. "Yes. Now that was a good role. A big part. I'd always wanted to work with Moretti. But there were three men nominated besides me, and the judging panel couldn't see past my boobs."

Her frank talk stunned him a little.

"Did you enjoy playing Queen Anelia?"

"And now we're back to *Starship XII*," she said, slapping at his arm good-naturedly. "Well, I don't know. Did I enjoy playing her? She seemed a bit one-dimensional to me. I couldn't really get into the method with her, because I didn't really know who she was. She was just some male fantasy figure. Not that they wanted method, it was just a case of hold this sword,

164

flash some leg." She laughed. "Now, before you ask me anymore questions, I did promise tea, didn't I?"

With a wink, she turned and left the room. Matt set his bag down beside an armchair and turned to the window in time to see a train passing along the tracks. Rather than one of the bright, modern Virgin trains it was dark green and flat fronted; of the type he hadn't seen since he was a child. He watched it until it had vanished out of sight, thinking of what Ava had said earlier. *Sometimes the trains thunder through here so fast I imagine them passing themselves on the way back.* Now that would be something. Hearing footsteps at his back, he turned and caught sight of someone— a young woman he thought—retreating out of the door.

"Hello," Matt said. But it was Ava, returning with the tea tray, who answered him.

"Hello, hello. Did you think I'd abandoned you?"

"No, I—"

"Don't worry, I talk to myself all the time too. It's one of the side-effects of living alone. Shall we get down to it?" She nodded towards two armchairs stood facing each other, before setting the tea tray down on a little table in between. Matt took a notebook from his bag then showed Ava his Dictaphone.

"Do you mind?" he said.

Ava gave a dismissive shrug. After she had poured the tea and Matt had taken the seat opposite her, she said:

"I suppose you want to talk some more about *Starship XII*?"

"Well..."

"Of course you do. I'd only just turned twenty when I worked on that film. If only I'd known then that I was going to spend the next fifty years talking about it."

"If you'd rather we discuss something else..."

"No, I don't mind really. I remember the pranks we used to play on that film. I was always a bit of a prankster. Still am. We had some wild parties too. Drink, drugs, sex. I don't think there was an actor working on that film who I didn't wake up in bed with at some point or other."

"Really? Even...?"

"Oh, not *him*. He's actually gay. Didn't you know? I thought everyone knew."

Watching his face, she raised a hand to cover her laughter. "I'm sorry," she said, when she regained herself. "Lately I've developed this twisted enjoyment in destroying people's childhoods. I'm so sorry."

"No..." Matt glanced up. Heavy footsteps were passing back and forth in the room above. As Ava continued, he found it hard to concentrate such was the commotion from above.

"It's wonderful to be successful with something, and *Starship XII* was a huge success. But after a while it becomes a bit of an albatross around your neck. You start to resent it, and then you want to destroy it. Does that make any kind of sense?"

"Of...of course."

"The films I did later on—when I no longer had to be a sex symbol—I enjoyed those so much more. It wasn't about taking my clothes off all the time. What a relief. Now I could be an actor and...my dear boy, is something bothering you?"

"No...it's nothing. Please. Continue."

"You seem very distracted."

"Guests?" he said.

Ava raised her eyebrows.

"That noise." He pointed his pencil towards the ceiling.

Ava flicked her gaze up then back to him. "It is only you and I here."

"But..."

"Just us."

Matt nodded, and decided not to press the matter. Ava was elderly after all. Didn't elderly people get confused? Perhaps she had some kind of dementia. And what was all that earlier about them having met before? Could she be thinking he was someone else? There was still a trace of disappointment in him which he couldn't quell. Why was it he thought she wouldn't have aged? Because on screen people didn't age? It was only in life that people got older. Inevitably, they got older. Wasn't that why so many actors and actresses submitted to plastic surgery, in an attempt to remain that beautiful young person captured on screen, some even turning themselves into monsters in the process? All because people like him expected their movie stars to remain forever young. Realising this, he felt a twinge of guilt.

Ava leaned forward in her chair. Reaching out, she nudged the Dictaphone towards his side of the table.

"I want to know about you."

"What?"

"I've always wondered who this Matthew really was."

"What do you mean?"

"Tell me about yourself. Are you married? Girlfriend. I already know you're not gay."

"I...I'm not sure...this is..."

She smiled. "Come on. It doesn't change anything. Not really."

Matt took a deep breath. "I had a girlfriend until recently. Julia. We moved in together last winter. But I left."

"Why?"

"I don't know. I suppose I was a bit overwhelmed by it all."

Ava nodded. "Too much reality."

"What?"

"Was she beautiful?"

"She was very attractive, yes."

"So...you meet this beautiful woman, you fall in love, you put her on a pedestal. Right? Then you move in together and suddenly you realise she's just a human being, with bras and knickers hanging over the bath. The makeup comes off. You get to see behind the curtain, and you don't like it. She's a real person. She's not some fantasy figure. Right?"

Matt felt a blush rising in his cheeks once more. For the second time since he entered the house he felt as if Ava had unpicked him.

She laughed now. "I'm sorry. It's not just you. We all do it. You're looking at a woman who's been married three times. I kept thinking I'd found my knight in shining armour, but then I realised they were all just actors. And not even good actors at that. The only mercy is I never had children with any of them. That would've been a disaster. Forgive me, I didn't mean to embarrass you."

"Shall we just continue with the interview?"

"Yes, but give me a moment." She struggled to get up from her chair, so Matt stood and offered her his hand. "Thank you. I'll only be a minute."

She left the room. Matt turned his attention to his notebook, flicking through the list of possible questions he'd written out on the journey from London. But he was thinking about Julia. In his mind he saw her sitting alone in the Croyden flat they had rented together. He pictured her wearing the baggy grey jogging suit she always changed into in the evening, the one she said she felt most comfortable in, and her hair was caught loosely, carelessly behind her head with a clip. He thought he should feel guilty about abandoning her, but remembering her this way he didn't. He just didn't.

At the sound of a train passing along the tracks, he looked towards the window. It took him a moment to understand what he was looking at. The train was sleek, dark red and windowless. Yellow stripes were painted along its sides. There were no carriages, just one long body. It looked like some kind of enormous insect and he felt a sudden shock and revulsion. Where the hell did a train like that come from? He'd never seen anything like it. It seconds it was gone and he sat blinking, wondering if he hadn't imagined it.

He waited a while longer, but when Ava still hadn't returned he went to the door and looked out into the hallway.

"Hello?"

He received no reply, but he could hear noises from above and wondered if he should investigate. Ava seemed to have been gone a long time. Perhaps she'd had a fall, and was in need of help. This was what he told himself. The truth was, he was curious to see how she lived and wanted to explore the house.

Cautiously, he climbed the stairs. On the first floor there were four doors, only one of which stood open on a room empty of all but a large made bed and a bedside table with a lamp and—he noticed—a small marble statue of Buddha. As he moved towards the set of stairs at the end of the hall, he briefly paused in front of the other doors to listen for a noise. He heard nothing. Reaching the stairs to the next floor, he found that he didn't dare ascend. After all, wasn't he already intruding? If Ava was anywhere, wouldn't she be somewhere below, in the kitchen, or maybe a study? It seemed unlikely that she would have left him downstairs alone.

Turning back, he realised that the door was closed on the room he had looked into a moment ago. And he hadn't heard a thing. Pausing before returning downstairs, he leant to listen against the door and heard what appeared to be the sound of a couple engaged in rigorous lovemaking.

A flush rising to his face, he steered himself away and crept down the stairs. When he returned to the sunny lounge he found that Ava had still not returned, and what's more he could hear the creaks and thud of the bed in the room above.

But surely it wasn't Ava? Surely a woman of her age couldn't be—? No, he decided. There was someone else here. He'd heard footsteps in the room above when he began the interview. He'd seen a young woman entering the lounge and then backing out again. Hadn't he? *Just us*, Ava had said. But no, that couldn't be right. To assure himself that he wasn't going mad, he rewound the Dictaphone and listened back, thinking that surely the footsteps above had been picked up when Ava talked. He turned the volume up as high as it would go but all he heard was Ava and himself.

168

Her voice: "You seem very distracted."

Then him: "Guests?"

A pause then him again: "That noise."

Ava: "It is only you and I here."

Him: "But..."

Ava: "Just us."

Another train passing along the tracks drew his eye back to the window. It was another of those old style trains, the kind that had been operating when he was a child. It seemed even more antiquated when he recalled the futuristic model he'd just seen blasting along the tracks ahead of it.

Hearing feet on the stairs, he switched off the Dictaphone and set it back down on the table. He waited a moment, expecting Ava to return to the room, but when she didn't he stood and went to the door. Outside the room, at the foot of the stairs, ready to ascend, he saw a slim young woman. He was so startled at the sight of her, he couldn't speak. Their eyes met briefly, before she gave a bark of laughter as if in the midst of a game—hide and seek perhaps—and darted up the stairs. He had time to see that she was naked from the waist up. Below she wore some kind of slip or lacy skirt, and her feet were bare. Long chestnut-coloured hair had obscured most of her face. He listened to her scurry up the stairs then crossed to the banister.

"Miss?"

Her footsteps halted in the hallway above. Matt climbed halfway up the stairs then stopped when he saw her standing at the top looking down at him, her hair hanging around her face. She was only there a moment before she shot to one side, laughing again, but he was struck by her resemblance to a young Ava **Candelaria**. Perhaps this was her daughter. No, that couldn't be right because hadn't she said she'd never had children?

"Excuse me, Miss."

Matt climbed two more steps then paused again. Hearing his name called from below, he shook his head and descended back down the stairs. On returning to the lounge he discovered Ava waiting for him in the armchair she had previously occupied. Beyond her, through the window, he noticed a train passing along the tracks, a red and yellow *Virgin* train. For some reason he felt reassured at the sight of it.

Ava glanced up. "Ready to continue?"

"I'm sorry," Matt said. "You'd been gone a little while and I was worried something might have happened to you."

"I was only gone a moment. Bathroom break. The curse of the elderly."

"It felt like you'd been gone quite a while."

Ava shrugged. "It's this house. It plays tricks with time."

"How do you mean?"

"Time's a bit...confused here."

"Confused?"

"Blame the old fairy fort."

"I don't understand," Matt said.

Ava pointed at his Dictaphone. "Shouldn't we finish the interview?"

"Yes, yes. Of course." Matt shook his head as if to clear it. After switching on the Dictaphone and setting it down once more before Ava, he wondered if he could trust anything she said. *All this strange talk*, he thought. *Her mind's gone.* As he ran through the list of questions he'd prepared, he made a show of listening and responding as Ava talked about her film career, but all the time he was thinking about the young woman he'd encountered on the stairs. There'd been something compelling about her. Despite having only glimpsed her, he wanted to know more. As time went on he found that he couldn't shift her from his mind.

He had neared the end of his list of questions, when Ava sat back, took off her glasses and rubbed her eyes.

"You okay?" Matt said.

"All this talking, it's worn me out."

"We can call it a day if you like. You've been very generous with your time already."

Something he'd said made Ava laugh under her breath. "More generous than you know."

He took her to mean that he had overstayed his welcome, and began hurriedly packing away his notebook and Dictaphone when she leaned forward and put a hand on his wrist.

"I hope I didn't offend you with those things I said about your girlfriend. All that stuff about bras hanging over the bath."

Matt shook his head. "Not at all."

"Touched a nerve, didn't I? I could tell by your face."

"You put it into words for me, that's all. Listen," he said then, no longer able to contain himself. "There are other people here, aren't there? Here in the house. It's not just us."

Ava held his gaze for a moment before glancing away. "Sometimes."

"I heard footsteps, and when I went looking for you, I saw a woman on the stairs. Do you mind me asking who she is?"

Ava was silent a moment. Then she said, "A woman? What did she look like?"

"Young. Slim. Attractive. Well, I didn't really see her face, but I could kind of tell, you know. I mean...she was..."

"Beautiful?" Ava gazed at him, a half-smile on her lips. "Oh her. She's just another fantasy."

"I...I mean...I hope this doesn't sound strange...but I'd be interested to meet her."

Ava laughed now. "You already did."

"No, I mean, I'd like to talk to her."

Ava drew in a long breath then as she let it out she shook her head. "What is it with men? Tell me. They glimpse some young thing and they lose their heads."

"I'm sorry."

"Don't be. You'll get to meet her. You just need to choose your moment."

"I really should be getting out of your hair." Matt gathered his things and stood, then held out his hand to help Ava to her feet. As one, they moved towards the door.

"Well, it was a pleasure," Matt said, offering Ava his hand again, this time to shake. Ava took hold of it in both her hands and once more held on to it.

"I like you, Matt. I'd like you to come and see me again one day. Would you do that?"

"Of course," Matt said, slightly taken aback. "I'd love to."

"Perhaps next time you won't be so disappointed in me."

"Ha, ha," Matt said, despite being confused. "You haven't disappointed me at all. You've been very generous. Very kind."

When they reached the foot of the stairs, he couldn't help glancing up towards the floor above. He saw no one.

"Don't worry," Ava said. "You'll see her again. When the time is right— ha ha."

"The time?"

"It's this house. It confuses things."

"I don't get your meaning," Matt said.

"Things aren't as locked down here as they are everywhere else."

"Things?"

"Time. I'm talking about time. It crosses, like the train tracks, and there are collisions. Sometimes. If you pick your moment right, you can...return."

"I see," he said, though he didn't. Not at all. He was already thinking how he'd describe her to his colleagues when he returned to the *Action!* office. *Fruitcake. Total fruitcake. No*, he thought, looking at her smiling up at him, *I won't say that*. Perhaps he would say she was wise.

Opening the front door, she stood to one side and smiled as she bid him pass.

"Well," Matt said, "Thank you again for your time. It's been an interesting day."

"You're most welcome," Ava said. "I know for certain we'll meet again."

"How can you be so certain?" Matt said.

She showed him that gamine smile then, the one she'd been charming cinema goers with for decades. Raising one hand, she tapped the tip of a finger against her temple. "Because I remember it?"

"Remember...?"

"Goodbye. For now. Oh, and don't touch the ground."

Matt stepped through the door of the house and the sunlight seemed now too bright. It dazzled him, and made his head feel light. He stumbled down the first few steps away from the house. When he reached the last step, he turned to look back at the house and ran his eyes across every window, hoping for one more glimpse of the young dark-haired woman he'd seen on the stairs. But all of the windows were blank.

He hesitated then as he made to step down from the last riser and place his foot down in the grass.

Don't touch the ground, hadn't she said?

He watched as one of those old-style trains emerged out of the distance and began careering towards him.

Choose your moment.

Turning, he began to climb the steps again in single bounds until he reached the front door of *Tír na nÓg*.

He pressed the doorbell and heard it chiming inside the house. Then he waited to see who would answer.

The Birdman of Bishopsbourne

IT'S A GOOD story how I got that name. I'm not often called it anymore though. People got tired of telling the tale, and it's only the older folk around here who remember. And, of course, my kids. I can still recall that day driving home from town with Noah in the passenger seat—he must have been around four or five at the time—when he turned to me and said, "Daddy, why do some people call you The Birdman?"

That made me laugh.

"It's because of something very, very stupid I did once, son."

I remember this kind of *surely not* expression, completely sincere the way kids are at that age—as if he couldn't be conceived of his old man doing anything remotely stupid ever.

"What did you do?"

"Built myself a pair of wings. Climbed to the top of Danver's Head and was about ready to jump of. Thought I could fly."

"Why didn't you jump?" Noah's face was all lit up.

"Your grandma stopped me. She got wind of what I was up to. I think one of the farmhands saw me leaving the house early with my wings, and they went and woke her up. She came running along the path in her dressing gown and slippers, the wind blowing her hair all wild, screaming at me not to jump just as I was getting ready for take-off. Good thing as well. It was a long way down. I could've died. Everyone who heard about it thought it was hilarious. After that, people started calling me The Birdman of Bishopsbourne. It's a joke, that's all."

Noah's wide eyes were fixed on me. His mouth hung open. "I think it would've worked. I've seen you build things. I think you could build anything you wanted to. Even wings."

"Aw. Thanks, pal. I thought so, too. At the time."

Noah's all grown up now, about the age I was the day I tried to jump off that cliff with nothing but some nailed together bits of plywood and some canvas sheeting to save me from plummeting forty feet. He went off to

University last July, but says he'll come home to help me work the farm next summer.

He's a good boy, but put him out of your mind for now. This story isn't about him. Nor is it the story about how I got that name, The Birdman of Bishopsbourne. No, the story is about the thing I found in the barn one morning, not so long ago.

In fact, it wasn't long after Noah left that it all began. I know it was the end of summer, because when I left the house that morning it was still daylight. It must have been, otherwise I wouldn't have seen what I did.

After breakfast, I'd ridden the motorbike up into the high field, as usual, to bring the cows in for milking when I happened to look back and notice a huge hole in the barn's roof, like something big had plunged right through. At first, I thought maybe a meteor or a piece of space junk. I couldn't think of anything else that could drop out of the sky and leave a hole that big.

Instead of shepherding the cows out of the field, I rode back down the track to the barn and opened it up. The smell hit me as soon as I got inside. I'm used to the stink of animals—it's something you get used to after a while—but this was different. This was a smell you could *taste*. The pungency of it burned my eyes, musky on top with an undertone of something rotten, like dead flesh; kind of how you imagine a person who hasn't bathed or changed their clothes in a month might smell, when the sweat and piss and grime get all mixed up. Once I'd got over that stench, I became aware that there was something there—something big—looking back at me from the shadows at the end of the barn. I think my heart stopped beating for a few seconds when I got sight of it. My thoughts died as well.

I must be fucking dreaming! But no, the smell alone would have woken me. Stupidly, I squinted and tilted my head from side to side. This thing lay there completely still, hunkered low to the ground with two giant wings spread out to either side of it. Though it couldn't possibly be, my first thought was: *dragon, a fucking dragon in my barn.* But it was more bat-like than reptilian, with a dark furry body, except it had these big eyes, both of which were fixed on me, a reddish glow in the gloom.

Fear hit me, and I backed away, sure that any moment this thing would pounce on me, but it didn't move.

I slammed the barn door behind me, whacked the chain and padlock on with shaking hands, and ran back to the house.

174

When Marie got up, she found me at the kitchen table. She waved at the hanging smoke as she came through. I'd smoked a whole pack of cigarettes without realising.

"Jack? What's going on?"

"Nothing. Nothing's going on."

She gave me a long look before checking the clock on the wall. "Shouldn't you be bringing the cows in? Mick and Billy will be here soon."

"Yes. I...I was just about to go."

I started to get up, but she stopped me. "Have you taken your pill?"

I met her gaze. "Uh...maybe I forgot."

"You're always forgetting."

Taking the pack of pills down from the cupboard's top shelf, she brought one to me with a glass of water. I swallowed it with a gulp as Marie stood over me with her arms folded. I got up and walked out into the yard.

Marie watched me from the kitchen window.

I don't know why I didn't tell her about the thing in the barn.

Perhaps I thought I'd imagined it.

Or perhaps, I hoped that next time I checked it would be gone.

I didn't tell the hired hands either when they showed up and started asking why the gate had been left open in the high field and why the cows weren't already in the milking shed. I couldn't think of anything to say.

Shaking his head, Mick went off with the bike to get the cows in whilst Billy went to prepare for the milking.

I stood in the middle of the yard, occasionally glancing over my shoulder towards the barn. There it was in my mind's eye: that great winged beast lying in the scattered hay like something from a nightmare.

THAT EVENING AFTER Marie and Ava were in bed, I went into Noah's room, sat down at the desk, and fired up his computer. As I waited for Windows to start, I took stock of Noah's room, of his shelves of books, the guitar propped by his bed, and the posters of rock stars on his wall none of whom I recognised. Although I'd always planned for Noah to take over the farm one day, as I'd taken it over from my father; more recently, I'd discovered he had bigger dreams and the will to realise them. We'd joked about it the day he left for University, after he'd told me he'd be back for the summer.

"You'd better," I remember saying. "This'll all be yours one day. Farming's in our blood."

175

"Yeah, Dad." Noah grinned. "But so is flight, remember?"

He referred to my Birdman nickname, but something else hid in his words, another meaning, and my smile faded. For some reason, I found myself thinking about that day I'd stood on the edge of the cliff at Danver's Head, before my poor Ma came screaming up the hillside. In that moment, I'd felt alive, truly alive, as if all my senses had suddenly woken up, and everything about me—the sea, the grass, the sky—seemed to sparkle in the dawn light.

I clapped Noah on the back.

Yes, son, fly. Get as far away from here as you can. I wish I'd flown when I had the chance.

That wasn't what he'd meant though, I knew that.

I opened the internet browser. All day I'd been thinking about the thing in the barn, and I remembered Noah trying to explain to me once about how these days everyone had a digital footprint. Pictures and information about you would be shared on social media whether you liked it or not. All you had to do, Noah said, was type your name into a search engine and see what the results were. I figured that creature in the barn had to have some kind of digital footprint.

A thing like that couldn't just exist without leaving some trace.

I tried various search criteria, including 'giant bat,' 'winged monster,' 'flying beast' and trawled through the results. A lot of it was useless until I found an article entitled:

"The demon of Idaho, terrifying image captured by unsuspecting photographer shows 'winged creature.'"

Included in the article were two blurry images, which purported to show this creature silhouetted in the middle of a haze of fog and streetlights. Although the article was sceptical, the images struck me. Had the monster in my barn raised itself upright, it would, I supposed, have looked like whatever had been captured in those images.

Narrowing my search to Idaho, I found what could have been another sighting. Seven-year-old Corey Heil, who lived in a town called Twin Falls, had gone missing whilst on a camping trip with friends. Some of Corey's friends claimed he'd been 'taken by a birdman' and described a huge flying creature resembling a giant bat, which had swooped down out of the sky and snatched Corey from his place by the campfire. Police dismissed these reports, the article said, and searches were still underway for the missing boy.

My heart beat fast when I read this, but Idaho was a long way away. The creature would've had to cross half of America and then the Atlantic Ocean in order to crash land in my barn.

Was this possible? Could I use the internet to track the beast's progress from Idaho to my farm?

After several hours trailing a string of missing children, stolen livestock, and odd sightings east from Middle-America to the English Lake District, I'd found nothing conclusive and was too exhausted to continue.

I NEEDED TO take another look.

I returned to the barn early the next morning, armed with a cattle prod and the shotgun I occasionally used to put sick or injured cows out of their misery. Part of me hoped the creature would be gone. Surely, it could have escaped out of the hole it had made in the roof? Another part of me hoped it was still there; because if it wasn't there, then where was it? Those articles I'd found on the web about missing children—whether related to my monster or not—had convinced me that I'd have to kill it. I couldn't have a thing like that at large on my farm. I had Ava to think of.

I knew it was still in the barn the moment I opened the doors and the smell hit me. The stench seemed stronger this time, and I had to tuck the cattle prod into my belt, so I could cover my nose and mouth with the scrap of cloth I used as a hankie.

The day was already bright, and a shaft of sunlight entered through the hole in the roof illuminating the far end of the barn where the creature lay. It appeared not to have moved since the previous morning, still crouched low to the ground with its great wings spread out to either side.

Its eyes remained fixed on me as I approached.

How wrong I'd been to think of it as a giant bat. Although its limbs were tucked beneath its body, the wings were attached to its back, as is the case with flying insects. I couldn't help but feel a little awed as I looked along the length of the wings. The span must have been fifteen feet or more. The creature's thorax muscles had to be huge. What would the damned thing look like as it sailed through the air?

The creature jerked up its head and barked like a seal, which scared me so much I turned and got the hell out of there. Once I'd got the locks and bolts back in place, I leaned against the barn door, panting.

My eye caught movement in the yard. Marie paused, cutting leaves from her little herb garden in front of the kitchen window. I waved at her, but she made no response.

How incredible it would be to see that flying creature airborne.

That heaviness I was so used to feeling in my chest—that feeling like a swallowed scream—wasn't there anymore. Gone.

I SAID I wasn't going to write about how I became known as The Birdman of Bishopsborne, but there's more to the story than almost throwing myself off Danver's Head, strapped to a pair of homemade wings.

I've been fascinated by flight since I was a child. I may not be one for small talk, as Marie likes to point out, but I can yammer on about yaw and pitch and flow fields and Mach numbers until the cows come home - literally!

As a boy, I made toy airplanes out of whatever was available: first paper and card, then balsa wood. The constructions became more elaborate. My greatest achievement was a model I knocked up in my Dad's tool shed when I was fourteen. I called it The Sky Rover. I'd just started to understand how an airplane wing works, and it took a lot of sanding to get just the right curve on the aerofoils.

Quite a crowd of people gathered to watch me launch The Sky Rover off Danver's Head, and to this day, I can still remember the combined gasp as my model plane flew a straight course over the sea towards the setting sun until the wind changed direction, spun it upside down, and sent it spiralling downwards. With a splash, it was gone. The crowd cheered and applauded either my achievement or my failure, I'm not sure which, but I prefer to think it was the former. For a good thirty seconds, my plane had *sailed* through the air. And I'd felt the world around me come alive again.

Shortly after, I told my folks I wanted to be an airline pilot or a flight engineer. I'd already looked at college courses.

Dad just laughed and said, "What you're going to be, son, is a dairy farmer just like me. Farming's in our blood."

IT KEPT ME awake at night, thinking about what that monster in the barn would look like in the air. Marie kept asking me what was wrong. She said I seemed distracted. She was always reminding me to take my pills. One morning, she sat down at the kitchen table with me and took my hands in hers, turning them palm up. I knew she was looking at the scars on my wrists.

"Think about Ava," she said. She kept her face lowered, but her voice had a catch in it. "She's only five. She needs you. We all still need you."

"I know, Marie. I know."

178

"I understand that it's hard. It's hard sometimes. The farm. The work. But you have to keep going."

"I know."

"Don't ever think about leaving us again. Don't..."

"Don't worry, love. Everything's fine."

"What is it then? Why can't you sleep? What's in your mind?"

"Nothing."

I didn't want to tell her about the thing in the barn, not then.

Every morning before getting the cows in, I took the cattleprod and the shotgun, and I paid a visit. The beast had slumped over on one side, its eyes half-closed.

Perhaps dying.

Encouraged by this, I dared to get close. One of the creature's wings was damaged.

One morning, planning to put the thing out of its misery, I pressed the shotgun against its furry head, but I couldn't pull the trigger.

What would it look like in flight?

How incredible would it be to see this thing lift off the ground?

I checked the length of the wing, which was torn and bent.

What could be done to fix it?

Similar to a butterfly's wing, though the shape was different, large tubular veins supported thousands of scales and hairs.

Mick kept a butterfly farm and always yammered on about the rare specimens he'd acquired. I'd ask him if he'd ever had to repair a wing.

Something would have to be done about the beast. It was probably hungry.

As the sun was going down, I led one of the older male cows from the top field down to the barn. At the smell from inside, the cow baulked, and it took a lot of effort to get it through the door. Once it was finally inside, I closed the doors and locked them.

When I returned the next morning, nothing remained of the cow. Nothing. The flying beast had found a new position in the far corner of the barn and seemed more alert. So I didn't linger.

When I saw Mick, I raised the subject of mending butterfly wings as casually as I could, and he told me the only method of repairing a wing is by gluing. What kind of glue would be strong enough to fix my creature?

THE NEXT MORNING, the thing rushed me as soon as I entered. It was fast, flapping the undamaged wing with a great whooshing to propel itself across the barn floor, but not as fast as it might have been had the damaged wing not been dragging behind.

The sudden tumult of its flapping wing and loud aggressive barks disorientated me.

Even in my panicked state, I managed to jam the cattle prod underneath its head as it attacked and keep it pressed against the soft tissue of its neck until it reeled away, shrieking, its undamaged wing flapping around and almost sweeping me off my feet.

As it recovered and settled, making a high-pitched mewling, it faced me and fixed me with a hateful glare.

How human its features were. The nose was flatter, more like an ape's, and the mouth wider and full of small saber-like teeth; but the eyes were like human eyes, the pupils so dark brown, they were almost black.

I held its gaze and laughed between gasps for breath. The sudden rush of adrenaline had made my whole body tighten, and my nerves were shredded, but I stood my ground.

I gained a minor victory over the beast.

"Hungry again, huh?"

The creature moved its head from side to side, contemplating me. I showed it the cattle prod, and it shrank backwards.

"Not me," I said, in what I hoped was an authoritative voice, pointing at myself with one thumb. I shook my head. "No. No. Bad. I'll bring you food, but you won't try to eat *me*. Bad. Bad. This is what you get if you try that again."

Moving forward, I jabbed at its shoulder with the cattle prod, and the creature lowered its head submissively and crabbed further back into the shadows at the far end of the barn.

Could I tame this monster?

And not just tame it, perhaps I could even saddle it.

I pictured myself astride it, sweeping over the fields, over the town. There he goes, the Birdman of Bishopsbourne, astride his great winged beast. A joke no more.

A ridiculous thing to be thinking, but the thrill of this idea set my nerves jangling all over again.

THAT EVENING, I did falconry research on Noah's computer. I figured it was a good place to start. I would treat the creature in my barn like a giant bird, tame it in the same way one might tame a kestrel. It was worth a try.

The first thing you were supposed to do was called manning, to get the bird used to you and its new environment. Well, I couldn't let that thing out of the barn, but I could go there and talk to it.

This I did, occasionally taking it a cow or a calf, and always with the cattle prod at hand. Sometimes, I thought it even understood what I said, or wanted to. It hunched there and watched me, moving its head from side to side as if it was trying to figure me out.

One evening when I left the barn, Marie played in the yard with Ava. Ava rode her trike around in circles, but Marie stood with her arms folded, watching me. In one hand, she held the canister of petrol we kept by the back door for filling the tank on the motorbike.

For the first time, I wondered if she knew something about my monster. What she was thinking?

THIS IS WHAT I remember.

I replay it often in my mind, trying to recall every detail.

We were flying, me and the monster. Or rather, it was flying, and I was astride it. And it was exhilarating, like nothing I could ever have imagined.

The wind rushed around us.

The creature dipped and swooped with ease, great wings beating the air like sails.

So, this was how it felt to fly!

But not just to fly, to dip and to rise.

My heart leaped up into my throat as we plummeted, then dropped again, down into my guts when we rose.

My head went light, but I held tight to the reins I'd fashioned for my steed. I crouched low against the beast's neck, my arms taut and my thighs aching where they anchored me against its ribcage.

And the view!

Fields and hedges for miles.

The curve of the earth over the horizon.

The world had come alive again.

I had come alive again.

The monster dipped its head as if spying something on the ground far below. It arrowed forward, and I was almost knocked from the saddle by the air rushing around me in steep descent.

I woke with a clutch of breath.

THAT MORNING, I knew something was wrong the moment I opened my eyes.

I smashed my palm against the alarm clock. The dark room meant there was still an hour to go before dawn. Winter mornings were when it was hardest to motivate myself, but since that flying creature had crash-landed in my barn, I couldn't wait to check on it. Fear that it had died or that it had escaped propelled me. I imagined opening the barn door and finding it gone. Always a relief to find this was not the case.

For as long as it lived, I lived.

As I lay blinking the sleep from my eyes, something was more acutely awry. I sniffed at the air.

Scrambling out of bed, I woke Marie. I banged on the overhead light and pulled on my clothes.

"What's happening?" Marie said, lifting her head from the pillows and squinting at me.

"Something's wrong."

"What're you talking about?"

"Can't you smell it?"

I didn't wait for an answer. Within a minute or so, I had my boots on and was at the front door. As soon as I stepped outside, the smell hit me stronger.

The fire had turned the sky a reddish-black. All that remained of the barn was the metal frame, which silhouetted against the sky.

I ran towards it, soot and smoke filling my nostrils and clinging to the back of my throat.

Too late.

I stopped running.

Nothing could have survived the blaze, not even my great winged monster.

My chest tightened and tears spilled from my eyes.

When Marie appeared at my back, I shot her an accusatory look, remembering how she had stood and watched me with the petrol canister in her hand.

She'd been signalling to me. A warning.

I was so choked-up I couldn't speak.

"Think of Ava," Marie said as I turned and walked back towards the house. "Think about your daughter, won't you?"

I was so angry and upset at what she'd done, I wouldn't even look at her. Not for a long time.

TO THIS DAY, I've never spoken with anyone about the winged beast that was trapped in my barn. Sometimes, I wonder if it was even real. For days after the fire, I searched the ashes, but I found no trace of it, no teeth, no bones, nothing.

I know it was for the best, but I can't help feeling angry that I never got to see it fly. I could have fixed that wing. I could have got the creature airborne again. It would have become a legend. The new Birdman of Bishopsbourne. I may have even ridden it, as I did once, in a dream.

I keep taking my pills. I don't dwell on what happened. I've got Ava to think of. My little girl is growing up smart. She's going to escape this life just like her brother did.

As bad as I felt about what Marie did, I don't blame her. That dream had an ending, you see, a part I didn't like to bring to mind at the time.

We were flying, and the creature began a sudden descent. I could see my farm far below, so far as to seem insignificant, and as the creature dipped, I could make out the farmhouse, the barn, the road up to the top field where the cows were gathered.

As we rushed towards the ground the creature seemed intent on something, and I could make out a figure in the yard of the house.

Ava rode her trike around and around in circles.

The beast didn't rise up again, making a course straight for her. She stopped then, my little girl, and her head craned upwards. I wanted to scream, shout, tell her to run, but the beast had picked up speed, and the wind buffeted my face.

An awful screeching, like terror and joy and hunger and need all wrapped into one. I beat one hand against the back of the beast's head and pulled upwards on the reins with all my strength, but its will was too powerful.

I couldn't stop it.

Ava's mouth fell open as a shadow descended on her.

The Pale Little Girl by the Side of the Road

*H*EARING A CRUNCH of gravel from the driveway in front of the cottage Harriett Redgrave let out a small exhalation, stood and crossed to the window. Though her husband, John, had got the log burner started shortly after their arrival, she still hadn't removed her coat. Neither had she touched the glass of white wine John had poured for her before he set about putting up the Christmas tree. She'd spent the last hour perched on the edge of the sofa, in good view of the vintage school wall clock on the wall, clasping and unclasping her hands. As much as she enjoyed spending Christmas with her four children, the anxiety she felt as she waited for each of them to arrive was unbearable.

"That'll be our Nicholas," John said. He had strung a set of Christmas lights around his shoulders in order to test them.

Harriett rubbed at the mist on the window and squinted to see through the swirling snowflakes outside. She recognised the green Volkswagen parked on the driveway as belonging to her youngest daughter.

"You're quite wrong," Harriett said. "It's Beth."

"Beth arriving before Nicholas," John said, frowning. "That's a first. Has she brought her chap with her? What was his name again?"

"No, she's alone."

Seeing her daughter move towards the front door, Harriett hurried to open it. Beth entered the cottage shaking snow from her hair and laughing. She kissed her mother then crossed to her father, looking around as she did.

"Love the cottage."

"Your father chose it. He wanted a sea view this year."

"Lovely," Beth said. "And snowing too. It's perfect."

"Get your coat off," John said. He pointed at the Christmas tree. "You can help me with this. How's Uni? Leave your mother. She's fretting like always."

"I worry about the roads in this weather," Harriett said. "Nicholas is normally the first to arrive and there's still no sign of him."

"Oh, he's here," Beth said. "I saw him."

Harriett, now at the window again peering out through the little patch she'd cleared in the condensation, turned to her daughter. "Whatever do you mean?"

"I passed him a little way down the road. He had parked up and he was having a snowball fight."

"A snowball fight? With who?"

"That kid."

"Kid? What kid?"

"A little girl. I assumed she belonged to that woman he's seeing now. Didn't you tell me she had a child?"

"Zoe had a little boy, but that was only a fling. It's over now." Harriett shifted her gaze to her husband. "Whatever can he be doing out there?"

"You know how Nicholas is," John said, and turned to his box of decorations.

"Funny," Beth said. She took a glass angel from the decorations box, held it up, and smiled at it. "They gave me the oddest look."

"Did they?"

"I saw them playing together on the top of a little hill by the side of the road. Looked like they were really enjoying themselves. I beeped the horn as I passed, and waved at them, and they just stopped what they were doing and stood watching me go by. I was going to stop but that look they both gave me made me feel a bit..."

"A bit what?" Harriett said.

"I don't know. A bit like I was intruding."

Harriett bit at her bottom lip. "Whoever can this girl be?"

"Pale little thing," Beth said. "Now I think about it, I don't know if she was even wearing a coat. Must live around here somewhere."

"There's nothing around here," Harriett said. "We're slap in the middle of nowhere. Aren't we, John?"

"More or less." John shrugged. He looked into his wife's worried face for a moment, then brightened and turned to Beth. "Listen, I thought we were finally going to meet this new chap of yours. Didn't you say you were bringing him along this year?"

"Oh, Patrick is coming. We travelled separately because he has to leave on Boxing Day. He'll be here soon, I expect."

"I hope he doesn't run into any trouble," Harriett said. "It's really coming down out there."

"Oh, he'll be fine." Beth noticed the bottle of wine her father had left on the dining room table and disappeared into the kitchen to find a glass.

Harriett resumed her position at the window and frowned at the thickly falling snow. Hearing the scrape of tyres on the gravel, she moved her face closer to the glass and could just make out a silver car pulling up alongside Beth's Volkswagen.

"It's Nick, at last," John said.

"It's Livvy," Harriett said. She watched her oldest daughter climb quickly out of her car, grab a small suitcase from the boot, and hurry towards the cottage. Harriett was at the door before Livvy had a chance to ring the bell. Her hair and shoulders patterned with snow, Livvy gave her mother a quick kiss on the cheek then hurried into the lounge where she parked herself on a footstool in front of the open fire.

"Olivia. Good trip?" John said.

"Bloody nightmare," Livvy said. She combed the snow out of her hair with her fingers. "Car's heater packed up a couple of miles back. Thought I was going to freeze to death."

"Want a drink?" Beth said.

"Something hot, please."

"There's some mulled mine somewhere," John said. "I'll go and boil it up for you."

"Grand."

"You didn't see your brother, did you?" Harriett said. "Beth said she passed him. She said he'd stopped to have a snowball fight with some girl by the side of the road."

"I did see a girl," Livvy said. "A mile or so back. She was just standing there. No coat or anything. I stopped to speak to her because she looked lost and I thought she might need a lift or something, but all she kept saying was that she wanted to show me something. She wanted me to go with her because she had something she wanted to show me. I told her she was going to catch her death wandering around without a coat. She already looked half frozen. But she just kept going on about this wonderful thing she wanted to show me. In the end I just left her there."

"You left her?"

"Yes. There was something off about her. I don't know. She gave me the creeps."

"And Nicholas?"

"I didn't see him."

"Did you see his car?"

"I don't know. I might have passed it without realising."

"What did she want to show you?" Beth said. "The little girl. What was it?"

"No idea," Livvy said. "Something really wonderful, she said. I didn't like the way she looked at me so I got out of there."

"How did she look at you?"

"King of hungrily. She had these big blue eyes and they were just fixed on me."

"Oh, I've just realised who she is," Beth said.

Harriett rounded on her. "Who?"

Bath smirked. "Why the little match girl of course."

Harriett shook her head. "Beth, really."

Livvy shivered and moved closer to the fire. "So, Nick's still out there?"

"He'll be here soon," John said, reappearing from the kitchen and presenting Livvy with a glass of mulled wine. He gave a measuring look to his wife. "Let's not start to panic. It's still light out."

Harriett glanced at the clock on the wall. "It won't be for much longer. It's almost four."

"I think you were right to abandon that little girl," Beth said to her sister. "When I was in India, they warned us about these children who would ask tourists for help and then lure them to a secluded spot where men waited to beat them up and rob them."

"For God's sake," John said, flicking his eyes to Harriett. "That's the third world. That doesn't happen *here*."

"It's happening everywhere now, Dad. Open borders and all that."

Harriett wrung her hands together. "John, I'm worried about Nicholas. Perhaps someone should go and look for him."

Before John could answer, the sound of a car engine was heard from the driveway. All four of the cottage's inhabitants hurried to the window. Harriett gave a startled gasp when she saw her middle daughter climbing out of a green Mazda.

"It's Andrea. I'd forgotten all about her."

They all watched as Andrea ran from the car towards the cottage. Harriett jumped at the sound of hammering on the front door.

"Somebody let her in."

Beth went. Harriett heard the front door open, then Beth saying, "Christ, what happened to you?"

Andrea came panting into the room. Her eyes were wild and she had a bloodied scrape on the left side of her forehead.

187

"What happened?" Harriett said. She began helping Andrea off with her coat, then took hold of one of her hands. It felt like a block of ice. She rubbed at it then steered her daughter towards the fire where she sat her down in an armchair and pressed Livvy's abandoned glass of mulled wine into her hand. The other members of the family clustered around.

"Girl," Andrea said, between gulps of wine. "Girl out there, wanting to show me something."

"You didn't go with her?" Livvy said.

"I was worried about her. She said she wanted to show me something so I followed her. We walked for a bit then I saw this glade of trees. There were people there, gathered in this little glade, but they didn't look right."

"Didn't look right? What do you mean?"

"They just didn't look *right*. They weren't dressed properly, for one thing. I think one woman was naked from the waist up. In that weather! I asked the girl who they were and she said they were all her friends. She said she wanted me to be her friend too, but I got scared and ran. That was when they all started chasing me."

"Chasing you?" Harriet straightened and looked at her husband. "John, call the police."

"Wait a minute, dear. Then what happened, Andrea?"

"I kept falling over in the snow. I hurt myself." She put her free hand to the scrape on her forehead. "I thought I'd lost my way, but then I saw my car. I only just made it."

"John, we should call the police. Nicholas is still out there."

Andrea gasped, meeting her mother's eyes. "He's not is he?"

"Beth said she saw him having a snowball fight with that little girl."

Andrea looked at Beth. "The same one? Pale? Long straight blonde hair, almost white. Big blue eyes. Kind of a...weird look in them?"

Beth shrugged and glanced away. "Not sure. I didn't stop."

"We have to go and look for him," Livvy said.

John said, "We can all go."

"I'm not going back out there," Andrea said.

"Don't be daft. I'm sure there's some reasonable explanation for all this."

"Call the police," Harriett said again.

"Now, now," John said. "Why don't we just go for a drive first and see if we can spot him. We'll be able to find his car at least."

Harriett went out into the hallway followed by Beth and Livvy and began distributing coats, hats and gloves. When Andrea got up and also

188

began putting her coat on, Beth looked at her and said, "I thought you weren't coming."

"I'm not staying here by myself," Andrea said.

"We'll take my car," John said.

As one the family exited the cottage and trooped out into the falling snow. Already, there was a couple of inches build up on the ground. Harriett glanced back towards the cottage and through the lounge window she saw the coloured lights of the Christmas tree and the orange glow of the fire. They should all have been enjoying their first glass of wine now, maybe some of the canapés she'd brought, and catching up on each other's news. Nicholas and his father would be talking about rugby, whilst Beth made her sisters jealous by telling them about everything she'd been up to at University. "Wait until you get out into the real world," Andrea would say, whilst Livvy nodded in agreement. "It's not all gap years and getting up at noon for a two o'clock lecture." It was Harriett's favourite part of the Christmas season, that moment when she could relax because her family were all together again.

Except they weren't together again, and she couldn't relax. Andrea had arrived at the cottage with some bizarre story about half-naked people hanging out around a glade of trees and Nicholas was still out there somewhere scampering about after some child. She thought of Beth's tale about children luring tourists to be beaten and robbed in Indian and she couldn't help but picture her son lying bloody and unconscious in a ditch.

"Hurry up, John," she said as she watched her husband fidgeting with the car keys.

"Oh my God," Beth said, suddenly. "What about Patrick? I totally forgot he was coming too."

"Who's Patrick?" Livvy said.

"My boyfriend. I'd better ring him. Damn it, he's not picking up."

"He's probably driving, dear."

"I hope so."

John eased the car off the cottage's driveway and reversed out onto the road. He drove slowly. The only sound was the swish and squeak of the wipers as they worked to keep the windscreen free of snow. After only a few minutes, Harriett found she could no longer see out of her side-window. For some reason, perhaps thinking to lighten the mood, John turned on the car radio. Maria Carey's voice squealed out of the speakers. *I just want you for my own, more than you could ever know. Make my wish come truuuuuuuue. All I want for Christmaaaaaaaaaas is yooooooooooouuuu...eeeee...*

"Turn that off," Harriett said. She had always hated that song, but now it was like a screwdriver in the temple. That voice. The shrillness of it. "Turn it off."

John glanced at her but said nothing. He switched off the radio.

Harriett tuned to look at her daughters who were huddled together in the back seat.

"This was a bad idea. We should have just called the police."

THEY FOUND NICHOLAS' green Hatchback parked by the side of the road about a mile from the cottage, but there was no sign of Nicholas. Climbing up onto the snowy embankment, Harriett began calling her son's name. Her husband and daughters joined in, all apart from Andrea who hung back by her father's car. When John called to her, she reluctantly went to him. The light was fading and the surrounding landscape had taken on a bluish tint. Harriett could almost feel the temperature dropping as she stood there.

"You said something about some trees, with people?" John said to Andrea.

Andrea's mouth opened and closed. She glanced at her mother. "You're not seriously thinking to go there?"

"Maybe Nicholas is with these people. We have to check."

"Did you not hear what I said about them? Something about them was just...wrong. I think Mum was right, we ought to just call the police."

"Well let's see if we can find these people first. You stay here if you want. Your mother and I will go."

"Dad?"

"Which way was it?"

Andrea grimaced, looked as if she might say something, but then simply pointed over her father's right shoulder. Beth began moving that way, wading forward in the snow.

"There's footprints," she said. "We can follow them."

"Wait, Beth," Harriett called. "Wait for us."

She wished she'd had the time to change into her Wellington's. The leather block heels she had on weren't made for walking through snow. Nevertheless, she hurried after Beth who was following a line of footprints.

"We'll have to be quick," Andrea said, glancing at the sky. "It'll be dark soon."

"These footprints," John said. He stopped to place his foot alongside one of the prints. His foot was almost twice as big.

"A child," Harriett said.

"The little match girl," Livvy said in a dull tone.

"And she was walking barefoot," John said. "Look, you can just see the indents of her toes."

"Her?" Harriett said. "How do you know it was a her?"

"That's weird," Andrea said, before her father could answer. "Isn't it? Don't you think that's weird? Who lets a child go walking around barefoot in the snow? I'm telling you, something's not right about all this."

"Well," Harriett said. She was trying to ignore her own churning unease. "I suppose we'll find out."

They continued in silence until they saw the copse of trees Andrea had described. The setting sun, obscured behind a blanket of cloud, was behind the trees, turning them to stark silhouettes, black against the blue. There was no sign of any people.

John turned to Andrea. "Are you sure about this?" He went on before Harriett could say anything to stop him. "Are you sure you didn't just imagine it?"

Andrea's features tightened. She flicked her eyes to her mother. "Of course I didn't. Why would I make up something like that?"

"You know sometimes you like to..."

"John," Harriett said. She gave her husband a warning look.

When the rest of them came to a halt, Beth had continued walking towards the trees. Now she scampered back to join her family. Her cheeks were red and she exhaled great plumes onto the cold air.

"There's a house down there. After the trees. Just beyond the slope of the hill."

"A house?"

"It looks pretty dilapidated. Abandoned."

"I'll go," John said, catching his wife's eye. "I'll take a look."

When he began striding down the hill, though, the rest of his family followed.

The house had no grounds or driveway. It was just *there*. It didn't seem to belong. It looked as if it had just been plonked there, or as if it had dropped out of the sky. Harriett made a little moan in the back of her throat on sight of it, so that Andrea gave her a look of foreboding. The house appeared just as Beth had described it. Dilapidated. Abandoned. The lower floor had two bay windows with a doorway in between. The front door itself was gone. In fact, Harriett thought she could see it lying on the ground in front of the house, half buried in snow. The bay windows were boarded over. There were three windows along the upper floor, two of which still appeared to have glass in them. The one on the far left, however, was just an empty black rectangle. It was this more than any other aspect that chilled Harriett, that open portal on the blackness inside the house.

"Oh John," Harriett said. Her lips were numb with cold and it was hard to form words. "Let's go back. Let's just call the police."

"Wait," John said. He gazed intently at the house. "Isn't there someone there? Can you see...?"

Harriett looked again at the house. She now saw that there was indeed someone standing in the doorway of the house–a small pale figure. As she squinted to better make out the figure, Harriett decided that it was a girl of perhaps eight or nine years old. The girl was doing something with her right hand, making some kind of gesture.

"What's she doing?"

"She's waving to us. Isn't she?"

"Not waving. Beckoning."

"She wants us to go in there? She must be joking."

"I want to go back," Andrea said. "Can't we just go back?"

AT THE FIRST sign of snow, Patrick Evans was already regretting agreeing to spend Christmas with Beth and her family. When she told him her parents always hired a cottage out in the country for Christmas, it had sounded like the perfect way to spend the holidays. Certainly preferable to spending Christmas with his family who would be bickering before the first gift was unwrapped. Once he was on the road, he'd soon realised that actually getting to the cottage in these weather conditions was going to prove difficult. He was also in two minds about whether he wanted to meet Beth's family. Their relationship was getting more serious than he was comfortable with, especially since he'd met Chloe. He'd spent one night with Chloe when Beth was away on a field trip, and now she wouldn't stop texting him. He liked her. She wasn't as serious as Beth, and not as committed to her studies. He could have fun with her. He wasn't sure that meeting Beth's family was the right move in the circumstances. From the look of things, though, he was going to spend Christmas Eve sleeping in his car by the side of some country road.

His mobile had been ringing, but he'd been too busy navigating a roundabout to answer it. He pulled over to check it and to look at the road atlas again. He saw that Beth had been trying to call him. Probably worried. He called her back but there was no answer. He looked at the road atlas and was relieved to see that he had almost arrived at the cottage. He started the car engine and was about to pull out into the road again when he saw her. She gave him a start at first, standing perfectly still as she was at the side of the road just inside the glow from his headlights. As if she'd just materialised there. It was a girl, about ten or so. She looked directly at him. He noticed she wasn't wearing a coat.

"Hey! What...?" He lowered his side window and shivered at a rush of cold air into the car. It was then that he noticed the other people. They stood grouped together further along the road, at the very edge of his headlights' reach so that he could hardly make them out. He returned his attention to the little girl who had shifted closer to his half-open window. There was something unnerving about her. The way she stared at him, unblinking, with a half-smile on her lips.

"Hey, aren't you cold?"

"Do you want to see something good?" the girl said.

"What? Where're your parents? Do you need help?"

"I want to show you something," the girl said. "I promise you'll like it."

"What?"

Patrick looked through the windshield again and saw the group of figures ahead moving forward fully into the beams of his headlights. It was a group of women and men. Something about the way they moved struck him as odd. *Were they drunk, perhaps?* Then he saw that one of the women was Beth. She must have come looking for him. She must have come with her family to find him because of the weather and the roads. He wondered who the little girl was. She backed up a little as he sprung the car door and lifted himself from the driver's seat. He placed one Converse trainer into the snow.

"Beth?" he said, leaning around the car door and waving. "Hey, Beth. It's me. I made it. I—"

Beth twitched her head up to look at him and he knew at once that he had made a terrible mistake. Some instinct made him retreat back into the car and pull the door shut. The people outside were moving forward now, clustering around the car and banging on it with their hands. The car skidded on the snow as he reversed onto the road in a panic.

"What the fuck? What the fucking fuck?" he was saying to himself over and over.

As he tried to turn around, the car skidded again and plunged into a ditch on the opposite side of the road. He was thrown forward and struck his head on the steering wheel. When he lifted his head he could see only blackness with snowflakes twisting through his car headlights. But then he saw her, ahead of him now, directly in front of the car. The little girl. Looking straight at him and smiling.

The Furthest Deep

THE HOUSE MADE noises.

Whenever the boiler was turned on there would be clanking sounds from the first floor. "Pipes," Vince would say. "Just pipes." Sometimes, when Aubrey was sat in the lounge reading a book, alone in the house, she would hear what sounded like footsteps crossing the room above. Vince told her it was just the house settling. And that odd scurry from the spare bedroom she sometimes heard at night was, Vince assured her, merely squirrels running across the garage roof.

But this, this was different. This was a definite crash. A loud, resounding crash, and it came from the attic. Aubrey, pausing and lifting her eyes from her laptop, wished Vince was at home to tell her what innocuous thing had occurred. Maybe a pigeon had got trapped in the eaves and had knocked something loose. Sure, Vince might say something like that. Then he would go take a look. And she wouldn't have to.

Vince, though, was in Italy, on tour with his band. He'd told her when they first met that he was away from home a lot; and Aubrey had been fine with this because her freelance work meant she could push on with her assignments whilst he was away then make time for him when he returned. Plus, she secretly felt that it was only the long stretches of time they spent apart that kept their relationship alive. She knew if they were together every day they would drive each other crazy. No, she was fine with all the time he spent on the road. At least, she'd been fine with it until they'd moved in to this house full of clanking pipes and footsteps and rooftop scurrying. She had too fertile an imagination be left alone in a place like this.

There was nothing for it, she would have to go and take a look. Her mind wouldn't rest until she knew what had caused the crash. Leaving her laptop open and her notebooks spread out on the kitchen table, Aubrey climbed the stairs trying to affect a casual air. *Just got to check this out,* she told herself. *Then I can get back to work.* She did her best to stop her thoughts from going places she didn't want them to go.

Finding the rod that unhooked the trapdoor in the ceiling at the top of the stairs, she got the door open and used the rod to flick the light switch. It took a few moments for the strip-light to stutter to life in the attic, and as she waited Aubrey thought how glad she was this had happened in the middle of the day. If that crash had woken her up at some ungodly hour in the middle of the night, there was no way she would've been able to investigate. She felt calmer once the attic light was on. Again using the rod, she hooked the retractable step ladder and dragged it down.

The attic contained stacks of boxes, furniture she and Vince had doubled up on when they moved in together a year ago, her suitcases, and bags of shoes and clothes. Standing on the ladder, with only her head inside the attic, Aubrey saw at once what had happened. One box had fallen from a small stack and on hitting the ground had split open and spewed its contents across the attic floor. Aubrey didn't waste time wondering how it had fallen. Most likely the box underneath had startled to buckle under its weight, tilting the one above until it fell. What else could have happened?

When Aubrey climbed up into the attic, she saw it was a box of her old vinyl records that had fallen. Despite the split in the box, the stack of records had stayed together. Only one had slid out across the floor as if being presented to her. She saw at once that it was Gabriel Black's final album 'The Furthest Deep'.

God, she thought, picking up the record and turning it over in her hands. *I haven't heard this in years.*

In fact, she'd stopped listening to all three of Gabriel Black's albums after her trip to Wringsham a decade or so ago. She couldn't. All she had to hear was a strum of Black's guitar and she was back there on that hillside, amongst those standing stones, desperately searching for...what had that guy's name been? That odd little man with the children's book? She couldn't remember. He'd been Hungarian or something.

Her eyes scanned the song titles on the back of the sleeve and she wondered why she'd kept the record. She'd sold her copies of Black's other two albums online. Shortly after her return from Wringsham, she'd met Vince and the soul and funk music he loved had started to dominate her own tastes. It was happy music. Upbeat music. It lifted you. Early in the relationship, Vince had encouraged her to get rid of what he called her 'teenaged-angst bed-wetter crap'. She did, and she hadn't regretted it. Gabriel Black had unfortunately fallen into that category.

She noticed something then that she couldn't remember having noticed before. Underneath the song titles was a dedication written in tiny text. It read: For AW.

AW?

Those were her initials.

AW. Aubrey Winehouse. No relation, so don't expect a song.

But no. It's wasn't her. How could it be? It was some other AW. Some girl, probably. Just some girl he'd known.

As she began packing the contents back into the box, she realised that amongst the records was a plastic zip file containing the notebooks and Dictaphone recordings from her trip to Wringsham. She'd never written the article she'd planned to write about Black for *Rollin'* magazine. She hadn't known what to write once she got back to London. In truth, after returning from Wringsham, she hadn't wanted to think about Gabriel Black at all.

One notebook had fallen open and before she could snap it closed and return it to the file she saw the words WHO DID YOU THINK WAS FOLLOWING YOU? written in her own tiny scrawl. She should get rid of all this stuff, she told herself. What was she keeping it for? It had been eleven years. She wasn't going to look through it. She wasn't going to write the article now. After a fleeting renaissance a decade ago, mainly centred around his first two albums, Gabriel Black had faded back into obscurity.

She closed the box and resealed the tape as best she could. Only when she arrived downstairs did she realise that under her arm was still tucked the record she'd picked up off the attic floor: *The Furthest Deep*.

Sod it.

She wasn't going through all the rigmarole of putting it back now. She had work to do. She left it on the stairs, thinking to put it back in the attic later, or tomorrow. But when she came across it again that evening, she couldn't resist sliding the record from its sleeve. Then she was placing it on the turntable. She set the needle down in the groove before the final track.

The song started. When the voice began, she had the acute sensation that the singer was somehow present in the room with her. She even looked around as if she'd see him there, somewhere. Sitting down in an armchair, she let the song work its familiar spell on her.

When the light falls at a curious slant, Gabriel Black sang, *and hopes are scant, you've reached the furthest deep. When shadows bend at the pathway's end, the furthest deep you've reached.*

2

September 2005

AUBREY HADN'T PLANNED on visiting the grave until after her meeting with Sierra Black. She'd imagined herself going on a little pilgrimage in search of the Holy Cross Church, then wandering amongst the headstones in search of Gabriel Black's name. There she would sit and commune with him. Perhaps, if there was no one around, she would talk to him and tell him what his songs had meant to her over the years. How she'd discovered his first album in a charity shop when she was sixteen, and bought it because she liked the cover. How, the first time she played it, she'd had to stop what she was doing, sit down and just listen. How when her father died she'd played 'Always, Dear' over and over again. How his second album, *Shadows Over the Sun*, had soundtracked her first romance, from the joy and optimism of it's opening track to the wracked and heartbroken finale.

The graveside commune would be one of the focal points of the article she planned to write, the end point of a twelve-year journey that began when she'd plucked her vinyl copy of *Rivers Run* out of that charity shop vinyl bin as a teenager. In all those years she'd never met a single person who'd heard the name Gabriel Black. This had made his music more special to her. It was her treasure, her find.

As it turned out, she stumbled upon the Holy Cross Church during the short walk from Wringsham train station to the centre of the village. The church was not as she'd pictured it in her mind; it was small and non-descript. In the little open graveyard the headstone of Gabriel Black was easy to find. Again, she was disappointed. She'd expected graffiti, maybe candles and little shrines like the ones she'd seen in pictures of Jim Morrison's grave. But there was nothing, just his name etched onto the stone with the dates: 1953 – 1982. There was not even a line from one of his songs. Something from 'Always, Dear' perhaps. The one line that still brought tears to her eyes.

If I'm in your thoughts, I'm always here, always near...always, dear.

"No," she said to herself, glancing around at the other graves, all as blank and unadorned at his. "This is wrong."

198

Checking her watch, she saw that she was due to meet Sierra Black in less than ten minutes.

"I'll be back," she said to the gravestone. As she left the churchyard she couldn't shake the profound sense of disappointment.

ONCE SHE GOT into the village, she found the streets were thin and winding. She had to ask directions to The Oddfellows Arms, and arrived ten minutes late, sweating and out of breath. The pub was almost empty, but even had it been bustling with people she still would have recognised Sierra Black. The woman sat alone at a table by one window. She had the same warm dark eyes Aubrey had seen in pictures of her brother, and the same abstracted, inward-turned expression. She also shared her brother's thick dark hair, but hers was streaked with grey. Though she had to have been in her mid-to-late sixties, she remained a good-looking woman who Aubrey imagined still caught the eyes of men. Shaking her hand, Aubrey was suddenly as star-struck as if she were meeting Gabriel Black himself.

"You're Aubrey Winehouse?" Sierra said, looking Aubrey up and down.

"No relation," Aubrey said, "so don't expect a song." It was a stock joke of hers to which Sierra only showed puzzlement.

"For some reason I was expecting a man."

"I get that sometimes. Can I get you another?" Aubrey pointed at Sierra's glass of white wine. Sierra shook her head.

"I saw your brother's grave," Aubrey said after returning from the bar and sliding into the chair opposite Sierra. "I passed the church on the way here, and I couldn't resist having a peek."

"Really?"

"I was surprised. I was expecting something grander. Some messages from the fans maybe. Something. Ever seen pictures of Jim Morrison's grave?"

"My brother wasn't Jim Morrison," Sierra said. "He never had that level of fame. And now..." She sighed. "Now he's all but forgotten."

"That's why I'm writing this article. I want to change that." Aubrey took her voice recorder from her bag and set it on the table. "Do you mind?"

Sierra shook her head again. "I don't think Gabriel wanted to be Jim Morrison. He didn't chase fame. He just wanted his songs to be heard. He felt like he had something to say to people. Another way of thinking about life, I suppose."

199

"I get that. I love all his songs, but it's on *The Furthest Deep* where I feel he's really trying to communicate something."

Sierra raised her eyebrows. "Really? People don't usually like to talk about his last album. It's so dark..."

"But beautiful." Aubrey took a notepad from her bag and began looking for the page where she'd scribbled some questions during the last leg of her train ride. "I think *The Furthest Deep* is his masterpiece. What do you think he's singing about on that album?" Setting her notebook down, Aubrey sang a few lines from the album's title track. *"When the light falls at a curious slant, and hopes are scant, you've reached the furthest deep. When shadows bend at the pathway's end, the furthest deep you've reached."*

Sierra was silent a moment, staring into her wine glass. She lifted her eyes. "Isn't it obvious?"

"Obvious...?"

"It's about depression. He was depressed."

"I never saw it that way."

"How could you not? Clearly, it's a metaphor. The furthest deep. He'd sunk as low as he could go. The only thing left for him to do was—"

"Have you listened to that album?"

"Of course I have. A long time ago."

"I never saw it as being about depression. He starts off singing about some kind of paradise he's found. It's only on the second side that it gets darker. I always saw the album as being like some kind of...some kind of a guide."

"A guide?"

"Yeah, it's like he'd giving directions to some place only he knows about." Aubrey started singing again. *"Where tall trees sway, you'll see the way."*

"Tree sway all over the place. That's hardly directions."

"And at the end of the song there's a warning. *Girl, don't go, don't go down to that furthest deep.* And what's that last line?"

"We..."

"Stay away, stay away, let the creatures sleep. Creatures? What do you think that means?"

"I think it means he was depressed," Sierra said. She gazed out of the window as if she'd spied something outside that interested her far more than Aubrey and her conversation. "It's a metaphor." She shifted her gaze back to Aubrey. "Can we talk about something else?"

"Of course." Aubrey, noticing the tone of reprimand in her interviewee's voice, sat up and nudged the voice recorder closer to Sierra. "I'm sorry; it's just that your brother's music fascinates me. It has done ever since I first heard it. That song, *The Furthest Deep*. I always thought it was kind of like his *Break on Through*."

"Jim Morrison again?"

"Only he's not saying 'break on through to the other side', he's saying 'don't, whatever you do, break on through to the other side, the other side is a damn scary place'. You know?"

Sierra let out her breath and shifted her gaze to the window again. Aubrey sensed that at any moment the women might get up and leave; and she'd take a whole section of the article Audrey planned to write with her.

To buy herself time whilst she thought about how to proceed, Aubrey said: "Do you mind if I smoke?"

Sierra shook her head. She watched Aubrey search through her bag. "Nasty habit."

"I know." Aubrey laughed. "It's Courtney Love's fault." She found a pack of Camels and tipped one out.

"Courtney Love?"

"Yeah. She was kind of my hero as a teenager. She always had a cigarette in her mouth. She made it look so sexy and cool. I only took up smoking because of her."

"You're not serious?"

"Sure. Didn't you have any teenage idols?"

Sierra shrugged. "Maybe Chopin."

"Chopin?" Aubrey supressed a smirk. "The composer?"

"Yes, well I obviously didn't have posters of him on my wall, but I loved his piano concertos."

"But did you know that Chopin—"

"I'm not interested in knowing about his private life," Sierra said. Her voice had a sharp edge. "That's the problem, you see. The music, the art, is never enough. The fans want to know all about the musician's private life when it's really not important or relevant. There's never any end to how much they want to know."

"I think that's only natural," Aubrey said. "When you love someone's music you—"

"And when it comes to people like your Jim Morrison and your Courtney Love, I think those people really were deranged. This need for fame, it's like a sickness in some people. The last thing anyone should do is emulate a person like that."

Aubrey glanced down at the cigarette in her hand, wondering what had sparked this outburst. Maybe Sierra'd had to watch her brother being hounded by fans; or perhaps she thought he'd been more deserving of attention than the people they were discussing. She exhaled and stubbed out the cigarette. "Too late for me, I suppose."

"These stars today, musicians–whatever they are–they're like the Pied Pipers of the modern world. Luring the children away like rats to be drowned in the river. I'm speaking metaphorically of course."

"In some versions of the story, he leads them away to a magical land."

"Well..." Sierra frowned. "The result is the same. They're gone." She held Aubrey's gaze a moment. "The grave. Of course you know he's not in there."

Aubrey blinked. "What?"

"My brother. He's not in there. After Gabriel had been missing for—"

"Missing? Hang on. I thought Gabriel committed suicide."

"We suspected he had, but we just never knew for certain. They found his car parked near the suspension bridge in Bristol. You know it? It's a popular spot for...well. It appeared that he'd been living in it for a while. After there'd been no word for more than a decade my parents decided to have him declared dead. Death in absentia they call it. We had the funeral and everything. 1994 I think it was. We needed closure, and we were quite certain he wasn't coming back."

"Wait." Aubrey clutched a hand to her brow. "This is...you mean to say he could still be alive?"

Sierra's face darkened. "There'd been no contact, no word."

"What about sightings? There are always sightings."

"He wasn't famous enough for sightings."

As Aubrey tried to process this new information, she was aware that Sierra had become irritated and might be close to ending the interview. The questions she'd scribbled in her pad now seemed trite. She racked her brain for a something that would set them on a different course.

"What about...was Gabriel always musical?"

For the first time since Aubrey had entered the pub, Sierra smiled. She met Aubrey's eyes. Aubrey saw the resemblance to her brother more clearly now.

"We were a musical family."

Once they got off the subject of *The Furthest Deep*, Sierra became more open and communicative. It was clear she cherished the memories of her early years, the loving family unit; the singsongs around the living room piano; long summers on the lawn strumming guitars. Aubrey found herself wondering how a childhood as idyllic as the one Sierra described could have resulted in her brother becoming depressed and eventually taking his own life before he reached his thirtieth birthday. If that, indeed, was what he'd done. It appeared now that there was some doubt. She didn't dare broach the subject again though. When the interview was over, Sierra thanked her for attempting to bring her brother's music back into the limelight, stood up and gave her a hug.

"You won't focus too much on that last album, will you?" she said. "It was such an unhappy time. It wasn't Gabriel, really, that record. Gabriel really was a gentle soul."

"Well," Aubrey said. "There's plenty to talk about, apart from that."

She wondered if Sierra realised she was being deliberately vague. Sierra gave a wan, questioning smile, wished her good luck and then left.

Noticing that it had started to drizzle outside, Aubrey remained at the table writing notes and sipping the last of her Guinness as she waited for the weather to clear so she could return to the cemetery for her planned commune with Gabriel Black. The old man from behind the bar came to her table and picked up the empty wine glass Sierra had left behind. He lingered there, looking down at Aubrey.

"Writing a book, are we, miss?" he said in a jovial tone.

Aubrey looked up. "Not a book. Just an article. For *Rollin'* magazine. It's about Gabriel Black. Do you know who that is?"

"Sure, sure. I used to see him around a lot when I was younger."

"You knew him?"

"I never knew him. I'm not sure anyone really knew him. Kept to himself a lot. You'd see him around, going about with that guitar case of his. He was always up in the hills, wandering about at all hours. Tall, good-looking chap. All the girls wanted to get closer to him, but none of them could I think. He had this air of being from another planet. Course then he went a bit mad, and it only got worse."

"A bit mad? What do you mean?"

"He got strange. By the end, if you did see him – which wasn't often — he looked like someone was always after him. You know, always looking over his shoulder. Looked like he wasn't taking good care of himself either.

Always dirty. Kind of unkempt. I don't think anyone was too surprised when he killed himself."

"Do you...?" Aubrey began, but the man spied a customer waiting at the bar and went to serve him. Aubrey glanced down at the notes she'd made on her pad. *Always looking over his shoulder*, she added. Then: *Who did you think was following you?*

Looking up and out of the window, she saw that it had stopped raining, so began packing her things back into her bag. Making to stand, she locked eyes with a young man stood at the bar. He'd been watching her, but he shifted his gaze when their eyes met. Though he appeared to be in his twenties or early thirties, his small stature and his clothes–duffle coat, baggy cords and Convese trainers–made him seem childlike. His scruffy blond hair fell in his eyes. She guessed he was not a local. When she stood up, he looked at her again, appeared for a moment to be about to speak, but then returned his attention to a book laid out on the bartop. Aubrey hitched her bag onto her shoulder and left the pub, squinting against the bright sunshine.

SHE FELT SELF-CONCIOUS and a little foolish sitting by Black's grave, and now that she knew his remains weren't even buried there she saw no point in attempting to commune with him. What she'd wanted was to feel him there, feel his presence somehow. But she felt nothing. Standing, she kicked at the overgrown grass. The article she'd so carefully constructed in her mind about her journey from charity shop vinyl bin to sitting beside her idol's grave was dissolving in her mind. What was she to write about instead?

When she began to feel hungry she returned to The Oddfellows Arms, thinking that was as good a place as any to rethink her article. Arriving, she first tried to call Noah from the payphone by the bar, but he didn't answer. Perhaps this time she'd driven him away for good. Probably, when she arrived back in London she'd find he'd cleared the flat of his things, the same way Ben had, the same way Steve had. The thought was so depressing she pushed it away. *No*, she told herself. *No, by the time I get back it will have all settled down.* But then she remembered him screaming 'Go to hell' into her face before he stormed out the door.

After ordering a pint and a burger, she took out her notebook but was distracted by a man setting up amps and a microphone on a small stage in a corner of the bar. The man looked to be in his sixties. He was skinny, with long greying dreadlocks, and he wore cowboy boots, a leather waistcoat over a plaid shirt, and sunglasses. As he continued to set up his equipment, a few locals entered the pub to occupy some of the tables. Aubrey tried to focus on rejigging her article, but the man on stage— apparently deciding he had a sufficiently large audience, although the pub was still mostly empty—launched into a version Neil Young's 'Heart of Gold'. He followed this up with some more current songs which weren't to Aubrey's taste, then a few Beatles numbers.

Aubrey checked her watch. She still hadn't decided whether she was going to look for a bed in the village or catch the last train back to Bristol Temple Meads. Finally deciding she should catch the train—what else was there for her to do here in Wringsham anyway?—she was preparing to leave when she heard the man on stage strum the opening chords to Gabriel Black's song 'The Furthest Deep'. She sat down again and listened. It was a poor version, the man lacking Black's vocal range and the original's strings were of course entirely absent. He inserted a few rock yeahs and yelps in between the lyrics which would have been comical had Aubrey not found his treatment of the song so offensive. He'd also changed the words, substituting some of Black's lines for different ones. And he left off the song's final refrain: *Girl, don't go, don't go down to that furthest deep, stay away, stay away, let the creatures sleep.* The song ended abruptly instead, to a smattering of applause, after which the man informed the audience he would be taking a short break. Seeing him headed for the bar, Aubrey slid from her seat and followed. On the way she noticed that the young blond man in the duffle coat who'd been watching her earlier was still here; sat alone at a corner table reading his book.

"Hi," she said, slotting herself at the bar next to the man who'd just left the stage.

He turned his head and scrutinised her for a moment before appearing to find something pleasing in her appearance—perhaps it was her leather jacket and Chrissie Hynde shag-cut and eyeliner—and slid his whole body around to face her.

"Hey, darlin'" he said. "What's happening?"

"Interesting version of *The Furthest Deep*," she said.

His expression tightened. "Familiar with that song, are you?"

"Very familiar. I'm a big fan of Gabriel Black. You changed some of the words."

"No so," he said, grinning and displaying a couple of gold front teeth. "The words to that song aren't fixed."

"What do you mean?" She frowned. "Not fixed?"

205

He drew back to assess her again. "Hey, what's your name? Let me get you a drink."

"I'm fine. What do you mean the words aren't fixed?"

"Every singer makes their own version of that song."

"Why not just sing it the way Gabriel Black wrote it?"

He laughed and patted her on the shoulder. "Gabriel Black didn't write that song, sweetheart."

"Of course he did. It's from his album—"

"No, no. That's a very *old* song. Very old. Black just recorded a version of it. *His* version."

Aubrey screwed up her face. "Not sure about that."

"It's true. Check the album credits. You'll see it's not credited to him. He didn't write it."

Aubrey tried to remember if she'd ever looked at the album credits. Had she done so, or had she assumed all the songs on The Furthest Deep album were originals.

"What are you saying; that it's a traditional song or something?"

He shook his head. "You know who that song's credited to? *Anonymous.* No one actually knows who wrote it. There's been other versions of that song. Lots of versions. All of them different. You didn't come to Wringsham because of that song, did you?"

"I'm writing an article about Gabriel Black. For *Rollin'* magazine."

His face lit up. "*Rollin'*, eh? Listen, I've got a CD with some of my own originals on it. Maybe you could take it back to the office with you, maybe—"

"I'm freelance, but I'll give it a listen if you tell me something useful about Gabriel Black. Something I can use in my article."

He nodded. "So you're interested in him. Not just that song?"

"I do love the song. It's one of my favourites."

"Oh Christ, you're in trouble."

"What do you mean?"

He did a little mime as if he were playing a flute then glanced over his shoulder and made a beckoning gesture. Audrey shook her head in confusion.

"Why are all the versions of the song different?"

"Because...everyone's given their own version, aren't they?"

His talk sounded like hippy-dippy nonsense to Aubrey. The kind of talk she heard from the old rockers who hung around Camden's back-street boozers. She pressed him anyway.

206

"Given?"

"Hey," he said. "Listen. I've said enough already."

"What do you mean?"

Instead of answering, he laughed then drew his fingers across his mouth as if closing a zip. When he made to move away, Aubrey stepped into his path.

"I thought we had a deal."

"Forget it, darlin'. I don't know anything about Black. Just playing the same tune, is all."

"You left off the end refrain aswell." She began to sing the lines for him, but he raised a hand to stop her. He turned away then and began looking around the other people gathered at the bar as if trying to find someone else to engage with.

"Hey," Aubrey leaned closer to him. "Why'd you leave off the refrain?"

He glanced at her. After a moment, he said: "Those lines aren't a part of the song. Never have been. Black added them. Some kind of afterthought. They were angry at him for including those lines."

"They?"

"It's a warning, isn't it? The song wasn't meant to have a warning. He added it." He downed what remained of his pint. "Got to get back out there," he said, pointing a thumb towards the stage. "Any requests?"

Audrey held his gaze.

"Anything," he said. "Anything you want. Anything but Tom Waits. Tom Waits for no man." He laughed at his own joke.

"Why don't you sing *The Furthest Deep* again the way Gabriel Black did it?"

The man gave an incredulous laugh; as if she'd asked him to perform some ridiculous or dangerous task he would never have contemplated attempting. Leaving her then, he went back to the stage and strapped on his guitar. When she heard the intro to 'Dirty Old Town' she took it as her cue to leave.

OUTSIDE SHE CHECKED her watch again. It was a quarter to nine. Plenty of time to walk to the station and catch the last train back to Bristol. From there she could get another train to London. Or perhaps when she got to Bristol she'd check into a hotel then tomorrow she could visit the suspension bridge where Gabriel Black was thought to have ended his life. Perhaps she could commune with him there. Walking away from the pub, she realised someone was following her. Looking over her shoulder she saw duffle coat man still looking as if he had something he wanted to say to her. She stopped walking and faced him.

"Not stalking me, are you, mate?"

He glanced back towards the pub. She saw that he held a book in his two hands.

"Something I can do for you?"

"Are you looking for the furthest deep?" he said. His spoke softly. His accent was not English. It sounded German, or Polish–somewhere Eastern Europe.

"What?"

"I heard you talking. You are looking for the furthest deep, no?"

"The song, you mean?"

He looked confused. "Song? Not the song. The place."

"Place?"

"Yes, yes."

He ushered her into a pool of light cast from a lamp over the entrance to the pub and showed her the book he held. It looked like a children's book. On the front cover was a colourful illustration of people gathered around a lake. It put her in mind of a kiddie-version of Hieronymus Bosch's 'The Garden of Earthly Delights'. Then she saw the title: *The Furthest Deep*. The author's name was below: Jesper Tobin. Taking the book from him, she began to leaf through it.

"What is this?"

Inside were more full-page illustrations of idyllic gatherings. There was barely any text.

"What year was this thing published?" Aubrey checked in the front of the book. "1967?" Gabriel Black would only have been fourteen years old then, she realised. Was it possible he'd got the title for his song and album from this children's book?

"Who is this Jesper Tobin? I've never heard of him."

"A wonderful illustrator. I understand he is from here."

Aubrey looked up. "From Wringsham?"

The man nodded. "I received this book as a present when I was a child. I loved it. I looked at it every day. One day, I realised—this book is like a riddle. You solve the riddle, you find the place."

"Place? This place, you mean?" Aubrey pointed at one of the illustrations.

"A kind of paradise."

"A..?" Aubrey laughed. "You mean you think this place really exists?"

208

He grew pensive, and took back his book. "It does exist. I just have to find it. I'm close. I only have to solve the last riddle."

"You mean you came to Wringsham all the way from...wherever...because of that book?"

He nodded. "From Bucharest."

"Bucharest? That's...Do you know Gabriel Black?" When he looked at her blankly, she added. "The singer-songwriter? The *Rivers Run* album? *Shadows Over the Sun*?"

He shook his head and shrugged.

"He was from here too. He had a song called *The Furthest Deep*."

The man became animated. He grinned. "Like my book!"

"Yeah," she said. She began to get a vague sense of the greater scale of the story she'd planned to write about Gabriel Black. "We should go somewhere and talk. We have to get to the bottom of this. What's your name?"

"Oskar," he said. "My name is Oskar."

THERE WAS ANOTHER pub called The Jolly Piper, in a room above which Oskar was staying. It was smaller and rowdier than The Oddfellows Arms. At the bar, Aubrey discovered that the landlord had a second guest room, which she booked for herself. *Rollin'* had agreed to pick up her expenses, so long as she could produce a printable article. Interest in Gabriel Black was beginning to stir. American indie-rock stars had started dropping his name in interviews and talking about his first two albums. The magazine wanted to be at the forefront of any resurgence.

Oskar found a table in a quiet corner where they sat and drank cider and leafed through Jesper Tobin's book. Aubrey saw now how vivid and unnatural the colouring was in the illustrations. Trees were painted with bright yellows, reds and purples. Grass was an almost luminous green. It made her think of the few times she'd taken LSD. Oskar didn't say much at first; he seemed internalised. But as he drained his pint, his tongue got looser. She guessed he wasn't normally much of a drinker.

"So what's the plan, Oskar? What're you going to do when you find this place? This paradise?"

His eyes focused and he sat up. "Stay there of course."

"Really?"

He nodded. "I think Jesper Tobin wanted me to find this place. If you read the clues in the book you can see his message. It says 'come, there is a place for you'. Look at the dedication." He flicked to the front of the book. "For OS."

"OS?"

"Those are my initials. When I was a child I used to pretend he made this book for me. I know that cannot be true, but I do know he made it for people *like* me, for sure."

Aubrey sipped her drink. "People like you?"

He shrugged. "Broken people."

"You think you're broken?"

He dropped his eyes and shrugged again.

"In what way are you broken, Oskar?"

"To me it feels like when we were children we were all given this *thing*. You know? Only mine was broken."

Aubrey raised an eyebrow. "Oskar," she said in mock reprimand. "Are you talking about your penis?"

"Not my penis!" he said, in a burst of childish anger which amused her. "Just a thing. Nothing specific. All through my childhood the other children point and laugh at me because what I had been given was broken, but theirs—theirs all worked okay. And for a long time I try to pretend it is not broken. I would try and fix it, but the tape would peel off and the glue would come unstuck and it is broken again. So in time I have to admit that the thing I had been given is broken and I must make the best of it. Patch it up somehow and make the best of things." He shook his head. "It never goes away though—the feeling of being cheated and the anger you have because you got given something broken." He looked straight into her eyes. "You understand or no?"

Aubrey nodded slowly. It was a moment before she could speak. What he'd said had connected with her so deeply she was sorry now for the penis quip. She'd always felt herself that she'd been held back and disadvantaged in some undefinable way since childhood. This persona she'd built around herself—it wasn't her. It wasn't who she was. It was just something she'd created to protect herself from bullies at school and a way she'd found of dealing with the death of her father. Only now it defined her. Something bitter, sarcastic, occasionally savage. *Caustic.* That's how her mother had described her when she was a teenager. *What did you become so caustic, Aubrey?* Until now, the only person she'd thought understood her true feelings was Gabriel Black.

"I think I know what you mean," she said. "Kind of like getting an orange for Christmas when all the other kids got dolls or games or new shoes and clothes."

She thought of that year when her mother had actually given her an orange for Christmas. It was to teach her a lesson. For being ungrateful, and sarcastic, and unruly. How old had she been? Thirteen? Fourteen? *Dad would never have done this to me!* she'd screamed at her mother that Christmas morning. Later, she'd found a bottle of some awful, treacle-like wine at the back of a kitchen cupboard, and was passed out drunk on the living room carpet by the time her grandparents, aunts, uncles and cousins arrived for dinner. But not before she'd puked in the pot of one of her mother's palm plants. Her mother hadn't spoken to her until well into the new year.

Oskar smiled now, nodding. "Yes, yes—just like that."

"And you think you won't be broken if you find this place, this paradise?"

He shook his head. "I will not be broken there. I will be someone else there."

Aubrey glanced down at the book. It was open on an illustration of a window looking out onto a beach. On the beach a circle of naked people, hand in hand, danced around what looked like a small pile of burning clothes.

"Aubrey," Oskar said, an odd urgency to his voice. "You are very attractive to me. I feel like I want to kiss you. Can I kiss you?"

Aubrey couldn't prevent herself from bursting out laughing. Seeing Oskar pout, she laughed even more. When she stopped laughing and dabbed the sleeve of her blouse to her eyes, he gave her a low look.

"That's strike one," she said. "You wouldn't want to get embroiled with me anyway. I'd only make you miserable."

THE NEXT MORNING she was woken by some kind of commotion in the street outside the pub. Raising herself, she listened to the odd cries, ringing of bells and repeated hollow clacking sounds. At the window, the sunlight was too bright and it took a moment for her eyes to adjust. She laughed when she saw what was going on in the street below.

"Jesus wept."

Directly in front of the pub, a group of men were Morris dancing. They wore green and blue tatter-coats, straw hats and carried what looked like sawn-off tree branches which they knocked together as they danced. An old bearded man wearing a pink nightie and a jester's hat moved in and out of the circle. He held a recorder to his lips on which he blew sharp tuneless blasts. Aubrey couldn't work out if he was part of the proceedings or if he was just some nutty bystander who'd decided to join in. Either way, watching him made her laugh again. Eventually, he left the dancing and fled down the narrow street, pursed by a few children drawn from the small crowd of onlookers.

Shaking her head, she moved away from the window and began stumbling about the room in search of her clothes.

Downstairs in the pub, she found Oskar sat alone drinking coffee, looking at his Jesper Tobin book whilst consulting the internet on his mobile phone. He grinned when she took a seat opposite him.

"I think I've solved the final riddle," he said.

"Hallelujah. Where can I get some coffee?"

"See this picture?"

Audrey squinted at the book. The picture Oskar showed her was of a man holding out one arm as if directing the viewer towards a gate which was opening behind him. Inside the gate could just be made out a blue lake with people sat around its edges.

"Yeah?"

"He is some kind of gatekeeper, yes? He shows the way."

"I suppose you could say that."

"See his nose?"

Aubrey squinted again. The man had been drawn with a prominent nose far too big for his face so that he looked like a caricature.

"Yes."

"I always wondered about this nose."

"Coffee," Aubrey said. "I need coffee."

"His nose is exactly the same shape as this." Oskar held up his phone. On the screen was a picture of what appeared to be a large standing stone. She looked from it to the illustration of the man and saw that Oskar was right. The stone fit the shape of the nose exactly.

"Where is that stone?"

"There is an avenue of standing stones on the hill above the village. West from here." He pointed.

"You're going there?"

"Today," he said, grinning again. "It must be the way in. That song you like so much. Is there any mention of stones like this?"

212

Aubrey tried to remember the lyrics to *The Furthest Deep*. Her mind was still fuzzy from all the alcohol she'd drunk the previous night.

"Following your nose..."

"What?"

"Following your nose along the avenue of stones. That's what he sings towards the end of the song. Following your nose along the avenue of stones. See the sun on a clear blue lake, and the smiles that welcome you in."

"That's it!" Oskar slapped a hand on the table. "We've found it."

"Hang on. Wait a minute. After that there's a warning." She sang it for him. *"Girl, don't go, don't go down to that furthest deep, stay away, stay away, let the creatures sleep."*

Oskar tilted his head. "We go today, no? To see the stones."

"Did you hear what I said? The warning."

He shrugged. "There are no...*creatures* in my book."

OSKAR ACQUIRED DIRECTIONS to the standing stones from Wringsham's tourist information centre. An elderly man, who had at first seemed friendly and helpful, became reluctant to offer information when asked about the stones. He looked from Oskar to Aubrey and instead began telling them about Wringsham's other attractions: a 14th century church and a woodland walk.

"We really just want to see the stones," Aubrey told him.

He held her gaze a moment before he frowned and nodded. He wrote directions down on the back of a paper bag and handed the bag to Oskar.

It was a forty minute walk to reach the stones. They had to cross a busy road to get onto the hills then find a path beginning near a clutch of high cedar trees that wound upwards and away from the village. It was a fine day but blustery. The wind shook the cedar trees and Aubrey wished she had something warmer than her leather jacket to wear. She hugged herself as she followed Oskar along the chalkstone path.

By the time they reached the stones, she was cold, tired, miserable, and wondering why the hell she'd volunteered for this expedition when she could be on her way to Bristol. Perhaps she was putting off the return home. Getting back to London and finding Noah and all his things gone from the flat. She couldn't face that. She didn't even want to think about it. The stones were lined up in a long flat dip in the hills. Each one was different in size and shape, the biggest being the one Aubrey had already began to think of as 'the nose'. She'd expected to be unimpressed but seeing them up close she found them eerie. They looked to her like sentinels. Though their shapes were not suggestive of human forms, she couldn't help but think of people turned to stone. She imagined Medusa stalking the stones. All you had to do was catch her eye and you were turned into a statue. One of her boyfriends had called her Medusa once. Which one—was it Steve? *You know what you are, Aubrey? You're like fucking Medusa!* She remembered a fairy tale were a group of princes, out looking for brides, were turned to stone by a giant after they passed too close to his castle. What was the name of it? She couldn't remember

"Hey, Oskar. What do we do now?"

He stood examining the last page of his book whilst the wind tugged at his coat. He didn't look up. Without acknowledging her, he turned and began to walk in and out of the stones. His lips worked but whatever he was saying was lost to Aubrey.

"Oskar?"

She looked around at the surrounding hills, noticing the low way the early autumn sunlight fell, the long shadows it gave the solitary trees and the standing stones. She wondered again what she was doing here. Her planned article about Gabriel Black had been derailed in all kinds of ways so that now she could no longer see what shape it might take. It had all seemed straightforward before: fan visits musician's place of birth, sits by his grave, chats to his sister, soaks up the local ambience, comes away understanding her idol a little better. Now it looked as though some of the things she thought she'd known about him were in fact false. Not the author of one of her favourite songs but an interpreter of it. Not dead by his own hand, but missing presumed dead. She wondered if that could be the focus of her article. How she'd thought she knew everything there was to know about Gabriel Black, but had come to Wringsham and learned there was more mystery surrounding his life and death. And somehow she'd got side-tracked into walking the hills with an odd Romanian guy searching for some kind of paradise described in a children's book. No, nobody would buy that.

Hearing a shout, she raised her head and looked around. Oskar was nowhere in sight. She began walking along the line of stones.

"Oskar? *Oskar*?"

There was no answer, and she couldn't see him anywhere.

She went up and down the line of stones a number of times, thinking he could be hiding behind one of them, but she didn't find him. Where the hell had he gone? He appeared to have simply vanished. Turning on the

214

spot, and shielding her eyes from the sun, she scanned the surrounding hills. Even if he'd set off running, he wouldn't have been able to reach one of the summits and vanish down the opposite side in the time since Aubrey had heard his shout. So where the hell was he?

She began to walk the line of stones again.

"Oskar? Where are you? Don't play silly buggers. Where are you?"

He was gone. Vanished. All she had was that single shout. She tried to recall if it had been a shout of distress or surprise, or if he'd been calling out to her, but she couldn't decide. She refused to entertain the idea that he'd found his paradise. It was too ridiculous. When she reached the final stone for the ten or eleventh time, she noticed something lying in the grass at its base. It was Oskar's book—The Furthest Deep by Jesper Tobin. It lay open as if dropped or hastily discarded. She picked it up. Dew had soaked into the pages. The book was ruined.

"Oskar!" she called one last time, as loud as she could. She listened to her voice echoing amongst the hills.

She went along the lines of stones a dozen times more. Then she began to walk back the way they'd come. *Maybe he has run off*, she thought with a flash of anger. Maybe it was all some elaborate joke he was playing on her. Lure her out here and then leave her stranded, let her think he'd found this paradise he talked about. Maybe he was just a nut. Maybe he worked for the village tourist board. Imagine if she wrote about this is her article. People would be flocking to Wringsham, looking for this mysterious place, The Furthest Deep. She wondered if she should go to the police and report Oskar missing. But what would she say to them? We were up on the hill looking for this imaginary paradise, when all of a sudden he just vanished. They'd think she was a madwoman.

She'd begun to climb the slope of a hill, walking fast against the wind, when she imagined she heard music. Halting, she looked back towards the standing stones. Squinting against the low sunlight, she thought she saw a figure there, leant against one of the stones. Thinking it was Oskar, she let out a sigh of relief, shook her head, and began to walk back down the slope. But then she stopped again. The figure looked to be thin and tall, almost like the shadow of a figure cut by the low sun than a real person. She could see a flag of hair; dark not blond like Oskar's. And the figure also appeared to be holding a guitar. Then she heard it again, dimly, the sound of a guitar being strummed and she recognised the chords as the introduction to The Furthest Deep. It was being picked out slowly, haltingly, as if to tease her. There was a voice then, just discernible, singing the words, words that reached her ears as if from a long distance away, like a song lost in static on a radio, barely there. Had she not known the words by heart, she wouldn't have recognised them as part of the song.

When the light falls at a curious slant, and hopes are scant, you've reached the furthest deep. When shadows bend at the pathway's end, the furthest deep you've reached.

Her breath caught in her throat. She wanted to say his name, but couldn't. That too got lodged inside her. She tottered a few more paces down the hillside, wanting nothing more than to go to him. Go to him because he knew her, he understood her. But then something told her to get away from here. Her breath caught when she saw other figures, all dressed in what looked like ragged clothing, appear from amongst the stones. They clustered together and began making their way towards her. The man with the guitar was blocked from sight, or lost amidst this shambling crowd. She heard a series of high, thin screams from beyond the slope of a hill somewhere on her left. She darted her gaze that way, but saw nothing.

The crowd of figures were advancing towards her.

Stay away, stay away, let the creatures sleep.

Turning her back to the crowd, she began to walk quickly away, but it wasn't long before she broke into run.

She ran all the way back to the main road, her heart in her mouth. Only once did she look back as she neared the road to see a line of figures stood at the crest of the hill behind her, clustered around the cedar trees; odd hunched and elongated silhouettes against the sky, their ragged clothes flapping on the wind.

Who are they?

What do they want?

They pursued me all this way. They pursued me because they didn't... didn't want to let me get away. Didn't want me to escape.

Girl, don't go.

Don't go down...

Down to that furthest deep.

Stay away...

It's a warning, isn't it? The song wasn't meant to have a warning. He added it.

He...

They were angry at him for including those lines.

They?

Back at The Jolly Piper, she collected her belongings together and struck out for the train station. Already, it had started to get dark.

The man who'd been singing in The Oddfellows Arms the previous day was busking outside the train station. Approaching, she heard him finishing off a version of Leonard Cohen's *Hallelujah*. He grinned, recognising her, and called out.

"Find what you were looking for, darlin'?"

She ignored him and carried on walking, but he called to her again.

"Hey! Did you ever think that perhaps Gabriel Black was singing that song just for you?"

Halting in her stride, she faced him. "What do you mean?"

"It got you here, didn't it?"

"Are you suggesting he recorded that song just so I'd come here asking about him? He didn't even know me. How could he?"

"It will never let go of you, that song," the man said. "*They* will never let go of you."

"They who? What're you on about?"

He gazed into her face for a long moment and nodded. "I think you know. I think you've seen them."

"I don't know what you're talking about," she said. Then before he could answer, she carried on walking. Climbing the steps to the station, she heard him picking out the intro to *The Furthest Deep* on his guitar and she shivered, remembering what she'd seen and heard on the hillside that morning. And all that awaited her in London was an empty flat. She felt close to tears.

"Shut up!" she shouted over her shoulder. "Just shut up!"

At once he stopped playing. Instead, he began to laugh.

3
March 2016

THE LOCAL NEWS said the police had found another body in the river.

Don't let it be her, Vince thought. *Please don't let it be her.*

His phone rang, making him jump. *That's them*, he thought. *That's the police. They've found her.* He didn't want to answer.

"Hello?"

But it was only his sister, Gina, calling from London.

"Any news?" Gina asked.

217

"They're pulling another body from the river," Vince told her.

A pause. "You don't think that's her. Aubery wasn't suicidal, was she?"

"She didn't appear suicidal, but then you never know what's in someone's mind, do you?"

"Aubery wasn't suicidal. She wasn't the type. You just have to be patient. She'll turn up."

"It's been two weeks, Gina."

"Do you want me to come up? I don't mind. Honestly."

"No, you've got the kids. I'm fine. I'll be okay."

"There'll be some silly explanation for all this. You'll see."

After he'd finished talking to Gina, Vince sat back on the sofa and went over everything in his mind again. How he'd arrived back from Rome expecting Aubery to meet him at the airport, only she never did. He hadn't been able to get through to her mobile for a few days so he'd texted her his arrival time. Then when he got home he found she wasn't in the house either. Her laptop had been sat on the kitchen table along with a scattering of papers, and there was a pile of dirty dishes in the sink. But no sign of Aubery. Her keys were missing and her car was not in the garage. Late that evening, he called a few of her friends and family, the ones he had phone numbers for, but no one had seen her. He waited until the next evening before he called the police.

Propped next to the record player he'd found the sleeve of an album he'd never heard of. The Furthest Deep by Gabriel Black. Vince had never heard of Gabriel Black either. He'd played the album over a number of times, as if he thought it might possess some clue to Aubrey's whereabouts. At first he'd dismissed it as some kind of pastoral folk rubbish with twee lyrics about fairy rings and the summer solstice. During the first few listens he couldn't help but imagine women dressed in kirtles skipping through fields waving flowers in the air. It wasn't to his taste at all. But, somehow on the fourth or fifth listen, it had taken hold of him. He found himself sat for hours examining the cover, turning it over and over in his hands whilst the record played. Who was this Gabriel Black? Was he some new discovery of Aubrey's? And if not, why hadn't she mentioned him before?

He noticed a small dedication on the back of the sleeve. For VC. VC? Strange. Those were his initials.

The day after he'd spoken to Gina, the police revealed the identity of the person who'd been pulled from the river.

It wasn't Aubery.

Publication History

"RAKING LIGHT" first published in SANITARIUM MAGAZINE ISSUE 1, Sanitarium Publishing, 2019.

"UNWRITTEN SONGS" first published in the magazine "NOT ONE OF US #59", 2018.

"THE STENCH" first published in "DARK LANE ANTHOLOGY VOL.5", Dark Lane Books, 2017.

"VISIONS OF THE AUTUMN COUNTRY" first published in the anthology "NIGHTSCRIPT IV", Chthonic Matter, 2018.

"THE HOLE" first published in the anthology "BUBBLE OFF PLUMB", Feral Cat Publishers, 2018.

"WOLVERS HILL" first published in "WEIRDBOOK #38", 2018.

"COMBUSTIBLE" first published in the anthology ON FIRE, Transmundane Press, 2017.

"COLLECTABLE" first published in "TURN TO ASH: Vol. 1", 2016.

"THE SIX O'CLOCK GHOST" first published in "DARK LANE ANTHOLOGY VOL.7", Dark Lane Books, 2018.

"THE GARDEN OF LOST THINGS" first published online in daChunha, 2018.

"GHOSTLIGHTS" is original to this collection.

"HEAR" first published in the anthology "CAT'S BREAKFAST". Third Flatiron Publishing, 2017.

"YOU WILL NEVER LOSE ME" first published online in SYNTAX AND SALT 2018:1, 2018.

"UNDER IRON" is original to this collection.

"SOMETHING'S KNOCKING" first published in THE ODDVILLE PRESS: SUMMER 2018, 2018.

"LAND OF YOUTH" first published in COLP: ISSUE 1, Gypsum Sound Tales, 2018.

"THE BIRDMAN OF BISHOPSBOURNE" first published in IN THE AIR, Transmundane Press, 2019.

"THE PALE LITTLE GIRL BY THE SIDE OF THE ROAD" first published in THE BLOOD TOMES: WINTER HOLIDAYS, Tell-Tale Press, 2018.

"THE FURTHEST DEEP" is original to this collection.

WITH THANKS FOR HELP, SUPPORT, ENCOURAGEMENT, FRIENDSHIP AND GENEROSITY: Martin Greaves, Isabel Hurtado, Sharon Chard, Liz Belringer, Sally Barnett.